Rogues Gallery

A Sebastian McCabe — Jeff Cody Case Book

Dan Andriacco

Paperback ISBN 978-1-78092-702-2
ePub ISBN 978-1-78092-703-9
PDF ISBN 978-1-78092-704-6

Published in the UK by MX Publishing
335 Princess Park Manor, Royal Drive,
London, N11 3GX
www.mxpublishing.co.uk
Cover design by www.staunch.com

This book is dedicated to

ERIN DWYER ANDRIACCO
and AMANDA ANDRIACCO

CONTENTS

Case One
Art in the Blood (7)

Case Two
The Revengers (63)

Case Three
Santa Crime (85)

Case Four
A Cold Case (105)

Case Five
Dogs Don't Make Mistakes (168)

ART IN THE BLOOD

I

"But I don't want to be dragged to an art gallery," I complained to Lynda about a week before the opening. "I had enough of that on our honeymoon."

"Now there's a sentence I never thought I'd hear Jeff Cody say—'I had enough of that on our honeymoon.'"

"Very droll. Don't change the subject."

She put her arms about me in a most distracting fashion. "I'm not dragging you anywhere, *tesoro mio*." But her husky voice shifted into persuasion mode. I love it when she's being persuasive. "I'm just saying you ought to go for Kate's sake. It won't kill you, Jeff."

My lovely wife was right about that. I wasn't the one killed.

Kathleen Cody McCabe, my big sister by thirteen months, is a successful illustrator, mostly of children's books. But the "Art in the Blood" exhibit at the Looney Ladies Gallery was the first public display of her stained-glass work. So when I saw how many people had turned out for the opening show of the new gallery that crisp mid-October night, I was glad I wasn't conspicuous by my absence on her big evening.

The industrial chic building, with open ductwork and track lighting, was packed from one open-brick wall to the other. In one corner of the former hardware store, a woman sitting at a harp played lighter-than-air music that seemed to float above the chatter of the crowd. At the other end of the room, bartender-for-a-night Justin Bird was dispensing locally produced wine and beer. You could tell this was a sophisticated operation because the beer required an opener and the wine a corkscrew.

In between those two action spots, there wasn't a lot of space to move around. I could only wave across the long, rectangular space to Aneliese Pokorny, my administrative assistant at St. Benignus College, and Dr. Trixie LaBelle, my urologist. Looking around the gallery, I quickly spotted Kate and Mac—that's her husband, Sebastian McCabe, who is hard to miss—chatting with Frank Woodford. Everybody knows Frank, editor and publisher of *The Erin Observer & News-Ledger*, where Lynda was news editor before she was boosted up the corporate ladder. Right behind him was the equally familiar Scrappy Smith, a local character with no visible means of support and a penchant for getting into fights. He was talking to a guy with a shaved head and a black goatee—nobody I knew.

"I didn't know there were this many art lovers in the whole town," I told Lynda.

"There aren't, darling." She took my arm. "This crowd is all about civic pride, the lure of something new, free drinks and snacks, and maybe a dash of safe feminism."

"Oh, that explains it."

And it did. Rosalie Hawthorne, a member of the Gamble banking family and wife of a well-known doctor here in Erin, had won plaudits from all quarters for turning an empty storefront on Mulberry Street into a gallery for showcasing art by women. Ms. Hawthorne happened to be one of the artistic women herself. Several of her sculptural pieces made of old bicycles were mounted on one of the brick walls. This struck me as a waste of perfectly good bicycle parts, not to mention wall space. I may not know art, but I know what I don't like. There was no disagreement about the glitzy new gallery being good for the town, though. That's why Mayor Saylor-Mackie was among tonight's crowd, absorbed in a conversation with the energetic Adam Mendenhall, director of the Shinkle Museum of Art.

"Let's congratulate Kate," I said to Lynda.

By the time we managed to make our way over to them, Kate and Mac were sipping drinks and exchanging pleasantries with Dr. Dante Peter O'Neill, interim head of the art department at St. Benignus. Though generally classified as a freelance illustrator and stay-at-home mom to the three young McCabe offspring, Kate also had a tenuous connection to the art department as an adjunct professor. That made O'Neill her boss of sorts.

Sebastian McCabe, inexplicably my best friend as well as my brother-in-law, is a big man—not especially tall, but wide—and bearded. He attracts an audience whether he is touting his mystery novels, performing magic, arguing, playing the bagpipes, or lecturing to his students at St. Benignus. And he loves it. Surrounded by people, he is in his element. But tonight he was subdued, figuratively stepping back as if to push Kate forward on her night. I loved him for that.

"Jeff!" Kate embraced her younger brother as if she hadn't just seen me that morning. She's nearly as tall as my six-one, with hair the same shade of red as mine but usually piled on top of her head. Tonight it was half up, half down, for a very feminine and attractive effect. Hugs were exchanged among the Codys and McCabes, one big happy family, and then I realized that Lynda probably didn't know O'Neill. I introduced her under the newly minted Lynda Teal Cody name, which she uses about half the time.

"I've heard a lot about you," O'Neill told Lynda in his deep voice as he shook her hand. Lynda responded with a conventional "uh-oh." She'd heard about him, too—from me—although she didn't say so. O'Neill was something of a *wunderkind*. Only thirty-two years old, he'd been hired away from the University of Cincinnati's College of Design,

Architecture, Art, and Planning a year ago. Although only department head on an interim basis, he was said to be a strong candidate for the job. One of the few people in the room I had to look up to, he stood about six-five but looked taller because of his slim build and three-button gray suit. The eyes behind his brown, horn-rimmed glasses were serious. He wore a mustache, but it was almost invisible against the black of his skin.

"I'm still a newcomer to the Erin community," O'Neill said. "In fact, I still commute the forty miles from Cincinnati every day. But I'm really impressed by what Ms. Hawthorne is doing here. I know there are a couple of other galleries, but the vision—"

He stopped dead, a look of annoyance on his face as if he'd been interrupted. At first I couldn't figure out why, and then I realized that a newcomer was standing next to me. It was the guy with a shaved head and goatee that I'd seen Scrappy Smith talking with earlier. He was of medium height, wearing a black turtleneck sweater, jeans, and a corduroy sport coat. In his right hand he held a glass of white wine.

"Good evening, Dr. Calder," O'Neill said to the man stiffly.

So that was the reason for the freeze-up. This was O'Neill's competition—one of the other two contenders for the position of department head. Thurston Calder was older than O'Neill by a decade or so and had written several books and dozens of articles. I'd heard that he was on campus for interviews, but I hadn't met him. He had been available for other opportunities, as someone had described it to me, since leaving the Warhol Art Institute in Pittsburgh about two years previously.

"Hello, O'Neill." Calder smiled, but not with his ice-blue eyes. "Enjoying yourself?" Somehow he made the question sound suggestive.

"Immensely," the younger man responded. He began the introductions.

"Oh, yes, the mystery writer," Calder sniffed at Mac's name. "Sorry, I don't read for entertainment." He showed considerably more interest in Lynda. She was tastefully attired for the occasion in a simple black and white cocktail dress with spaghetti straps, which I thought made a nice contrast with my colorful Bugs Bunny tie. Her gold necklace and matching earrings set off the naturally curly, honey-blonde hair swept behind her ears. But Calder, professing himself to be charmed, wasn't looking at the hair or the jewelry. His eyes were roving a little lower, where there is plenty to see. Obviously he wasn't a leg man. I was about to say something subtle— *"How would you like a bust in the mouth, Calder?"*—when O'Neill pointed out that Kate was one of the artists whose work was on display.

"The stained glass?" he repeated. "Oh, yes. I saw that—the Art Deco birds. Echo Deco, rather, since it's new. Nice little pieces. More craft than art, of course, but very nice. Have you worked in glass long, Kate?"

"Actually, the style is closer to Art Moderne," Mac said, oozing charm. "However, the distinction is a rather subtle one." *Nice one, big guy!*

Without a glance at her husband, my sister answered for herself. "Not very long, Dr. Calder. We're all just hobbyists here, you know." As a professional artist, not to mention an adjunct professor, Kate was being modest.

"Well, it's nice to have a hobby, I suppose. So, Jeff, I gather you're responsible for public relations at St. Benignus?"

"That's right." *Want to make something of it?*

"Well, you certainly have your work cut out for you. I'd never heard of your little school until I was asked to apply for the position." He sipped his white wine with an expression that suggested it was gall. "Given the state the art department is in and the meager resources available here,

I'm not sure that even I can help much. Ah, well. We'll see. Excuse me. I'm supposed to mingle."

When he'd left, I looked at O'Neill and said, "What a charmer. I hope you don't wind up having to work for him."

"Don't worry about that." The interim department head looked determined. "I will never work for Thurston Calder."

"He is not only thoroughly unpleasant," Mac said, emerging from his uncharacteristic reticence, "he is not even clever about it."

"I wonder who invited him," Lynda said.

Kate held up her hands, one of which included an empty wine glass. "Not me! That was Rosalie's idea."

The effort involved in not punching Calder in his patronizing mouth had made me thirsty. I turned to Lynda. "Glass of wine?" She prefers bourbon, but that wasn't on the bar menu.

"Sure."

"I shall accompany you," Mac said, taking Kate's glass with his left hand and holding up his empty beer bottle in the right.

With Mac's substantial bulk clearing the way, it was easier to get to the bar than if I'd been on my own, but it still took a while. And there was a long line once we got close.

"We should be happy it is so crowded in here, old boy," Mac said as we waited.

I knew what he was thinking: The obvious success of the opening show was good news for the gallery, for the artists, and for the city of Erin. "Maybe so, but it could have been just as successful with two bartenders."

Justin Bird, a troubled young man who seemed to be straightening out his life, smiled in recognition when we finally made it to the head of the line. Lynda's best friend, Sister Mary Margaret Malone, had made Justin's redemption something of a project[1]. Mac engaged him in cheerful banalities while he, Justin, served up a glass of water for me, a bottle of Moerlein OTR Ale for Mac, and a glass of red wine from Erin's Silk Stocking Winery for each of our spouses with admirable efficiency. Maybe Justin had found his niche.

On the way back we passed within three or four feet of Thurston Calder. He was standing in front of one of the exhibits, an oil painting of flowers, lecturing a tall woman with cottony white hair. He stuck his head close to the painting. "Those brush strokes remind me of . . ."

"I wonder if Calder realizes to whom he is speaking?" Mac mused when we were out of earshot.

He must have seen a blank expression on my face, because he expounded:

"That is Lillian Peacock, Beryl's grandmother, and that is her painting." We knew Beryl Peacock from Beans & Books, a local coffeehouse where she was a server. I had noticed her among the throng earlier in the evening.

"Does it matter?" I said. "I'm sure Calder thinks he knows more about the painting than the artist herself." Okay, I was being judgmental—Lynda says I'm good at that—but not without good reason in this case. Besides, I didn't like the way Calder had looked at Lynda.

When we got back to Kate and Lynda they were alone in the crowd, happily talking to each other. They'd been good friends while I dated Lynda, and then while I wasn't dating Lynda for a while, and their friendship had even survived the wedding planning. Now they were more like sisters. Mac and I joined what turned out to be a conversation about the state of journalism today as viewed from Lynda's perch as editorial director for Grier Ohio NewsGroup, the chain that owns *The Erin Observer & News-*

---

[1] See *The* 1895 *Murder*, MX Publishing, 2012.

Ledger. That was such a depressing subject that I was relieved to hear a new voice say:

"Where's the blood?"

Later, in view of what happened, I would remember the question with a chill. But at the time I recognized it for the witticism that Lesley Saylor-Mackie intended. Elsewhere I have described our mayor as elegant, but classy and dignified would do just as well. A noted historian and head of the history department at St. Benignus, she is a solidly built woman in her late fifties. If her sandy, gray-streaked hair has ever had a strand out of place, that's news to me. On campus or at City Hall she dresses for business, but tonight she was strikingly attired in a red dress with a black border. The design was vaguely Egyptian, as was her necklace.

"You mean the blood in the title of the show," Kate said. "We thought that might get some attention. It was suggested by a quote from Sherlock Holmes. 'Art in the blood is liable to take the strangest forms.'"

"Of course," Mayor Saylor-Mackie said, "from the opening scene of 'The Greek Interpreter.'"

I fought back a sinking feeling. *Et tu, Saylor-Mackie?* Was I the only non-Sherlockian left in the whole bloody world? Even my own wife . . . but that's another story, and a grim one[2]. Sebastian McCabe, BSI, belongs to half a dozen Sherlock Holmes societies and writes highly popular (except to Thurston Calder) mysteries of the amateur sleuth variety. I, on the other hand, prefer my streets mean and my detectives armed with guns instead of wordplay. Those are the kind of stories I write. So far every publisher I have been able to track down in the English-speaking world has deemed them totally resistible. They remain unpublished.

"Mac thought of the Holmes quote when I told him that all of the artists in the show are related to other artistic

---

[2] See *The Disappearance of Mr. James Phillimore*, MX Publishing, 2013.

women in one way or the other," Kate said. "Their family members aren't all sculptors and painters, but that's the whole point of the quote—artistic tendencies get expressed in many different ways."

Our mother is the poet Cornelia Randall Cody. (If you were forced to read her poems in school, I'm sorry, but it was good for you.) Rosalie Hawthorne's mother plays with the Cincinnati Symphony Orchestra; in fact, she was the harpist here tonight. Lillian Peacock had been a bit vague about her artistic antecedents, but her granddaughter had earned a degree in art history from St. Benignus.

"So, of course, Beryl is waiting tables at Beans & Books two years after graduating," Lynda said.

Before I had a chance to point out that a journalism degree wouldn't have been any more practical in these days of media downsizing, a commotion erupted several feet away at the bar.

"What the hell do you mean you can't find it? What kind of bartender loses the flipping corkscrew?"

Scrappy Smith, living up to his pugnacious nickname, was yelling at Justin Bird. Neither of those dudes was wound too tightly, so I was paying close attention to the row. Scrappy's age was a mystery, like everything else about him, but he was probably between fifty-five and sixty-five, with stubble of a gray beard and thinning hair cut badly. He had a powerful physique, which tonight was covered in a blue blazer I was pretty sure I'd passed up buying at the St. Vincent de Paul store last week. He was also wearing a pale blue shirt and a white silk scarf tied around his neck like an ascot.

The room grew quiet, except for the incongruous sound of the harp music. All eyes were on the brewing confrontation.

"I'm s-s-s-sorry, sir." Justin gulped. Despite the snake tattoos all down his arms, the body piercings, and the shaved head, he looked cowed. But considering that he had once shot up a school bus because he was mad at his ex-girlfriend, I wasn't sure what he might do.

"Well, this isn't boring," I whispered to Lynda.

"Sorry doesn't cut it, kid," Scrappy fired back at Jason. "I need a drink."

But by this time, Mac had made his way to the bar. "I believe I may be of some assistance," he said loudly enough for everybody to hear. With a minimum of dramatic flourish (for a change), he produced a Swiss Army Knife with a corkscrew and started opening the bottle of Silk Stocking Roadhouse Red in Justin's hand.

"More like it," Scrappy announced.

The conversational hum quickly returned to the previous level. Within about ten seconds the only people looking at the bar were the ones in line for a drink. Later I tried to figure out how much time Lynda and I spent circulating after the drama was over, but that was hopeless. All I know is that we had just started to talk with Mo Russert, an old friend who was bubbling with plans for her long-dreamed of mystery bookstore, when we heard the scream.

The harp fell silent, making the alien cry seem even louder and the room smaller.

I don't know why I was the first to respond. If I'd thought about it, I might have been more cautious. But I didn't think about it. I just pushed my way through the crowd of stunned onlookers to the source of the scream. It was coming from an alcove at the end of the long room, the area where the restrooms were located.

Lillian Peacock, the elderly artist, was kneeling in the little hallway in front of the restrooms. She had found the corkscrew. It was embedded in Thurston Calder's right eye.

II

An hour later, although it felt like much longer, Oscar Hummel was doing his best to look unimpressed.

"Through the eye right into the brain," he said. "We had a case like that once in Dayton. A man shoved a filet knife into his wife's eye. And then he killed himself. I kind of like it when they do that—no loose ends and you don't have to worry about what some defense attorney may do at a trial."

Before coming to Erin, Ohio, as police chief, Oscar had been a desk sergeant in Dayton. But he hadn't *always* been a desk sergeant, and he occasionally liked to relive past glories. Oscar looked older than his forty-eight years and could stand a little exercise with me at the gym. He's vain enough to usually wear a cap—tonight it was the Cincinnati Bengals—to hide his bald head.

"Fingerprints?" Mac asked.

Oscar regarded him scornfully. "Of course not. Wiped clean."

"Look on the bright side, Oscar," Mac said. "The circle of suspects is limited. As soon as I realized that something serious had happened, I asked Popcorn to keep an eye on the only door to make sure that no one left."

That was a shrewd move. Give Aneliese Pokorny a task and she will execute it flawlessly. If she said nobody had left, Oscar could bank on it—and he knew it.

The chief looked sourly around the room. Oscar's assistant chief, Lt. Col. L. Jack Gibbons, and the rest of his troops were talking quietly to the assembled art lovers, notebooks in hand. "There are eighty-seven people in this room, Mac, not counting my cops. I figure they're all suspects. And one of them happens to be Her Honor the Mayor. Unless somebody confesses soon, I think I'm in deep guano. I don't suppose anybody wants to confess?"

Oscar was just venting. We all knew that what he really wanted most—next to the cigarette that he knew he wasn't going to get—was for Mac to identify the murderer in time for Oscar to get back to whatever game he'd been watching on ESPN. That didn't seem likely, though.

"What have you been able to find out about the disappearance of the corkscrew?" Mac asked.

Oscar sighed. "Justin says he was in the can a few minutes before Scrappy Smith asked him for a glass of red. The murder weapon might have been taken then. It's small enough to palm and nobody would have noticed. The bar area was pretty crowded, wasn't it?"

"Very," I said. "You don't seriously suspect Justin, do you?"

"No more than anybody else. Not this time." He meant in contrast to the time he *did* suspect Justin, which I'm surprised that Oscar would allude to, considering that it had not been his finest hour.

Oscar had already gotten our take on the evening's festivities right after questioning Lillian Peacock and Justin. We'd reported everything we'd seen and heard, verbatim, including our unpleasant encounter with Calder earlier. Kate and Lynda, meanwhile, were on the other side of the room, queued up to talk with the unflappable Gibbons.

Mac nodded toward Mrs. Peacock, who was sitting on a couch in a corner with her granddaughter. "Did she see anything?"

"Just the body," Oscar said. "As you might imagine, she was pretty wigged out by the whole thing. I could barely understand her through the sobbing. She was on her way to the bathroom when she found him."

Beryl held her grandmother's hand, the family resemblance between the two tall, pale women obvious as they huddled with each other.

"Next up, I have to talk to the gallery owner, Rosalie Hawthorne," Oscar went on. "You guys might as well stay."

Why not, we're practically unpaid deputies at this point. Although disdainful of Mac's mystery novels featuring magician and amateur sleuth Damon Devlin—and I'm with him on that!—Oscar had been forced by experience to a reluctant appreciation of Mac's real-life abilities as a crime solver.

Rosalie Gamble Hawthorne, a slim, attractive woman in her mid-forties whom I'd seen working out at Nouveau Shape, looked shell-shocked when she joined us at our low table in response to Oscar's beckoning wave.

"I just can't believe this," she mumbled.

Clad in jeans and a vest, with her auburn hair hanging shoulder length below a fedora, she gave the impression of being a woman who didn't expect to have her perfect plans ever go awry. With her youngest child recently moved into a dorm at St. Benignus, she had immersed herself just recently in art and artists. Is there anyone more unstoppable than a determined woman with a lot of time and money? But at the moment she looked more vulnerable than formidable.

"I understand you invited Mr. Calder here tonight," Oscar said. "Is that right?"

"Yes. I'd heard he was in town for a couple of days."

"He was a friend of yours?"

Give Oscar credit, he asked it without a hint of innuendo. Still, the question seemed to give pause.

"I guess so," she said finally. "We didn't exchange Christmas cards or anything like that, but we served on the Defense of Free Art Committee together." I'd heard of that outfit—some kind of trendy anti-censorship group. "I greatly admired Thurston's criticism." She shook her head. "This is horrible. Just horrible. The gallery will never live it down. Who could have done such a thing?"

"And why?" Mac added softly.

III

The rest of the evening was spent in the painstaking process of Oscar and his men talking to everyone present, the sort of dogged police work that Oscar will tell you solves maybe 98 percent of all criminal cases. Chalk up another 1 percent to luck. The final 1 percent is where Sebastian McCabe comes in.

Nobody had seen anyone pocket the corkscrew or walk away with Thurston Calder. The art lovers had all been too busy chatting, drinking, or gaping at stained-glass birds, paintings of flowers, or bicycles on the wall.

"Or perhaps the killer lured Calder away while Scrappy had everyone else's attention with his temper tantrum," Mac mused the following day, pulling thoughtfully on his beard. "That is something to ponder."

We had gathered with our coffee cups in his study after brunch on Sunday, the heat of the fireplace pleasant in the mid-October chill. It's the finest man-cave I've ever seen, but women are welcome, too. Married less than six months, Lynda and I treasured our Sunday mornings alone together after Mass. But we needed to talk this out with Mac and Kate, so an older habit had reasserted itself. Besides, we still lived just a few feet away in my carriage house apartment over the McCabes' garage.

"Frank did a good job on the story," Lynda said with a note of pride in her voice, pointing to the Sunday morning edition of *The Erin Observer & News-Ledger*. Frank Woodford had once been a reporter, going all the way back to the days of manual typewriters, but he'd been editor of the paper for so long that Lynda hadn't been sure he could still write. His specialty now was community engagement, and he was great at it. There wasn't an important club in town he didn't belong to or board he didn't sit on. Frank had hired Lynda out of journalism school, but now she was a rung above him on the Grier Ohio NewsGroup organizational chart.

"Based on what we observed ourselves and on what Oscar and his men learned in their initial inquiries, I would agree that Frank's article appears to be as accurate and as comprehensive as possible at this point," Mac said. "To summarize, everyone at the gallery last night had the means and the opportunity. Unless we can find a way to narrow that down a bit, perhaps motive is the most promising line of investigation."

"There was no love lost between Calder and Dante Peter O'Neill," I pointed out. *What am I saying? What kind of college PR director tries to finger an employee of his own institution for Murder One? I need more sleep.*

Lynda, sitting next to me on the love seat, took a sip of her high-test coffee. "I only spent about five minutes with the late Mr. Calder, but my guess is that if everybody who didn't like him is a hot suspect, then the only possibility you've ruled out is suicide."

I wish I'd said that.

"Maybe I have some books that would help," my sister said. She left her chair and returned a couple of minutes later with three fat volumes, one of them a coffee table book.

"When I heard that Calder was a candidate for head of the art department, I bought some of his books," Kate explained. "He's also famous for his biting criticism in articles, but I wanted to read the books." She picked up the coffee table tome, *LaDonna McQueen: Her Violent Life and Vigorous Art.* "He was always a controversialist. This was his first book. It started out as the dissertation for his doctoral degree in art history at Stanford."

"Shows you what I know about art," I said. "I've never even heard of this LaDonna McQueen."

"Nobody had until Calder discovered her," Kate said. "Or rather, everyone had forgotten her. LaDonna

McQueen was an obscure urban guerrilla who was part of a gang that shot and killed a guard during a bank robbery in 1970. She was no kid like Patty Hearst; she was a thirty-year-old art teacher in San Diego who fell in love with one of her radical students and ran away with him. She never surfaced again after the robbery, but she left behind a cache of watercolors and oils. Decades later, Calder became fascinated with her story and tracked down her work." Kate held up the book. "This was the result. Basically he argues that she was a tortured genius."

Kate opened the book and paged through so that we could see the art. The subjects all came from nature—flora and fauna, mostly the former—but made bolder and brighter than real life. "There is certainly energy in these paintings," Mac said.

"Creative violence, Calder called it," Kate replied. "The family of the guard killed in the bank robbery was outraged at his book. They compared it to praising Adolf Hitler's artwork." She put that volume to one side and picked up the next one.

"*Andy Warhol: A Post-Post-Modern Assessment,*" I read out loud. "I guess that's better than a pre-post-modern assessment."

Lynda rolled her eyes.

"This is one of Calder's later works, a revisionist, rather negative view of the art of Andy Warhol," Kate explained. *Oh, now I get it.* "It's probably no coincidence that he quietly left the faculty of the Warhol Art Institute shortly after it was published."

So maybe an irate Andy Warhol fan . . . No, I just couldn't see it.

"It's been a couple of years since that book and he hasn't had an academic post since," Kate continued. "He's been busy, though." She picked up the third book, *The Sincerest Form of Fraud: America's Strangest Art Forger.* "This just came out earlier this year. It's fascinating. You crime writers should read it. Calder was a bit of a sleuth himself. He was working a side job as a consultant to a small museum in Wheeling, West Virginia, a few years ago when he began to suspect that one of the paintings was a fake. It turned out that he was right, but there was a much, much bigger story there. Calder eventually found that a man named Carl Banks had donated more than a hundred watercolors and sketches, supposedly by minor but collectable artists, to at least fifty museums over twenty years. They were all forgeries and all by him."

"But he *donated* them?" Lynda said.

Kate nodded. "He didn't even claim a tax write-off on his income tax."

"Then what was the point?" I asked.

"When Calder interviewed him for the book, Banks said he wanted to show that he was as good an artist as any of them, good enough to fool the museums. It also might be worth mentioning that Carl Banks has been hospitalized in mental institutions several times."

"Mentally ill or not," Mac said, "he managed to successfully perpetrate art fraud on a massive scale until Calder uncovered it. So Calder's evident self-esteem was not without foundation. That is most revealing, Kate."

The doorbell rang. It was Oscar, dressed in Sunday clothes and a panama hat. After he joined us in the study and Kate shoved a cup of caffeinated coffee into his hand, I expressed surprise that he wasn't having lunch with his mother at the Bob Evans restaurant.

The chief scowled. "She's on a date with some old geezer she met at Kroger's. They went pumpkin picking, which will be followed by dinner. I told him he'd better keep his hands on the pumpkins. Anyway, I've been on the Calder case, working the domestic angle. The first thing I wondered was whether the victim had a wife, or girlfriend, or both. Or maybe even a husband and/or boyfriend, whatever. I didn't find any current romantic attachments, but there is an ex-wife."

"That is promising," Mac said.

Oscar shook his head. "I'm afraid not. Her name is Cherise Steele and she has an iron-clad alibi—she was taping a show for WSTV, that wine and spirits cable network, in front of a live audience in Pittsburgh."

"Oh, I love that channel!" Lynda said.

"Surely her alibi is irrelevant," Mac observed. "I presume we already know she was not among the crowd in the gallery last night. That is of no consequence. The media have been replete lately with stories of people attempting to hire hit men to deal with their spouses. Apparently that is cheaper than divorce."

"That's true enough," Oscar said. "But these two were already divorced, and according to Steele she was getting a decent monthly alimony check from Calder that just got cut off. If that checks out, she doesn't seem to have much of a motive."

"Then who does?" I said. "That's what we were talking about a few minutes ago, Oscar. Who benefits?" Then I had a brainstorm. "Why don't we look at it this way: What's changed by Thurston Calder being dead?"

I thought that was clever, if I do say so myself, until Lynda responded, "For one thing, he for sure won't get to be head of the art department at St. Benignus."

She had uttered two words I didn't want to hear in connection with the murder—"Saint" and "Benignus."

"Maybe I'm being selfish," I said, "but I'd really rather this has nothing to do with the college."

"Good luck with that, Jeff." Lynda's gold-flecked brown eyes looked bright over her coffee cup. "St. Benignus was Calder's only connection to Erin."

"Not exactly," Oscar said, beating me to it. "Rosalie Hawthorne invited him to the party where he was killed.

She knew him from some national arts committee they were on together."

"Rosalie wouldn't harm a fly even if it were in her Marvini," Kate said. "Maybe there was something else Calder was going to do here that got prevented by his death—give a lecture, or meet with somebody, something like that."

"If so," Oscar said, "we'll find out eventually. Somebody will know. Or it will be recorded on his calendar."

"I presume the next step is another round of interviews with those among last night's guests most likely to know or to have seen something that did not surface in the first round," Mac said.

"Bingo. I also want to make sure we didn't miss anybody the first time." The chief reached into the side pocket of his coat and pulled out a spiral-bound book, about six inches by five, with ruled pages. "You might recognize this as the guest book you signed when you came in. I borrowed it from Mrs. Hawthorne. It took us half the night, but we talked to everybody in this book. I want you to look at the names and see if you can remember anybody being there last night whose name doesn't show up."

He handed it to Lynda and me, the closest to him.

With Lynda looking over my shoulder, I quickly ran down a list of familiar names, people whose faces I had seen last night—Fr. Pirelli, Lafcadio Figg, Adam Mendenhall, Josiah Gamble, Amy Quong, Trixie LaBelle, Tony Lampwicke, Sister Mary Margaret Malone . . .

"Who the heck is Reginald J. Smith?" Lynda asked, putting her finger on the name.

"Better known as 'Scrappy,'" Oscar said.

"Oh, sure," Lynda said. "I never knew his first name. Well, he seems more like a Scrappy than a Reginald."

"He's earned the nickname, all right. Scrappy's the most entertaining of all my frequent guests at the lockup, but for his sake I wish he'd stop getting into fights. One of these days he's going to lay into the wrong person."

"Well, that did not happen last night," Mac said. "Justin was obviously quite shaken by their contretemps. Surely Scrappy cannot be a serious suspect, either—a killer would hardly call attention to himself or to the missing corkscrew that turned out to be the murder weapon."

"Isn't that just what a clever killer would want us to think?" I suggested.

Oscar snorted. "Only in one of Mac's books." The look on his face showed what he thought of my cleverness—and Mac's.

"Wait a minute," Lynda said. "We don't know exactly when the murder took place, but it could have been during that little set-to with Justin. That's a very convenient distraction."

Oscar regarded Lynda. They had not always gotten along during his first year in town, when she had been news editor of *The Erin Observer & News-Ledger*, but that hatchet had been long since buried. "So, Teal, you think maybe the killer somehow caused Scrappy to yell at the bartender?"

My beloved shrugged. "I'm just throwing it out there."

Oscar sipped his coffee. "Well, I'm not sure that Scrappy ever needed an excuse to start a fight, but it's worth asking him about. We'll start looking for him. He moves around a lot." Translation: Scrappy had no permanent address, i.e., was homeless, apparently by choice.

Looking through the guest list, we noticed that several names of attendees were missing, but they were all folks that Oscar's people had talked to. Frank Woodford hadn't bothered to sign in, for example.

"I've already debriefed him," Lynda said, "but he didn't hold anything back from the readers. It's all in his story, everything he saw."

That led to a discussion about which of the eighty-seven attendees should be contacted again.

"Justin was rather shaken up last night," Mac observed. "Perhaps in a day or two he will remember more. In light of our history, I would like to be the one to talk to him."

Their "history" included Mac's efforts to save Justin from a murder rap, and then hypnotizing him to get some key information after Justin had almost been killed himself. As a side project, Mac—a champion cigar smoker—had also helped the young man kick the cigarette habit.

"I'll talk to O'Neill," I volunteered. "He might know some gossip that would be helpful." *Like whether he'd killed Calder, for one thing.* "Hey, I should talk to Popcorn, too. Maybe she saw something while she was watching the doors but it didn't register with her last night."

Oscar studied the guest book, not looking up. "I'll ask her."

"I'll see her at work in the morning. You don't have to make a special trip—"

"I won't. We're having dinner together tonight. Like I said, Mom won't be home."

Mac raised an eyebrow, and rightly so. I'd often thought I detected sparks between my diminutive administrative assistant, a widow with a penchant for steamy romance novels, and Oscar Hummel, a life-long bachelor. They were about the same age. *Go for it, Oscar!* Kate and Lynda exchanged sisterly woman-looks.

My brother-in-law cleared his throat and changed the subject. "Lillian Peacock not only found the body, she may have been one of the last persons to talk to Thurston Calder before the murder. Jeff and I overheard him lecturing her on her own painting style not long before the murder. Certainly she is worth a second interview."

Oscar slammed the guest book shut. "Okay, then, let's have at it."

IV

Lillian and Beryl Peacock lived in a brick Cape Cod home on Lindner Street about two miles from downtown. Beryl had grown up in the Chicago area, moved in with her grandmother while she attended St. Benignus, and stayed on after graduation while casting a wide net elsewhere for a job in the art field.

Lynda and Kate had elected to stay behind at the house on Half Moon Street. I regretted their decision when Beryl opened the door and I saw the look on her face as she beheld the all-male trio of the police chief, Mac, and me on her doorstep.

"What's wrong?" she said. "Has something else happened?"

Beryl looked like a frightened bunny rabbit, although I've never seen a rabbit in a tie-dyed T-shirt that looked like it was old in 1970. Her blue eyes were wide behind her rimless spectacles. With her strawberry blond hair pulled off her high forehead and braided, she looked too young to be out of college. She wasn't wearing makeup.

"No, no, nothing new," Oscar assured her hastily. "We'd just like to talk to Mrs. Peacock."

"Grandma's upstairs lying down. She's still very upset by what happened last night. But come on in."

The door opened into a cozy living room, with a quilt above the mantle and a watercolor of a sunflower field moving in the breeze on the opposite wall. The sunflowers looked very professional, but I'd have bet it was one of her grandmother's paintings. We sat down in matching wicker chairs.

"She's been so upset by what happened," Beryl said, "and I feel awful. She didn't want to show her paintings, but I pushed for it. Ever since I was little I've loved Grandma's art. It inspired me. So when Ms. Hawthorne was talking about starting her gallery and a show of women's art, I thought of Grandma." She shook her head. "If I hadn't talked her into it, she wouldn't have found—"

"It's not your fault, child." Lillian Peacock stood on the staircase, her thin frame almost lost in a fluffy bathrobe. "You didn't kill that man. I insist that you not feel guilty about it."

She finished descending the stairs. Oscar, Mac, and I stood up and each said something soothing and meaningless. Mrs. Peacock joined her granddaughter on the sofa. Again I was struck by the similarity of their features. Their eyes, for example, were the same shade of cornflower blue. But Mrs. Peacock must have been in her seventies, with cottony white hair. She reminded me of Miss Marple. *Maybe she can solve this case!*

"So why have you gentlemen come to visit an old lady?" she asked, although she must have known.

"We just want to ask a few follow-up questions about last night," Oscar said.

"I don't know what else I can tell you. I haven't thought of anything that might help. You said to call you if I thought of anything I forgot to mention, but I haven't. Not that I've been thinking about last night. In fact, I've been trying hard not to."

"That is quite understandable," Mac said. "Our intrusion is unforgiveable. However, it is also unavoidable. Jefferson and I observed you in conversation with Thurston Calder not long before you found his body. You may have been the last person to talk with him, other than the murderer." Lillian shivered slightly and drew her fluffy robe around her more tightly. Her granddaughter hugged her.

"May I ask what you talked about?" Mac said.

"Talked about? Why, art, I suppose. What else would we talk about? It was an art show. I didn't know the man, you understand."

"You were in front of one of your paintings," I prodded. "He must have said something about it." *Actually,*

I know that he did because I heard him, but I don't want to admit that I was eavesdropping.

"Oh, yes, I remember now. He made it clear in no uncertain terms that he didn't think much of my work. I wasn't surprised. I'm sure my perspective was flawed and my composition hopeless. Heavens, I'm no artist. I have no training whatsoever. I've never taken a class or even watched one on PBS. I just picked up a brush." Beryl started to say something, but her grandmother glared at her. "It was very kind of Beryl to suggest that I exhibit my work, but I was foolish to let her talk me into it."

That wrapped up Mac's questions, but Oscar wasn't finished. "Let's go through the finding of the body again," he said, "just so I'm clear."

A day after the murder, Lillian Peacock could still barely get the words out as she described her utter shock at the grisly horror that lay in the alcove in front of the restrooms. Just watching her relive the moment was hard. By the end, tears were streaming down her wrinkled face. She buried her head in Beryl's shoulder.

"I'm sorry we had to do this, Mrs. Peacock," Oscar said. "I hope we won't have to trouble you again."

V

"How was dinner?" I asked Popcorn when I got to work the next morning.

"Oh, fine. I love meat loaf and mashed potatoes."

So that's how we're going to play it. All right, Popcorn. If you don't want to talk about your date with Oscar, I'm not going to pry. Just how long has this been going on?

Popcorn followed me into my office with a cup of decaf coffee. She put the coffee on my desk and sat in the chair in front of me. Her blond hair looked freshly dyed and

I hadn't seen the white pantsuit before. *Primping for Oscar?* "Want to hear some gossip?" she said.

"Am I allowed to say no?"

"No. Thurston Calder wrote an extremely nasty review of Dr. O'Neill's book, *Walt in Daliland: How Walt Disney and Salvador Dali Changed Each Other.* He called it, quote, 'simplistic, naïve, and uncritical to the point of fawning over his two right-wing subjects,' unquote." *Well, that was clear.* "The review appeared in *The Atlantic* and got a lot of attention."

I lifted my eyebrows as I sipped the java. "You surprise me, Popcorn. I didn't know you read *The Atlantic.*"

"Not on a bet, Boss. Shirley Diebold told me. Dr. O'Neill's admin. She likes him and she's hoping he gets to strike the 'interim' off his job title. After Shirley found that review in an online search, she was worried that Calder would get the job. She thought he'd make Dr. O'Neill's life hell. So she's glad that Calder's—" Popcorn stopped dead. "I mean, she's glad he's no longer in competition."

Well, that was interesting. "Since you're so connected with Shirley, why don't you see if she can set up an appointment for me with O'Neill as soon as possible?"

"Sure. What shall I say it's about?"

"Let him use his imagination on that."

Later that morning, Lynda sent me a text saying that the *Observer* was desperate for new angles on the murder to keep the story on life support. *Good luck,* I texted back. Today's *Observer* piece, hastily written on Sunday by news editor Bernard J. Silverstein, was mostly a "Who Was Thurston Calder?" kind of story, with a few unmemorable quotes from the chief and Dante Peter O'Neill. The investigation of the crime was ongoing, and ditto the search for a new art department head.

Popcorn managed to get me an appointment with O'Neill at eleven o'clock. I was outside his office about five minutes early and he motioned me in. Defying every stereotype of the messy artist, the place was about as chaotic as O'Neill's pinstriped suit, rep tie, and button-down collar.

"I know why you're here," he said as I sat down. *You do?* "I realize I shouldn't have talked to the newspaper without clearing it through you, Jeff. But it seemed harmless to acknowledge to the paper that Calder was a candidate for department head and that the search process continues despite this tragedy."

I dismissed his concern with a gracious wave. "Your comments were fine. But what *didn't* you say?"

O'Neill allowed himself a half-smile, a wordless admission that he hadn't volunteered anything to Ben Silverstein in their weekend phone conversation. "Calder was one of three finalists. It's within the discretion of the search committee to reconsider one of the formerly rejected applicants if they aren't happy with the remaining two."

"Do you think they will?"

Hands up. "That would be pure speculation on my part."

"Okay, then, purely speculate."

"Well, my sources tell me that the committee will probably stick with the final two candidates."

"And you're one of them."

He nodded. "I have that honor. My interest in keeping this position has been no secret on campus from the day I was appointed as interim head. I'm sure you know that."

He was buttering me up, but I didn't deduct any points for that.

"Tell me about the other hopeful." Although I'd known about the search for a new art department head from day one, I hadn't focused on the details until now.

"She's a very strong candidate—Dr. Sheila Dunfrey. Dr. Dunfrey works at a very small college in Maine, even smaller than St. Benignus, but she's published a lot and is very well known in the field both as an artist and as an academician. She's teaching in Italy this semester."

"Are you sure she's there right now?" I said. "I mean, she's not off for some Italian holiday or something?"

"I spoke to her this morning to inform her about the situation here and she mentioned having a class tomorrow." He frowned. "Of course, I was talking to her on a cell phone. In theory, she could have been down the street for all I know. You don't think—"

"No, I don't." I smiled. "That would be a bit far-fetched. But I read a lot of mysteries, and I've written a few, too. That sometimes makes my mind go in devious directions that probably don't mean anything. For instance, I can't help remembering that you seemed awfully sure on Saturday night that you would never work for Thurston Calder. Those were pretty much your exact words."

O'Neill regarded me through his horn-rimmed glasses. Somehow it felt like he was getting taller than ever even though he didn't move from his chair. I'm going to avoid the temptation to say he assumed an air of injured dignity, because he wasn't assuming anything; it was the genuine article.

"I wasn't posturing," he said. "I meant it. Confidentially, Jeff, I've had an offer from my alma mater to assume an endowed professorship at DAAP. I'd rather stay here at St. Benignus if I can remain department head and move the program forward, but if not . . ." He shrugged. "Well, the offer was a very generous one. Even without it, though, I wouldn't have stayed if Calder had become department head. I suppose I shouldn't speak ill of the dead, but I simply had no respect for the man."

"Was that because of his charming personality or because of his poison-pen reviews—including the one he wrote about your Disney-Dalí book?"

O'Neill was either puzzled or a very good actor. His eyebrows wrinkled behind the horn-rims. "What?"

"I was referring to Calder's scathing review of *Walt in Daliland* that was published in *The Atlantic.*"

The young academic shook his head. "If I read it, I don't remember. I pay very little attention to negative reviews. Frankly, I find negativity a drain on creativity." *Hey, that's good—even though it sounds like a line in a rap song.* "No, it had nothing to do with that. Calder was thoroughly unsuited for any college campus, but especially a faith-based institution."

I stared at him blankly, trying to read between the lines when I couldn't even find the lines.

"Let's not be coy, Jeff. I refer to the reason for his hasty exit from the Warhol Art Institute."

"His book on Andy Warhol?"

"Hardly." O'Neill emitted a grim chuckle. "I assumed you knew. Calder was forced to leave the Institute because of a tawdry affair with one of his students, a nineteen-year-old female. Apparently the Institute only avoided a sexual harassment lawsuit by reaching an out-of-court settlement. The business cost Calder his marriage as well as his job."

This sounded like one of those romance novels by Rosamund DeLacey that Popcorn is always reading. It could even have some bearing on the case, I thought. "How much of this is guesswork or gossip?"

"None of it. Check *The Chronicle of Higher Education* around the time Calder departed the Institute. It's all there. The story even mentioned the financial settlement, albeit without naming a dollar amount." O'Neill turned his chair slightly to look out the window at the trees instead of at me. "Gossip, on the other hand, would be if I told you that this wasn't an isolated incident and that Calder had a reputation for dalliances with young women."

"Well, I'm sure you wouldn't want to spread gossip, and I certainly wouldn't want to hear it. If all this was so public, how did Calder ever wind up as a finalist for head of our art department?"

"That's an excellent question, but you'll have to ask the provost."

"Ralph?" I'm sure the name came out as an incredulous gasp.

O'Neill nodded. "I understand from someone who would know that Dr. Pendergast insisted to the search committee that Calder be among the final three."

VI

Ralph Pendergast, provost and academic vice president of St. Benignus College, has been the bane of my existence—and Mac's—since his arrival on campus two years ago with a mandate to tighten up the ship. He hates bad publicity and my brother-in-law's high-profile antics, especially when said shenanigans involve murder. Ralph seems to find homicide, however remotely connected to the college, just plain unseemly. Not surprisingly, he has closer ties to the board of trustees and to the business community than to the faculty or staff of St. Benignus.

So I was turning over in my mind the news that Ralph had essentially forced Thurston Calder on the search committee, wondering if this mess contained a silver lining, when I got back to my office and found a surprising visitor waiting for me.

Lesley Saylor-Mackie was sitting in the stuffed chair in front of Popcorn's desk, chatting away with my administrative assistant as if they were old friends. Maybe they were, but Saylor-Mackie had never been in my office before. She was professionally dressed in a blue pinstriped suit set off by a simple red pin and an equally red Bakelite bracelet like the one that I'd seen in an antique store recently priced at three hundred bucks.

She rose from her chair and we exchanged banal greetings.

"Who are you this morning," I said when that was out of the way, "Mayor Saylor-Mackie or Professor Saylor-Mackie, head of the history department?" Town and gown get along well in Erin, so the two titles aren't usually in conflict. Still, I thought it would be good to get straight at the beginning whether this was a professional visit or a political one.

"I wanted to talk to you about a press release."

Professional, then.

"You've come to the right place, Professor."

We moved into my office. Instead of sitting behind my desk, I sat in a chair facing her. In about sixty seconds flat I figured out that the press release she wanted—about an upcoming lecture on James Rankin and the Underground Railroad—was all smoke and mirrors. This was the kind of thing I handled routinely without a personal visit from the head of the history department. I nodded politely, made reassuring comments about my ability to get the job done, and waited for her to come to the real reason she'd dropped by.

"Thanks very much for your help," she said finally. Now I was watching her hazel eyes and they told me she was about to spring it. "Well, I guess you've been very involved with the murder."

"I'm afraid so," I acknowledged. "There was a St. Benignus connection." Talking without saying anything is a real art, and I'm pretty good at it. I watch *Meet the Press* for pointers.

She cleared her throat. You'd think that a politician would be better at what she was about to pull. "Yes, and that's so unfortunate. How lamentable that Dr. Pendergast chose to bring Thurston Calder to campus."

It was coming into focus now. Apparently the rumors that Professor Saylor-Mackie would like to add another title in front of her name—Provost—were on the money. She was trying to undercut the current occupant of that post by tying him to the Calder murder.

"You mean unfortunate because he got himself killed? That's hardly Ralph's fault." *Wait a minute! Is that really me I hear defending Ralph?*

"Of course not," Her Honor said dismissively. "But he should have known about the scandal following Calder. It seems that young women were not safe around that man. Due diligence would have turned that up."

"How did you happen to know about Ralph's involvement and Calder's amorous adventures, if you don't mind my asking? Art isn't your department." It hadn't bothered me quite so much that O'Neill knew this and I didn't, but I was put out that the stately Lesley Saylor-Mackie was up on the gossip that had eluded me.

She smiled. "Let's just say I have friends."

The way she said it made me want to be sure that I was one of them. This was not a woman I wanted to be on the outs with.

VII

It was time to compare notes with Mac. On the way over to his crowded office at Herbert Hall, I mentally prepared myself for the possibility that he already knew that Ralph had pushed for Calder and that Calder had been a cad with young ladies. *Why* shouldn't *I be the last to know everything? I'm only the public relations director.*

The dragon at the gate—that would be Mac's officious administrative assistant, Heidi Guildenstern—was nowhere in sight, so I just walked in on him.

He was sitting behind his desk, which was piled high with papers as usual, smoking a cigar and reading a book called *How to Read Lips for Fun and Profit*. The air was thick with illegal smoke from his Fuente Fuente Opus X. Without wasting my precious (and threatened) breath on a health lecture, I opened a window.

"I've been hard at work on this case, talking to witnesses all morning, and you're sitting on your rear end cozied up with a book on lip reading?" I suppose Mac might have called my tone accusatory.

He looked up. "I am increasing my skill set. When I found this book in an antiques store in New Albany, Indiana, I was immediately persuaded by the back cover that reading lips could come in handy for eavesdropping at a distance."

With a sigh, he closed the book, took off his reading glasses, and gave me his full attention. "However, your implication that I have been otherwise idle is quite unfounded, I assure you. I interviewed Justin at length, and I am convinced that he saw nothing. The simplest explanation, and therefore the most likely, is that he was absent from the scene when the corkscrew was taken. Or else he was simply too absorbed in the task of pouring wine to notice. Obviously, the killer would have taken pains to be sure that the corkscrew was not under observation when he or she stole it. I also spoke with Lenore Gamble on the off chance that her perch playing the harp in the corner might have afforded her a view of Calder stepping into the alcove with someone. Unfortunately, she was absorbed in her music making and not looking in that direction. As a musician myself, I completely understand."

"You're not a musician," I snapped. "You play the bloody bagpipes." The tarantula-like instrument in question lay flopped over a file cabinet. "So the bottom line here is that you didn't come up with anything. I sure hope Oscar is doing better with Scrappy. "

"It is true that my inquiries were not productive except in a negative sense. What have you learned?"

"For one thing, I found out that our mayor has talons that I've never seen unsheathed before. I guess Ralph brings out the worst in everybody. But let me give it to you in chronological order."

I did so, starting with my unsuccessful attempt to ply Popcorn for details about her date with Oscar. Mac couldn't complain later that I'd left anything out.

"Well, this is interesting indeed," Mac said at the end of my report. He smoked meditatively, exhaling the pungent smoke. I stuck my head out the window and breathed deeply in silent protest. "Ralph's involvement certainly adds a level of irony if nothing else," Mac went on, ignoring me. I knew what he meant. Ralph always acted as if we were constantly creating situations in which people got killed and St. Benignus was involved so that negative publicity followed. Well, actually, we did do that. But this time Ralph was the one who had had a major hand in bringing the victim to campus. "You need to confront him and find out what was behind his sudden interest in the art department. It is quite out of character for Ralph."

"Don't be so sure about that," I said. "Remember, I once ran into him at Beans & Books on jazz night and he was really into the music. Who knows what he thinks about the fine arts? He might surprise you."

Ralph disdained the popular culture department, which Mac headed, considering it not sufficiently serious and academic. But I'd never heard him hold forth on the arts one way or the other. For all I knew, he could be the world's greatest fan of paintings by 1970s terrorists.

"And why do *I* need to confront him?" I added. "He hates me."

"He hates me more."

You win! "Okay, I'll see if I can get an appointment today. But please don't tell me this is the best lead we've got." I kept hoping that Mac would pull a rabbit out of his hat, solve the murder, and get this story off the front page of the *Observer & News-Ledger* quickly.

"I would not be so pessimistic as to say that." Mac sat back and regarded his cigar thoughtfully. "Perhaps Oscar's interview with Scrappy will turn up something interesting. And yet . . . I have a nagging feeling that we have already been pointed in the right direction and somehow missed the arrow."

VIII

Going to Ralph's office in the Gamble Building was a surreal experience. I'd never made that trip before. He'd always come to my office or called me on the phone, and it had never been a social call or a good experience. Ralph had long labored under the much mistaken notion that I had personal influence over every news story published or broadcast about St. Benignus. Therefore, any such report that was less than positive—and he was a tough grader on that—had to be my fault. He thought this even before I married Lynda and even before she became editorial director of Grier Ohio NewsGroup.

Now that I thought about it, it was kind of odd that Ralph wasn't already on my back about the Calder murder in his usual charming fashion.

"Yes, what is it, Cody? I have another appointment in fifteen minutes." He turned away from his computer, a look of only mild annoyance crossing his face. With his slicked-back dark hair and rimless glasses, Ralph looks a bit like Dennis the Menace's father—never mind that he has a personality more like the grumpy neighbor, Mr. Wilson.

But I wasn't looking at him. I was gaping at his digs. In an era of budget cuts for which he was the chief advocate, Ralph had equipped his office handsomely with walnut bookshelves, hardwood floors covered with thick rugs, and a handsome wood desk approximately the size of an aircraft carrier. It made the modest office of "Father Joe" Pirelli, the legendary and much-loved president of St. Benignus, look like a tarpaper shack.

With great effort, I pulled myself back to the subject that had brought me there. "I think we may have a problem."

Ralph emitted the sigh of the long-suffering servant. "*We* usually do when you and McCabe are involved. I presume this is about the murder of Professor Calder. Well, I must say I'm glad you're on it."

Did I hear that right? And if so, was it sarcasm?

"It's not the murder, Ralph." He hates it when Mac and I call him Ralph. I sat down, invading his space. "I mean, the murder didn't happen on campus, Calder wasn't yet employed by the college, and there's no reason at this point to believe that St. Benignus was involved in his death at all. What I'm worried about is that some enterprising reporter working on a profile of the victim might find out that he left the Warhol Institute under the cloud of scandal."

"Oh, I see." Ralph blanched. "I didn't know about that until it was too late. By the time Dr. O'Neill called that unfortunate situation to my attention, Dr. Calder had already been short-listed. We had to go through with the interview, but I assure you that he was no longer a serious candidate."

"That may be, but the problem is that he was ever a candidate at all."

"I told you I didn't know!"

"Why not? It was reported in *The Chronicle of Higher Education*." *As if you ever read it.* "And that means it would turn up in a half-way competent Internet search, the kind some reporter is going to do." Ben Silverstein, a good newshound, had already written that quick Monday morning profile of Calder without touching on the scandal. But if he or another journalist decided to probe deeper, they would strike gold. I shuddered to think what Sylvester Link, the aggressive reporter for our student newspaper, *The Spectator*, could do with it.

Like a politician in a debate, Ralph ignored my point and went on the counter-attack. "Surely that distasteful business at Warhol can't have anything to do with Calder's murder!"

The way his voice rose in pitch and loudness almost made me feel an unfamiliar twinge of sympathy for the provost. But I shook my head. "Actually, we don't know that at all, Ralph. He could have been killed by a former lover, an angry parent, who knows. But that's beside the point. The fact that our proudly Catholic college was even considering a man of his rep for a position, well, it just doesn't look good."

Ralph stared at a set of fountain pens on his desk before he said, "I know we've had our differences, Cody"— *like Cain and Abel had a spot of sibling rivalry*—"but I hope you can put that aside for the good of the college and do what you can to prevent the media from playing up this angle."

I felt like throwing something. Why could I never make him understand how it works? "There's no way to control something like this, Ralph. The best I can do is try to get ahead of it—be prepared to react or maybe even take a pre-emptive strike against bad news. And if I'm going to have any chance of that, I have to have all the information. So level with me, why were you so hell-bent on Thurston Calder making the cut for the art department headship?"

"I wasn't." He paused, as if considering how much to tell me. "A good friend of St. Benignus felt strongly that he deserved serious consideration."

"Are you going to tell me who, or are you going to make me guess?"

For a minute he looked like he was going to resist, then gave it up. "Oh, very well. It was Mrs. Hawthorne."

Actually, I *could* have guessed. Rosalie Hawthorne knew Calder and she'd invited him to her gallery opening. I didn't even need Ralph to remind me that her father, Josiah Gamble, was on the St. Benignus board of trustees and that the building in which we were sitting had been named after her great-grandfather. She was in the top tier of the local gentry and the St. Benignus alumni—the folks that Ralph had been cultivating ever since the trustees had hired him.

"In that case, I'm sure you realize I'll have to talk to her again."

The protest I was expecting didn't happen.

"You can do that right here," Ralph said. "She's my next appointment. I believe she has some other thoughts on the search process."

Come into my parlor . . .

At first I was surprised at this generous gesture of accommodation. But then I saw what Ralph was up to. If I interviewed Rosalie in front of him, he could stay in the loop and possibly head off any embarrassing statements she might be inclined to make. So it was a bit of a devil's bargain I was being offered, but I decided to take it. There was something in it for me, too: This way, I got to talk to her before Ralph briefed her on our conversation. Forewarned is forearmed and all that. "Thanks. I'll try to keep it brief."

Ralph grunted.

The next few moments were awkward. I was out of questions for Ralph and he'd been out of small talk since the day he was born. But Rosalie was on time, wearing round sunglasses with white frames on her head and a smaller, rectangular pair of regular glasses on her nose. She'd dressed up a bit for her trip to campus, wearing khaki slacks and black pumps. Her auburn hair was pulled back and tied with a red bow.

"Jeff! What a surprise!" From her body language, it didn't seem to be an unpleasant one. I was her friend Kate's brother, never mind that she'd last seen me when Mac, Oscar, and I were asking her questions on the night of the recent unpleasantness.

"We were just talking about Thurston Calder," I explained.

"Poor Thurston. Such a tragedy! What else is there to say?"

I'm glad you asked. "A car accident is a tragedy," I said. "This was murder. On the surface it looks like a crime of opportunity, a spur-of-the-moment thing, but maybe it wasn't." That was something I'd been thinking about. "Maybe the killer planned the murder in advance, but used the corkscrew to make it seem unplanned. Who else knew that Calder was coming that night?"

"Whoever he told, I guess, and whoever they told. I only mentioned it to the artists, but it wasn't a secret. I suppose dozens of people might have known."

So, no help there. I moved on. "I gather from Dr. Pendergast that you were really interested in seeing Calder become head of the art department here."

"I sure was!" She sat down with ease, as if she were used to pulling up a chair and shooting the breeze with old Ralph. "Thurston was fab. He wouldn't have been popular, but he would have brought some attention to the department."

Oh, I'm sure of that—on both counts.

"Did you know that he was terminated at Warhol for an unethical relationship with a student?"

She waved her hands airily. "Oh, well, artistic temperament, you know. One must make allowances. Look at van Gogh."

I'd rather not, thanks.

"As for him not being popular," I plowed on, "have you thought of anybody who might want to kill Calder?"

She chuckled. "Probably just about everybody whose art he ever reviewed. He was a tough critic with a sharp tongue. But nobody would murder a person for that, would they?"

Thinking of Dante Peter O'Neill, I sure hoped not.

How much of this should I share with Lynda? That was a dilemma. When she was a working journalist, there'd always been a tension between her job and mine. That's one reason—though not the only one—that we'd dated for about four years, didn't date for four weeks (her idea), and semi-dated for about five months before we got engaged (her idea again). I know why Facebook has a relationship category called "It's Complicated." Eventually we worked it out that some things crossing my desk stayed at my desk, with no offense taken by my beloved newshound, and some things I told her on an "off the record at this time" basis.

Now, as editorial director of Grier Ohio NewsGroup, Lynda acts like a kind of circuit rider consulting on writing and reporting with all the Grier newspapers and television stations in the state. But she still has her office at *The Erin Observer & News-Ledger*, and it would be against the natural order of the journalist species for her not to pass on news tips to Frank Woodford and/or his troops. I didn't want her to do that with Thurston Calder's rascally reputation, but I was finding it harder not to share things with her now that we were married. Plus, maybe she would have some thoughts on where to go from here. Mac hadn't given me any new marching orders when I'd reported back to him.

"Can we go off the record?" I said as we carved a pumpkin for Halloween that evening at our tiny kitchen table.

She looked up from the pumpkin, curiosity on her oval face. Her fingernails were painted yellow, orange, and white to look like candy corn. "What did you find out?"

"Off the record?" I persisted.

"Yeah, yeah, the usual arrangement. The *Observer* gets the story first when you're ready to give it."

"That would be never, but your ace reporter might get this on her own if she does a little digging." I was thinking of Maggie Barton, the pink-haired septuagenarian on the St. Benignus beat. "It's about the reason Calder was forced to leave the Warhol Art Institute, and it had nothing to do with his book. There's some juicy St. Benignus campus politics involved, too."

I gave it to her more or less chronologically, taking her through my day with Dante Peter O'Neill, Lesley Saylor-Mackie, and Rosalie Hawthorne, just as I had earlier with Mac. She immediately saw the embarrassment to St. Benignus in Calder's background—and especially to Ralph—but she was more interested in the implications for the murder.

"So maybe Calder tried to put the moves on some young babe at the gallery," Lynda said. "She stabbed him in self-defense, and then panicked and ran when she realized she'd killed him."

"And she just happened to have stolen the corkscrew and had it on her when he got aggressive?"

"Oh, yeah, the corkscrew." Undaunted, Lynda thought a moment. "Okay, maybe it wasn't self-defense. But it still could have been a jilted lover or a jealous husband who killed him with malice aforethought. Or even an angry parent if he preferred student-age females. What did Mac say when you told him this?"

"Pretty much the same thing, but he used bigger words. He's going to pass the info on to Oscar as something to keep in mind when he circles back on the people who were at the gallery on Saturday."

Lynda held up her freshly carved jack-o'-lantern for me to admire, which I did. The smile looked deliciously evil, like Ralph Pendergast laying somebody off.

"It sounds like Rosalie Hawthorne was very forgiving of her friend Calder's romantic peccadilloes," Lynda said.

Before I could say that was part of Rosalie's pretention to open-mindedness, my cell started playing "You're So Vain." It was my new ringtone for Sebastian McCabe.

"I hope this is good news," I told Lynda as I picked up the phone.

It wasn't.

"I just received a call from Oscar," Mac said. "He and his men have been looking for Scrappy Smith all day in his usual haunts—the public library, the art museum, every bar in town. No one has seen him. It seems that he has disappeared."

IX

That was on Monday. By Wednesday, with Scrappy still missing, Mac had taken to muttering darkly that perhaps Scrappy was the hoary old cliché of the Man Who Knew Too Much and had to be eliminated. In other words, maybe he'd actually seen something and tried to blackmail the killer, who responded with extreme prejudice. That began to seem more and more likely as the days passed and Scrappy didn't turn up.

Oscar's official line was that the investigation was moving forward, but I didn't see how. The only thing new was the coroner's autopsy report, which confirmed that the corkscrew had been jabbed through Calder's eye in an upward motion that carried it into his brain.

"If the killer was jabbing upward, then he must have been shorter than Calder," I told Mac with some excitement. That would narrow the suspect list considerably because Calder was only of medium height.

"By no means, old boy," Mac said, "although it may indicate that the killer knew what he or she was doing. Going through the eye socket, an upward thrust is necessary to reach the brain no matter the height of the attacker. A downward stroke would only damage the eye and sinus cavity."

I bet he Googled that.

Life went on and the murder became background noise. Maggie Barton wrote a follow-up story about the search continuing for a new art department head in the wake of the murder, accompanied by a brief "murder investigation continues" sidebar by young Johanna Rawls, and then dropped it. For a couple of days I was tied up on a crisis involving the St. Benignus La Crosse coach. One night, while on a road trip to Boston, he had too much to drink. So he called a cab—good move. But he got into a fight with the driver—bad move. On that story I was dealing with ESPN and *The Boston Globe* as well as Maggie, who is easily the most energetic septuagenarian I know. Even that skydiving accident hadn't kept her down for long.

I'd just hung up after a conversation with Maggie, in fact, when I received a text message from Mac:

Meet me ASAP at Shinkle.

Grinding my teeth at Mac's assumption that I was always at his beck and call, which especially irritated me because it was true, I told Popcorn where I was going on the way out of my office.

The Shinkle Museum of Art is a wonderful old brick and stone building on Front Street with turrets and towers. A nineteenth-century Cincinnati pork baron named Nicodemus Shinkle had built it as his twenty-room country home. Decades later, his great-granddaughter had created a foundation to which she had gifted the house for use as an art museum.

Mac was outside the museum, pacing and smoking a cigar.

"What's up?" I demanded.

"I have an idea." *That's great! Or a disaster. It could go either way.* "This morning at home, looking at Calder's books and at the guest book from the opening, I suddenly saw a possible link between them: Adam Mendenhall—art museum—art fraud."

Calder's last book had been about forgeries donated to a large number of art museums. And Adam Mendenhall, director of the Shinkle Museum of Art, had been among the gallery crowd on the night of the murder.

"So your theory—"

"I do not have a theory, old boy, only a nascent idea. However, I must say that all along I have had the feeling that the solution to the murder was within our grasp. Perhaps we now stand on the verge of unveiling it. I thought you would be interested."

In other words, he thinks I'm his Watson and he wanted me on hand to record another triumph of Sebastian McCabe. Well, he asked for it.

Mac knew Mendenhall through Kate, who was a docent at the Shinkle. He explained this to a skeptical receptionist at the front desk. After a brief phone conversation, she told us we could see the director right away. She pointed to his office down a hallway.

Mendenhall was a little younger than me, mid-thirties, about Mac's height of five-ten or so with longish brown hair. He was wearing a pink bow tie with matching suspenders and a white shirt with the sleeves rolled up. That made two too many bow ties in the room so far as I was concerned; I've seldom seen Mac wear any other kind of neckwear, although never pink. The energy that Mendenhall had brought to the Shinkle with his arrival three years ago was much on display as he came out from behind his white, kidney-shaped desk, pumped our hands, and asked what he could do for us.

"Perhaps nothing, Adam, but one has hopes," said Mac. "I noticed that you were at the Looney Ladies Gallery on Saturday."

Mendenhall's smiling face turned solemn. "I'll never forget it."

"Had you met Thurston Calder before that night?"

"Why, yes. He was here on Friday, as a matter of fact. He came to look at our collection and he asked to see me."

"And did he by any chance suggest that a work of art in your collection was fraudulent?"

The wide-eyed look of surprise on Mendenhall's boyish face would have done Roger Rabbit proud. "Wow, you really are a detective, Mac—and a magician! That's exactly what happened. Calder claimed the Andy Warhol in our Pop Art collection wasn't genuine. He wasn't particularly nice about it, either."

What a surprise.

"And how did you react?" Mac asked.

"With great skepticism, as you might imagine. The piece is on loan from the Cleveland Art Museum, a fine institution. But I figured Calder should know something about Warhol since he wrote a book about him, so I called Cleveland right away. They said they'd send somebody down to look at it, but nobody's shown up yet. I guess we're not high on their priorities. Say, you don't think that had anything to do with his murder, do you?"

"Most probably not," Mac said in a low voice.

As we walked down the front steps of the Shinkle a few minutes later, he told me what he'd been thinking: "Hiding an art fraud might be an excellent murder motive for Adam. According to his easily verifiable testimony, however, he did not try to hide the fraud—if there was one. Rather, he immediately alerted more competent authorities of the possible problem. Ergo, he had no motive."

Mac seemed more ready to give up on his own theory than I was.

"Maybe Mendenhall's call to Cleveland alerted somebody else that Calder was a threat," I said. "This could be about a lot more than one painting here in Erin. The guy that Calder wrote his last book about scammed a whole bunch of museums."

"That is certainly a reasonable speculation, except for one flaw," Mac said gloomily. "In that event surely Mendenhall would have been silenced as well as Calder. No, Jefferson, I am afraid my theory simply won't wash." He stuck a cigar in his mouth and lit up.

Sebastian McCabe in defeat is not a pretty sight.

X

A couple of days a week Lynda and I manage to grab lunch together. Thursday was one of those days. We ducked into Beans & Books, the combination coffee house and used bookstore. It's the kind of place where the server asks if you need a menu. Most people say no.

"So what's new today in the world of spin and half-truths?" Lynda asked as we waited for a server.

"Why ask me? You're the one who works in the news business."

And so forth.

"Hi, guys." I looked up to see Beryl Peacock wiping an errant strand of strawberry blond hair off of her high forehead. She'd waited on me maybe fifty times while she was in college and since graduation, but somehow she was a different person now that I'd been in her house talking to her grandmother about the dead body she'd found. I asked Beryl how the older woman was doing.

Beryl shook her head. "I'm not sure she'll ever really be the same, Mr. Cody. She's not as old as she looks but she's kind of frail. And now she seems, I don't know, nervous all the time and kind of distant. I'm getting worried about what happens if I get a job out of town. My parents don't see her all that often and my grandfather died when Dad was little."

"She's such a sweet lady," Lynda said.

Beryl took our orders—Caffeine-Free Diet Coke and a low-fat tuna salad sandwich for me, Mountain Dew and a bowl of chili for Lynda. *No French fries with the chili?* She hadn't been married to me half a year yet and Lynda was already becoming a health-food fanatic by her standards.

She watched as Beryl hustled away with the order. "She's a cute kid."

"Oh, really? I hadn't noticed."

"You're married, Jeff, not dead. You noticed."

Okay, I noticed. "Is there a point to this?"

"Just that I bet Thurston Calder noticed, too."

Within a few minutes Beryl brought us our drinks. "Here you go!"

"Thanks, Beryl," Lynda said. "I've been wondering something. We've learned that Thurston Calder was quite a ladies' man. Did you happen to see him talking to any young women that night at the gallery?"

"No, I don't think so. I really wasn't looking at him. We never met."

"So he didn't, for instance, come on to you?"

"Of course not!" Beryl fled.

"What do you think?" I asked Lynda.

"I really don't know. Maybe she was just embarrassed at being asked the question. But I'm still wondering."

That evening after work, I barely had time to drop my briefcase on the floor and start wondering when Lynda would be home when the doorbell rang. I was startled to see

Lillian Peacock standing at the door. She was wearing a blue housedress, about the same cornflower shade as her eyes and Beryl's. It contrasted nicely with her pure white hair.

"May I come in, Mr. Cody? I'd like to talk with you about the murder."

"You'd be most welcome, Mrs. Peacock, but I think it would be a better idea if we go next door and see Professor McCabe. Whatever you have to say, I'm sure he'd like to hear it."

Her eyebrows knitted together. "You live next door to your brother-in-law?"

That's when I realized it was time for Lynda and me to move out of Mac's carriage house that had been my bachelor pad. We needed our own place. I would still pedal my bicycle to work, though; that was a non-negotiable.

"It's just temporary," I said hastily. "Let's go see Mac."

A few minutes later we were sitting by a fire in the McCabe study.

Lillian Peacock sat primly with her hands folded on her lap. "I came to see Mr. Cody because I'm concerned about my granddaughter. You were asking Beryl some questions about Thurston Calder. Surely you can't suspect her of some involvement in that awful murder?"

She stared straight at me, blue eyes piercing. I wanted to fall through the floor. *Technically, Lynda was the one asking the questions. I just happened to be there.*

Mac also looked at me, quizzically. I hadn't told him about our talk with Beryl because there wasn't much to tell.

"We've been asking a lot of people a lot of questions, Mrs. Peacock," I said. "Mr. Calder had a reputation for pursuing young women. Lynda and I were trying to establish whether he brought that habit with him to Erin. If he did, that could be significant."

"I see. So you suspect a crime of passion?"

"There certainly seems to have been some passion involved in the delivery of the blow," Mac observed.

Lillian Peacock nodded. "I see that, but still . . ." Her eyes fell on the three Calder books that lay on the coffee table. "Mr. Calder wrote that book about art fraud. I read about that in *The Erin Observer*. Perhaps he became aware of something like that here in Erin."

Miss Marple on the case!

A dark cloud passed over Mac's face as he recalled the fiasco in Adam Mendenhall's office. "I can assure you, Mrs. Peacock, that possibility has been explored to no avail."

"Oh, well, it was just a thought. I'm no detective. At any rate, I'm quite sure Beryl didn't know that man, Mr. Calder."

When Mac's cell phone burst out with its *Ride of the Valkyries* ringtone, it seemed like a reprieve.

"Yes? When? Where? We shall be right there. Thank you for calling."

He disconnected and returned the phone to his sport coat pocket. "That was Oscar. One of his officers found Scrappy Smith."

I felt the hair rise on the back of my neck. "Dead?"

"On the contrary, old boy. It is Scrappy's good fortune and ours that he is still alive and apparently as pugnacious as ever. I suspect that we are not far from a solution to the murder of Thurston Calder."

XI

Scrappy had changed jackets, but his clothier appeared to be the same—the St. Vincent de Paul store. With his beard growing out he looked closer to seventy than sixty this evening, but I still wouldn't want him to hit me— which he looked like he wanted to do.

"He's been staying at the presidential suite in the Harridan," Oscar said, naming one of Erin's two elegant old hostelries. "He paid cash in advance."

"Where did you get that kind of money?" I blurted out.

"From the ATM machine, moron," Scrappy retorted. "Where does anybody get cash these days? What century are you living in?"

"Naturally," said Oscar, "I was a bit suspicious. It's never been entirely clear to me how Scrappy makes a living."

"I'm retired, Barney."

"Well, that could be," the chief allowed. "But the fact is, I was suspicious. So I ran his prints. It turns out our friend here is actually Mr. Reginald Fortesque III, who disappeared from upstate, the Canton area, about five years ago."

"And what heinous crime did he commit that caused him to pull this vanishing act?" Mac rumbled.

"I won the damned Ohio lottery," Scrappy said gloomily. "Sixteen and a half million dollars."

"Scrappy Smith," homeless and belligerent, was actually a millionaire? *We're not in Kansas anymore, Toto.*

"I know it sounds like a crock, but it's actually true," Oscar said. "I checked."

"If you didn't do anything wrong," I said to Scrappy, "then why use the phony moniker?"

"It's my pen name, not that it's any of your business."

"Pen name?" Mac perked up. "What do you write?"

"Graffiti."

Oscar poured himself a cup of coffee from the pot behind his desk before offering the caffeinated concoction all around. We declined. "Let's take this from the top. Explain yourself, Mr. Fortesque."

"I don't have to explain myself to you or to anybody else." He pointed at himself. "I'm a free man, see? I always have been, always will be."

"You're as free as any other witness in a murder investigation. You want to call in a lawyer?"

Knowing Oscar, I'm sure he only asked because he was confident of the answer.

"Hell, no, I don't want a lawyer! I hate lawyers."

"Then talk."

"Oh, all right, all right. Crap! It's like this: Do you know what happens when you win big in the lottery? Your name and your mug are all over the newspapers and TV for days. All of a sudden you got friends you never knew you had, relatives you never even suspected. And they all want something from you. You'd be amazed at how many jackpot winners are bankrupt a few years later. You can look it up. The dumbest thing I ever did was buy that lottery ticket. I was perfectly happy as a barber."

Maybe that's why his haircut looked self-administered.

"So you left Canton and changed your name," I said. "Why didn't you just give the money away to charity?"

"That's one of the easiest ways to go bankrupt! Happens all the time, believe me. So, you see, I'm stuck. I don't want the money, but I'm afraid to get rid of it. So I keep it; I just don't use it. But I think maybe I've been making a mistake. I kind of like the Harridan."

Better than the homeless shelter or Oscar's lockup? There's a surprise.

"I believe that brings us up to date on your life story," Mac said. "However, there is still the matter of Thurston Calder's murder."

"I had nothing to do with that!"

"Oh, yeah?" Oscar said. "We think you might have been arguing with Justin Bird, creating a big hullabaloo that got everybody's attention, right when somebody was shoving a corkscrew into Calder's brain by way of his eye. Heck of a coincidence, don't you think?"

Reginald J. Fortesque III just shrugged.

"Let me be more blunt than the chief," Mac said. "Did someone ask, bribe, cajole, intimidate, coerce, or otherwise induce you to start a fight with the bartender?"

Scrappy jumped up. "I don't know what half those words mean, but I know my rights. There wasn't any damned fight—I was just defending my rights and nobody told me to do it."

Life, liberty, and a free glass of wine . . .

Mac sighed. "Well, it was a thought."

"I've got my own thought on this caper," Scrappy said, sitting down again.

"Like what?" Oscar's broad face was full of skepticism.

"I think the murder was what they call performance art. Somebody was making a statement. Maybe it was a feminist thing. 'Art in the Blood' was an all-woman show, you know."

I didn't want to think about that, so I found my mind wandering instead to the first time I saw Scrappy that night at the gallery. He was talking to somebody . . . the man I later learned was Thurston Calder.

"What did you and Calder talk about at the opening?" I asked.

"Oh, he was raving about some paintings of flowers. He was full of crap, though. They were okay, but not the hot stuff he claimed. I spend enough time at the Shinkle to know better."

"Those are Lillian Peacock's paintings," Mac said. "Jeff and I saw Calder later talking to Mrs. Peacock about them. He was commenting on the brushstrokes . . . the brushstrokes! Hell and damnation, I have been a fool! Scrappy, are you absolutely sure his comments about those paintings were so admiring?"

"I heard what I heard! He was gaga over them. What difference does it make?"

"All the difference in the world, I am sorry to say." Mac stood up. "I know who killed Thurston Calder and why."

XII

Mac was in a grumpy mood, hardly saying a word to Oscar and me, all the way to the house on Lindner Street. He muttered something about "perspective," but I didn't catch it and he wouldn't repeat it.

Evening had closed in and the front porch light of the Peacock house was on. Mac rang the bell. I had a moment of déjà vu as Beryl Peacock opened the door and Mac said we were there to see her grandmother.

"She went to bed early," Beryl said with a hint of exasperation. "Can't this wait until tomorrow?"

"I am afraid not," Mac said. "We are concerned about Mrs. Peacock. Please wake her up."

Beryl went upstairs, something in Mac's tone prompting her to take the steps two at a time. Two minutes later, she was back, a frantic look on her face.

"Something's wrong! I can't wake her."

While Oscar and Mac charged up the stairs, I whipped out my phone and called 911.

"You expected this, didn't you?" I said to Mac as we sat at St. Hildegard of Bingen Hospital waiting for word on Lillian Peacock's condition. The early betting was that she had taken an overdose of sleeping pills.

"I expected something."

"You don't mean that Beryl—"

He looked at me as if I had three heads. "Certainly not. Mrs. Peacock tried to kill herself—just as surely as she stabbed Thurston Calder to death."

Maybe you saw that coming, but I was a mile behind. Even now I didn't get it, and neither did Oscar. "She killed Calder?" the chief said. "How do you figure that?"

"It all came together for me when Scrappy insisted that Calder was so enthusiastic about her paintings. You will recall that she had told us exactly the opposite. She lied, and it was a lie too small to be insignificant."

"That's it?" I said. "That's all you've got? That wasn't a real lie; she was just being modest."

"No, Jefferson. She was quite adamant, well beyond the traditional protestations of modesty. She did not want us to know that the normally negative Calder was quite taken by her paintings. And no, that is not all I have."

"Wait a minute," Oscar protested. "Are you saying she killed the man because he liked her paintings? Hell's bells!"

"Not because he *liked* them Oscar, but because he *recognized* them. Jefferson and I overheard Calder saying the brushstrokes reminded him of something. I am quite sure they reminded him of her earlier work."

Before he could say more, an even paler than usual Beryl Peacock came into the waiting room.

"Grandma's conscious," she said. "I told her that you were here and she asked me to send you in. But she wants me to stay out here. What the hell is going on?"

"I am sorry, Beryl," Mac said. "That is not for us to say. I assume that your grandmother will want to speak with you in a few minutes."

Lillian Peacock's face was almost as white as her hair and the sheets of the hospital bed. Her blue eyes looked about a hundred years old, and sad. She didn't waste time.

"How much do you know?" she asked Mac.

"I know the following," he said. "Your real name is LaDonna McQueen. You were once an urban terrorist. You have been a fugitive from justice for more than forty years. And five days ago you murdered Thurston Calder to keep that secret."

She turned her head away from Mac and looked at the ceiling. "I'm not LaDonna McQueen, but I used to be. She was a woman who fell in love with the wrong man and the wrong cause. She died a long time ago, when I came here with Beryl's father and got the job in the flower shop. Who would look for LaDonna McQueen in Erin, Ohio? I told people I was a widow, and that was close enough. My lover was caught, went to prison. Maybe he was the lucky one. He did his time and moved on while I was still looking behind me all the time. Last I heard he owned a health food store in Kansas."

Her voice faded away.

"Eventually, however, you forgot about being on the run," Mac said. "You became comfortable in Erin."

"That's right. Oh, I got really scared a few years back when Calder's book came out—scared and proud both. But when nobody outside of an elite artsy crowd paid it any attention, I thought I was really home free, that nobody cared any more. And then Calder came to Erin. If I'd known that was going to happen I never would have let Beryl talk me into exhibiting the oils and watercolors I'd been doing for my own enjoyment.

"Calder recognized my technique. He didn't think right then in the gallery that it was actually my work, just a similar style. I knew he would figure it out someday, though. I panicked. I picked up that corkscrew when I saw that nobody was looking. And as soon as Calder wasn't talking to someone, I asked him to come with me to that little alcove."

She closed her eyes. "Then I did what I'd learned how to do years ago, in a manual, but I'd never done before. I did it for Beryl, you know. I mean, I didn't want her to ever know who I had been, before I became who I am."

XIII

"I honestly think she was more upset about facing Beryl than about being arrested," I told Kate and Lynda later that night in Mac's study. "That's why she tried to kill herself."

Beryl had turned out to be more resilient than her grandmother expected, however. She'd already hired Erica Slade to mount Lillian's defense. Erin's most prominent criminal defense lawyer, who is also not coincidentally the county prosecutor's ex-wife, was probably in Oscar's face right now despite the lateness of the hour.

Mac, standing at his bar, tapped himself a beer. "Doubtless you have realized that one of Thurston Calder's books held the solution to his murder after all—that one." He nodded toward *LaDonna McQueen: Her Violent Life and Vigorous Art*, still sitting on the coffee table where Kate had left it on Sunday. "It was right there when Lillian came earlier this evening. I believe that was the impetus for her suicide attempt: She saw the book and became convinced that someone else would eventually expose her identity."

Lynda sipped her Manhattan. "Did you really figure out the whole thing just from Calder admiring Lillian's painting and from knowing about his LaDonna McQueen book?"

"There were a few other indications," Mac said. "For example, Lillian told another lie. She said that she had never been trained as an artist. In fact, in an effort to distance herself as far as possible from her background as an art teacher, she overreached and claimed that she had never so much as watched an art instruction program on television. And yet, in describing her own deficiencies she talked in terms of perspective and composition. Those may not necessarily be art-school graduate terms, but they do indicate a level of knowledge she earnestly wished us to believe she did not have."

"She also 'found' the body," I pointed out, "and Mac and I saw her near the bar when Calder was looking at her paintings, which wasn't long before Scrappy threw his temper tantrum because the corkscrew was missing." *No flies on me . . . now.*

"It still seems like quite a stretch to me," Kate said with a yawn. "I think you just got lucky."

Mac quaffed the last of his second mug of beer. "Let us say, rather, that I made an intuitive leap that took me to the correct solution on what may seem to be thin evidence. I make such leaps all the time when I am writing a mystery novel, connecting characters and incidents in ways that I never foresaw in the plotting stages. I never know where it comes from. Perhaps intuition involved in the solution of a mystery is actually deduction carried on at the subconscious level. For example, my subconscious may have taken a cue from the story of Scrappy Smith, another person who came to our community under false colors.

"You look skeptical, Jefferson. Well, I don't insist upon it. In fact, there is another possibility that I find even more satisfying. Sherlock Holmes at the dawn of his career talked about the science of deduction. In later years, he referred to the art of detection. Perhaps my ability to create fictional crimes and solve real ones is simply another case of art in the blood taking the strangest forms. My mother was once a rather well known soap opera actress, you know."

THE REVENGERS

"Mrs. Peel, we're needed."

My feeble attempt at a suave British accent sounded lame even to me.

Undaunted, I considered myself in the hallway mirror of our apartment: Bowler hat, rakishly cocked. *Check.* Edwardian suit. *Check.* Black umbrella, full-size, not the kind that fits in a pocket. *Check.*

I was ready for an "Avengers" night, all right. I just had no idea then what that would involve. By the end of the evening my beloved wife and I would be nearly blown up, but it was almost worth it to see Sebastian McCabe pull off one of the neatest bits of deduction in his sleuthing career. Almost.

Enigmatic smile. *Check.*

Okay, I didn't actually look like the debonair John Steed, what with my red hair and all. But at least most of the other guests at the party would know who I was supposed to be, especially since I would be accompanied by—

The bathroom door flew open, propelled by the kick of a long, well-formed leg. Lynda Teal—known as Mrs. Cody here at home and in several other places—burst into the hallway flinging body parts with the skill of the taekwondo master that she is.

She was wearing a shoulder-length auburn wig over her curly honey-blond hair and a black leather catsuit over her shapely body. The suit was the sort of tight-fitting garment with lots of pockets and zippers that I always associate with Mrs. Peel, although she sometimes wore much softer outfits on the late 1960s TV show.

When Lynda paused to catch her breath, I moved in for a husbandly kiss.

"Very nice outfit," I murmured appreciatively. "I'm glad you talked me into the Steed and Mrs. Peel gig."

Originally, when Maureen Russert invited us to the party, I'd thought of dressing in an outfit more reflective of my own tastes. That had been about two weeks earlier as I was prowling the mystery shelves of Pages Gone By, the used bookstore on High Street where Mo works as a clerk and dreams of starting her own shop devoted to mysteries.

"Hey, Jeff, I want you and Lynda to come to my Halloween costume party." Mo has a few years on me, putting her north of forty, but she doesn't look it with her freckles and dark bangs. She also dresses young, on this particular day wearing a pumpkin-colored blouse, black slacks, high-heeled boots, and a chocolate scarf.

"I'm too handsome to be a vampire," I objected.

"You don't need to be," she said, totally ignoring the opportunity to agree with me. "The theme is TV detectives. You'd be perfect as Monk."

What do you mean by that? I had no idea what she meant by that.

"And you'll know most of the people there—Mac, Chief Hummel, Serena Mason, Fred Gaffe, Sister Polly . . ." This laundry list went on until she got to my sister and my administrative assistant.

"Am I the last to be invited?"

"Actually, you're one of the first. I've only mentioned it so far to friends and customers I happened to see. The invitations go out today. But I'm sure most of them will come."

That Sebastian McCabe would go I had no doubt. The chance to hold forth as a Great Detective would be too perfect an opportunity for my brother-in-law—professor, magician, mystery writer, and amateur sleuth of some experience—to pass up. But which detective? Mac was too rotund and too bearded to credibly assume the iconic deerstalker and pipe of his hero, Sherlock Holmes. He'd once shaved to portray Mycroft Holmes in a play, but he couldn't diet himself down to Sherlockian proportions by Halloween—if ever.

"Isn't your apartment kind of small for a party of that size, Mo?" *Or even for Mac by himself?*

"Yeah, but it isn't going to be at my apartment. We're having it at Jonathan's new place, a great atmosphere for Halloween." I was fast enough to pick up that she meant Jonathan Hawes, of Hawes & Holder Funeral Home on Market Street, which had just acquired a big old river captain's house outside of town for a second location. But my face must have shown that I didn't get the connection to Mo, because she quickly added, "We're dating."

"Oh! I see. Well, I hope it works out. He's a nice guy." How's that for a clever response? My etiquette book is missing the pages that explain how I was supposed to react to such news from a sort-of former flame. Mo is a divorcée, thanks to Arthur Bancroft Russert being a total jerk who traded her in for a younger model. A common interest in mysteries had brought Mo and me together for a few casual dates during a period when Lynda had given me my walking papers. But that was almost two years ago, and the walking papers had since been traded in for a marriage license. I barely remembered that Mo and I had dated, and I certainly never thought about it. But still—

"So are you," Mo said, snapping my mind back to the present. A nice guy, she meant. It seems her taste in men is good. "The party is Saturday, October 27."

"Unless my bride has something else planned for us, we'll be there."

I brought up the subject the next morning as Lynda and I were working out at Nouveau Shape, the fitness center not far from my office. After a few chuckles and totally unwarranted comments about Mo's suggestion that I come as the obsessive-compulsive and multi-phobic TV sleuth Adrian Monk ("How will they tell that you're not just being you?"), she said a Halloween party sounded like fun. Then we got down to the serious business of discussing our costumes.

"I want to be Mike Hammer," I said.

Lynda shook her blond curls as she lifted a barbell. "I don't think so." Her husky voice showed no strain from the exercise. I was breaking out in a sweat watching her, but that had nothing to do with the shape I'm in. It had to do with the shape *she's* in.

"Why not?"

"Because I think we should be Steed and Mrs. Peel. We could call ourselves 'The Revengers.' You'd make an adorable Steed."

Adorable. Oh, well, sure. If you put it that way . . .

I was familiar with the old British TV series *The Avengers*, not to be confused with the Marvel Comics superheroes of the same name, because it was one of Lynda's favorites. She'd brought her boxed DVD set of all fifty-one episodes featuring Emma Peel to our marriage.

"But you're too curvy to be Mrs. Peel," I objected, studying the evidence.

"I can fix that."

"Don't!"

I don't really remember ever agreeing to Lynda's costume suggestion, but somehow I wound up buying an umbrella and a bowler hat at the St. Vincent de Paul store in downtown Erin. Lynda bought her catsuit online. Standing in the hallway of our apartment, I admired it again in some detail.

"We'd better go," Lynda said.

"Are you sure we can't—"

"Yes. I'm sure. We can't." She punctuated the end of each sentence with a kiss. Talk about mixed messages!

"Mac still won't tell me who he's coming as," I said as I slipped into the passenger's seat of Lynda's bright yellow Mustang. My sister, Kate, was teaming up with Sister Mary Margaret Malone (AKA Triple M or Sister Polly) and Mo Russert to be Charlie's Angels, so that was no clue as to what identity her husband would be assuming. He could hardly be Charlie, the disembodied voice, and he would never settle for being the second banana on the show, Bosley.

"I hear that Lafcadio Figg is coming as Nero Wolfe, so that's out," Lynda said, buckling her seat belt.

Or maybe not. I smiled at the thought of those two peacocks both showing up in yellow shirts as Nero Wolfe. The subtle fireworks would make quite a show.

The way out to the new Hawes & Holder Funeral Home location seemed a bit creepy to me that fall evening. Our car was the only one on the road most of the way. Houses were far apart, and most of them dark.

"Half of these old homes look abandoned," Lynda commented.

"Probably not half, but there have been a lot of foreclosures out here in the country, just like in town. The good news for us is that home prices and interest rates are a real bargain right now."

We'd already decided to buy a home, but hadn't moved into the shopping phase yet. I was still mapping out our strategy for that.

"Look!" Lynda pointed down the road about a hundred yards on the right. A figure in green scrubs and a surgical mask was waving to us like mad. It had seemed to come out of nowhere. The effect was a little eerie in the gathering gloom. "I bet it's somebody going to our party. Who do you think he's supposed to be—Quincy? House?"

She put on her turn signal and slowed the car.

"You're going to stop?"

"Of course I am. It has to be somebody we know."

"Yeah, like maybe the Grim Reaper."

Even in the limited light I could see Lynda roll her eyes. "This is Erin, Jeff, not New York City. You aren't afraid to pick up somebody in trouble, are you?"

Now that you mention it . . . "No, I'm not afraid. I'm just cautious. And that's not a bad thing."

"No, it's not, but for a guy who's been through a lot of adventures, you're not very adventurous."

That's because I've been through a lot of adventures.

By this time Lynda had stopped the car. Dr. Whoever wordlessly climbed into the back seat. I was just about to turn around and see whom we had here when I felt something press against my neck, followed by a strange feeling that went through my whole body. My muscles seized up. I couldn't move and I tingled all over, not a fun tingle but more like what you'd expect if you stuck a wet finger into an electric socket. Then I felt a needle in my neck. Then nothing.

I woke up on the floor of a dark, empty house, my brains replaced with cobwebs. Disoriented, it took me a while to remember the first part of the evening—assuming it was the same day. Judging by the darkness outside the dirty windows, I was pretty sure that it was.

Lynda! My panic lasted only about two seconds. Looking around, I quickly saw that she was right next to me on a wicker couch, the only furniture in the room. But she was tied up. At first I thought she was bound in place with rope. On closer inspection, I realized that wrapped around her were several plastic-covered cables with a combination lock on the end, similar to what I use to secure my bicycle when I park in town. Why was she shackled like that? And since she was, why wasn't I?

"Welcome back," Lynda said, stretching her neck to peer down at me. "Thank God you're okay. I was afraid you were—"

"I'm fine. How about you?"

"Slightly embarrassed and very pissed."

"What the hell happened?"

"Dr. Grim Reaper tasered us, then injected us with something to put us to sleep."

"Tasered!"

"Absolutely. I was tasered once for a story when I was a reporter, so I know what it feels like."

I won't say I warned you not to pick that guy up.

"You warned me, Jeff. This is all my fault."

"No it isn't. It's the fault of the whack job who did this." I looked around the empty room. "I bet this house is in foreclosure. Our masked doctor must have broken into the place."

Lynda shook her bewigged head in puzzlement, a very limited range of motion because of the chains around her. "We know some crazy people, but we don't know anybody crazy enough to pull a stupid joke like this. Do we?"

"I don't think it's a joke, Lyn." While we had been talking, I'd noticed two things: An envelope lying on her stomach, tucked under a cable, and something attached to the wicker couch behind Lynda's head. I rolled over to get a closer look.

"I don't believe this," I muttered. But my body believed it, because I was starting to get warm and I was shaking. I breathed deeply to steady myself.

"What? What is it? What's wrong?"

"I've never seen a stick of dynamite in person, but I think there's one locked to the couch. It's wired to a small electronic alarm clock and a battery." I stuck my face up close. *Oh, crap.* "We've been out a couple of hours, Lyn. It's about nine-forty. And it looks like the alarm is set for ten o'clock."

"Thank God your hands are free to turn the alarm off."

How to put this delicately? "I don't think that should be our first option. Defusing a bomb is not something I want to try to learn on the job."

"Call 9-1-1."

I reached into my pocket. It was empty. "My iPhone's gone." *Now I'm really mad.*

"Run and get help."

I shook my head. "I'm not leaving you. Besides, I presume we're still in the country. We could be quite a distance from the nearest house. I don't know where your car is and I don't think I should waste time looking."

Lynda doesn't usually use the kind of language that came out of her pretty mouth at that point, but I can't say I blamed her.

She started wriggling her body, which in normal circumstances would have been fun to watch, but didn't do much good. "This is . . . just so . . . bizarre."

"Like an *Avengers* plot," I agreed. Looking back now, I can see the blessing of that. The total unreality of the situation staved off total panic. I removed the envelope tucked between Lynda's stomach and the cable binding her to the couch. "I suspect that this will tell us what's going on here."

Later, I realized I should have held the envelope with a handkerchief and slit it open with my Swiss Army Knife to preserve any fingerprints. Instead, I ripped open the envelope and quickly scanned the typed message, unsigned.

It was a poem:

How do I loathe thee? Let me count the ways.
I loathe thee to the depth and breadth and height
My soul can reach, when feeling out of sight
For the ends of Being and ideal Grace.
I loathe thee to the level of everyday's
Most quiet need, by sun and candle-light.
I loathe thee freely, as men strive for Right;
I loathe thee purely, as they turn from Praise.
I loathe thee with a passion put to use
In my old griefs, and with my childhood's faith.
I loathe thee with a loathe I seemed to lose
With my lost saints, -- I loathe thee with the breath,
Smiles, tears, of all my life! --- and, if God choose,
I shall but loathe thee better after death.

"That doesn't tell us much," I said. "We already knew that somebody doesn't like you—which I find hard to believe, by the way."

"Thanks, but it also tells me that our nutball is not very creative. That's a straight rip-off from Elizabeth Barrett Browning's famous poem, 'How do I love thee,' with 'love' changed to 'loathe' throughout."

"I thought it sounded familiar."

"Who do I know—oh!"

"What?"

"Do you remember Pete Duffy?"

"Refresh my memory."

"All of this happened shortly before you and I met, so it must have been about seven years ago. It was a story that I covered for the *Observer & News-Ledger* as a reporter. Pete Duffy was an eleventh-grade English teacher at Malcolm C. Cotton High School. He was having an affair with one of his students, a girl named Kathleen Bell. I remember that she was a pretty girl and smart, but very romantic. She was into Jane Austen novels. Pete used to send her love poems that were recycled from Mrs.

Browning's *Sonnets from the Portuguese.* Somebody—I always
suspected it was the football player that Kathy dumped for
Pete—found out what was going on and told her parents.
They went to the police."

This was sounding vaguely familiar. "There wasn't a
trial, was there?"

"No, Pete copped a plea so Kathy wouldn't have to
testify. I forget the length of the sentence, but the
prosecutor made it clear in public statements that he drove
a hard bargain because Pete showed no remorse at all in
interviews with me. I wrote a whole series—three stories, I
think. He was obviously still obsessed with the poor kid,
and full of himself to boot. His attorney thought it would be
a good idea to talk with me to show that he wasn't a pervert,
just a guy who happened to fall in love with and seduce an
underage student. The attorney was way wrong.

"The Bell family left town to put all this behind
them, even though Pete went to prison."

"I bet he isn't there anymore." I picked up the
combination lock. Just like mine, it had letters instead of
numbers. I started spinning them. "He's out and looking for
revenge on you. And he left this little love letter so you'd
know who's behind it before the bomb goes off."

"What are you doing?"

"The combination to this lock is five letters. Given
the unimaginative nature of our friend, I'm sure that it's the
name of his young lady love." I clicked in the Y of KATHY
and tugged. The lock didn't give. I said a bad word.

"Pete called her Kate in his letters," Lynda said. "It
was a pet name kind of thing." That kind of creeped me out
because Kate is my sister's name, but I gave it a try.

KATEB
BKATE
KATIE
KBELL
BELLK

No dice.

Damn! I'd been so sure. Despair settled on me. I was afraid to look at my watch. How would Mac solve this? He'd probably remember some Sherlock Holmes story that would provide a big clue. That was no help.

"*His* name!" Lynda shouted. "Try the name of his true love—himself."

I quickly moved the letters on the combination lock to PETED. *Nothing.* DPETE. *Nothing.*

"What was her pet name for him?"

"Peter."

"How original."

PETER

Click.

The lock opened. I shouted something inarticulate. Despite trembling hands—chalk it up to fear and excitement both—I had the other two locks off within seconds. Lynda stood up awkwardly, wobbling a bit on her stiff legs.

"Thanks."

I grabbed her hand and we started running. The house was set well back from the road. When we finally reached the pavement, we looked back. Lynda's Mustang was parked in the driveway on the side of the house. We stood in silence for a while, breathing a little hard and holding on to each other. Did we dare go back for the car? I didn't think so.

I looked at my watch: ten o'clock.

After another couple of minutes, I ventured, "Maybe after all that it was just a—"

The boom sounded more like a firecracker from where we were standing. It didn't take down the house and it didn't even shake the Mustang, but it was a real explosion. The bank would need to have at least a few rooms remodeled before they could sell the place. If we'd still been inside at the time we'd have been killed.

"No," Lynda said, "it wasn't just a joke."

Having no access to a cell phone and not knowing how many doors we'd have to knock on to find somebody home, we decided to go to Mo and Jonathan's party to report our near-death experience. Oscar Hummel, Erin's police chief, would be among the guests. And so would Mac. The GPS gizmo plugged into the Mustang, which has spoken with an English accent ever since shortly after we returned from London, got us there in about five minutes.

The old mansion that in a few weeks would become a funeral home was lit up and alive with noise. I felt warmer as we approached the front door.

Jonathan Hawes, the friendly undertaker, answered the door. Tall and lean, he looked right in the deerstalker cap and Inverness cape. Still, I thought it was a bit of a copout to wear his costume from the play *1895* in which he had starred as Sherlock Holmes. The deerstalker had been a big bone of contention between Lafcadio Figg, the director of the drama, and Sebastian McCabe, who wrote the play and co-starred as the smarter and lazier Holmes brother, Mycroft. Mac resisted the headgear because it was never mentioned in any story, but Figg insisted because it had been good enough for the actor William Gillette. Figg won.

"Where the hell have you been?" Hawes roared. His first drink of some adult beverage clearly had not been his last.

"Hell is exactly where we've been," Lynda said grimly.

She looked like it, with her wig askew and the catsuit somewhat the worse for all the wriggling she'd done in an attempt to slip her bonds. I didn't look like the cover of *GQ* myself, mind you. I'd found my bowler hat and umbrella in Lynda's car, but I was in no mood to dress for a party.

"What have you done with her, you beast?" Triple M yelled. But her perennially cheerful face fell when she saw us. I'm sure we didn't look like the jaunty Steed and Peel she'd been expecting for some time. Instead, our appearance must have reflected what our bodies and minds had been through over the past couple of hours.

Hawes got it. "Come on in."

Joining the party was like falling through a TV screen into The Mystery Channel, that cable network with all the old detective shows from the past sixty years. Some of the costumed guests were in the huge hallway, some in one of the rooms on either side of it. I'm sure there were also a few partiers in the kitchen where I couldn't see them.

Figg, as promised, was dressed as Nero Wolfe, with a yellow shirt and an orchid in his lapel. He had the figure for it, and he'd sacrificed his muttonchops for the sake of authenticity. My sister Kate's scarlet hair was teased like one of Charlie's Angels, but I'd never learned their names. Bob Tucker, the bald-headed principal of Malcolm C. Cotton High School, sucked on a lollipop as Kojak. Beth Bennet, a newcomer to town whom I'd run into a few times at Pages Gone By, wore a three-piece suit, a bow tie, a homburg, and a pointed mustache. She made a cute Hercule Poirot in the manner of the BBC productions with David Suchet, not the Peter Ustinov rendition.

Don't get the idea that I consciously made this inventory as soon as I stepped into the house. That didn't happen. Once in the door I looked around for Mac and Oscar. To my astonishment, Mac wheeled himself our way.

"There you are at last!" he thundered. "I was about to suggest a search party."

Lynda and I both stared at the wheelchair.

Mac, following our line of sight, answered our unasked question. "I am Robert T. Ironsides, Chief of Detectives, Retired, NBC, 1967 to 1975, television's most famous sleuth on wheels, not counting the car in *Knight Rider*." Mac spoke with some impatience, it seemed to me. *How was I supposed to know this trivia?* "I am quite certain he would have grown a beard eventually. Raymond Burr, the actor who played the part, did. And why, may I ask, are you two so late?"

"We've been tasered, drugged, kidnapped, and almost blown up," I snapped. "So I'm sorry we're late for the party." Mac is my best friend—has been for about twenty years— but once in a while I have to assert myself.

"Excellent!" he said. "You are obviously the Avengers, disheveled by your ordeal, and you have brought us a mystery suitable for a house full of detectives."

Sebastian McCabe's a genius, I'll admit that, but he was way behind everybody else on this one. Lynda had to spell it out for him.

"We're not just role-playing, dammit. Jeff just saved both our lives."

Hey, I guess I did at that.

Mac looked as if my bride had socked him in his considerable gut. "Indeed? That is most distressing!" Behind the beard, his broad face registered a combination of shock and concern, and maybe a measure of chagrin at misreading the situation. I hadn't seen Mac look so unnerved since Kate was abducted in London earlier that year. I bet he really needed a cigar just then.

"What happened?" Oscar Hummel was right behind Mac. "I mean, besides everything you said." He bit down on an unlit stogie. The thirty-year-old tan trench coat alone was enough to signal that Erin's top cop was Detective Lieutenant Columbo of the Los Angeles Police, never mind that Oscar was maybe fifty pounds too heavy for the part. He also wore a three-dollar wig of curly dark hair to cover his bald head.

Lynda put her arm around me. Now that the crisis was over and we were safe among friends, her body was trembling. "Can a girl get a drink first?" she asked Hawes. Her throaty voice was shaky.

"Bourbon if you've got it," I specified.

"I've got it." He left, cape flapping, before I could tell him to make it two, on the rocks. I don't drink alcohol very often, but tonight I needed something stronger than my usual Caffeine-Free Diet Coke.

"You'd better sit," Kate said, leading Lynda over to a sofa in what must have originally been a living room or parlor. By now partiers were drifting in from other rooms, murmuring quietly as if they were, well, at a funeral home.

Aneliese Pokorny (AKA Popcorn), my dyed-blond administrative assistant at St. Benignus College, had a look of concern that fit well with her role as Jessica Fletcher of *Murder, She Wrote*. Serena Mason, heiress and philanthropist, made an attractive Miss Marple—although she's a bit young, her hair still having a few dark streaks. Fred Gaffe, the white-haired author of the "Old Gaffer" column in *The Erin Observer & News-Ledger*, was just the right age for the septuagenarian (at least) private detective Barnaby Jones.

What I didn't see was anybody dressed in green scrubs.

"You have obviously had quite a shock, my dear Lynda," Mac said. *Oh, now it's obvious!* "If you are not ready to talk about it—"

Lynda shook her head. "No, we're ready. Oscar has to hear this."

"Damn right," the chief muttered.

With a considerable track record as an amateur sleuth, Mac occasionally needs reminding that Oscar represents official law enforcement in Erin.

Hawes came into the room with two glasses of brown liquid floating in ice. He gave one to Lynda and one to me, even though I hadn't asked for it. *You're a good man, Hawes. Remind me to see you for all my funeral needs.*

Lynda grabbed the glass as if it were a lifeline. She drank about half in a swallow. She didn't even ask what brand, a mark of just how shook up she was. "On our way here there was a hitchhiker dressed like a doctor in green scrubs. We figured it was somebody coming to this party."

With a journalist's eye for detail and the training to tell a story concisely, Lynda recounted our adventures of the evening. Before she even finished, Oscar called 9-1-1 to get the Fire Department to the house in the country. We'd had the presence of mind to get the address on our way out. By the time Lynda finished, Mac and everybody else knew just as much as I did. Even those who hadn't lived in Erin seven years ago were up to speed now on the backstory of the wayward English teacher.

"So there was a crime, but not exactly a mystery for you, Mac," Lynda said. "It had to be Pete Duffy."

If Mac was disappointed that he wouldn't be called on to play detective, that didn't last long. Hawes shook his head, looking professionally mournful. "That's not possible, Lynda."

"Parole boards—" I began.

"That's not what I mean. Pete died in prison about, oh, four months ago."

Silence.

I don't know what our friends were thinking, but I was getting ready to look around for Rod Serling. I mean, it was a *Twilight Zone* moment. Finally, Sebastian McCabe, bless him, stirred in his wheelchair to ask, "How do you know that, Jonathan?"

"Hawes & Holder handled the services," Hawes said. "The funeral was private with no public visitation. We didn't even place a death notice in the *Observer*. The family wanted to avoid any media attention at all." He ignored the darts Lynda shot him with her eyes over the bourbon glass. "Only family and a few close friends like Bob were there."

All eyes turned to bald Bob Tucker. He took his lollipop out of his mouth. "I guess as principal of Cotton High I shouldn't have gone to the funeral because of what he did. But I couldn't do that to Pete. We were friends from the time we both started teaching. His relationship with that student was totally unprofessional and immoral, as well as illegal. It was right that he paid the price. But he was still a human being, and he was still my friend."

"How did he die?" Mac asked.

"Stabbed," Hawes said curtly.

"Prison is a terrible place," Tucker said. "I visited him three or four times a year at first. I hadn't seen him in a while. I feel badly about that."

"You should," Fred Gaffe said coldly. "He asked about you all the time."

"You were also a friend of Duffy's?" Lynda asked. When she'd been news editor of *The Erin Observer & News-Ledger*, before she'd moved up the corporate ladder at Grier Ohio NewsGroup, Lynda had edited Gaffe's nostalgic column.

"Pete was my nephew—my late wife's actually. I can't believe this had anything at all to do with him."

"There has to be some kind of connection," I pointed out. "The combination to the lock that Lynda was tied up with was his name."

"*Eh, bien*, this must indeed be the deed of someone close to Monsieur Peter Duffy," Beth Bennet said, staying in character with a passable Poirot voice. She didn't seem to understand that the party was over and it was time to get serious. "It is to avenge his untimely death that this terrible thing has been done. Use the little grey cells, *mon ami.*"

"Indeed." Mac regarded her shrewdly.

"Maybe the combination on the lock was a red herring, a false clue," Gaffe said.

"That's not very likely," Oscar said, "given that the lock was supposed to blow up along with Lynda and Jeff." Oscar has a built-in bias against solutions that he considers "too cute" or overly complicated, the kind that show up in Mac's mystery novels. This time I thought his skepticism was well placed.

"If all of this is about revenge," Mo said, "why not kill Kathy's ex-boyfriend who presumably exposed the affair?"

"His family left town years ago, the summer after all that happened," Tucker said. "I remember because the boy was in my history class at the time. So maybe the would-be killer couldn't find him, or maybe he's next, or maybe he's already been done in. How would we know?" He sounded very depressed for a guy with a lollypop in his mouth.

"Let us not neglect the obvious," Mac said. "Sherlock Holmes never did. Lynda and Jefferson, think back on the costumed hitchhiker you picked up. How tall?"

"About average height," Lynda said. I concurred. Not much help there.

"Male or female?"

Lynda and I looked at each other. We'd been assuming male, but the costume covered almost everything and there was nothing telling in his or her movements.

"We don't know," I admitted.

Mac stroked his beard. "The androgynous costume was most likely no accident. That is in itself indicative. So is the fact that the assailant flagged you down on your way to this party. Surely it is a reasonable assumption that she knew about this party, and only slightly more adventurous to posit that she is here among us now?"

"Pfui," Lafcadio Figg retorted, using Nero Wolfe's favorite word. "She? You're grand-standing, Mac."

It wouldn't be the first time.

"There's nobody here in a costume like that," Mo pointed out. "That would mean this fruitcake changed clothes. Why do that when she—to use your pronoun—didn't expect Lynda and Jeff to be alive to make an identification based on the costume?"

Where others see a door, Mac sees a window—and climbs through it. "Because the perpetrator could hardly guarantee that no one else would see her near the scene.

Surely Oscar's men would make inquiries. Someone wearing green scrubs and a mask a mile or two away from the house where Jeff and Lynda were held might not go unnoticed even this close to Halloween."

"But why wear such a distinctive and easily remembered costume to begin with?" Lynda asked. "Most of us are dressed pretty simply with just a prop or two." *I'd certainly remember your costume, Lyn!*

"That, my dear Lynda, was the most crucial clue of all," Mac said. "Why wear a concealing costume unless the person behind that mask was afraid that if you saw her you might be either wary or so surprised that you would be fully engaged in talking to her, and therefore no easy victim?"

Oscar, a fat cigar between his first two fingers, scratched his wig. "Where is all this going, Mac?" He wasn't the only one who wondered.

But instead of moving ahead, Mac shifted into reverse. "Jefferson was right a while ago when he said the combination proves a connection to Pete Duffy, but it is not the kind of connection most of us would think of. The combination was PETER. Who called him Peter? None of his friends did—not Bob Tucker, not his Uncle Fred Gaffe. You heard them refer to him as 'Pete' tonight. So far as we know, only Kathy Bell referred to him by his proper name —Kathy Bell and you, Miss Bennet."

She was standing right beside his wheelchair. Her eyebrows shot up. I half expected her to say "*Alors!*" as Poirot often did. But she didn't say anything. Neither did anybody else for ten or fifteen seconds, which can seem like an eternity in a situation like that.

"So I don't use nicknames for people I don't know," she said finally, skipping the accent this time. "What's your point?"

"My point is that I am rather sure you did know him, and that is the reason you called him by what has been described as a 'pet name.' I find names quite interesting.

You prefer to be called Beth, invariably a shortened form of Elizabeth. Elizabeth Bennet is a rather famous name from the classic novel *Pride and Prejudice*, one well known to devotees of Jane Austen—such as Kathy Bell."

In one fluid movement, he stood from his wheelchair and pulled off both her hat and her pointed mustache.

"Kathy!" Bob Tucker cried. He almost swallowed his lollipop.

"Yes," Lynda said slowly. "She hasn't changed much. I saw her on the streets a few times back then, although her parents would never let me talk to her. I probably wouldn't have recognized her if I hadn't known that's who she was, but she couldn't know that for sure. That's why the scrubs when she flagged us down."

"There's nothing illegal about changing my name before I came back to this narrow-minded town," Kathy/Beth said. "And you can't prove I did anything else."

"We'll see about that," Oscar said. "There may be some physical evidence at what's left of the crime scene. I'd like you to come with me to answer a few questions."

I had my eye on the Poirot walking stick leaned against a wall behind Kathy Bell, alert for any quick movement in that direction. But she just crossed her arms over her flattened chest. "I'm not going anywhere or saying anything until I get a lawyer."

"May I recommend Erica Slade?" Mac said. "She revels in difficult cases."

"Well, we sure know how to throw a party, don't we, sweetie?" Mo Russert raised a glass of red wine to Jonathan Hawes and downed it.

It was past midnight. The McCabes, the Codys, and the lovebirds were the last holdouts, sitting around a coffee table. Lynda had removed her wig, giving free rein to her honey-blond curls. Mac was ready to do what he does best —quaff beer and fill in the blanks. But this time there wasn't much left to tell.

"The whole town, certainly including her parents, considered Kathy Bell a victim," he said. "But she didn't. She romanticized her relationship with Pete Duffy into a forbidden but genuine love, a perspective that apparently only grew through the years. And as it did, so did her bitterness at those involved in putting Duffy in jail. Perhaps she especially hated you for the stories you wrote, Lynda, because you were a woman."

Lynda wisely avoided commentary on Mac's amateur psychoanalysis and stuck to the facts. "I remember several widely reported cases around the country in recent years of female teachers who were convicted of having sex with a minor student, then resumed the relationship after serving prison time."

Instead of noting that I'd never been that fond of any of *my* female teachers, I said, "So after Pete Duffy died, she went totally round the bend and came back here hellbent on revenge. And Lynda was her number one target. She adopted a phony name and avoided people that she thought might recognize her."

Mac had beer in his mouth, so he just nodded.

"I must have told her that Lynda and Jeff were coming to the party, although I don't remember that," Mo said. "I do remember that she told me she was a nurse. That explains where she got the scrubs and the anesthesia or whatever sleep-inducing drug she used. But how could she become a nurse under an assumed name?"

"I think it more likely that she was a student nurse somewhere far from here under her real name," Mac said.

"And how and where did she get the explosives?" I wondered.

Mac shrugged. "We may never know, old boy."

"I'm worried about that old boyfriend who blew the whistle on Kathy and Duffy," Kate said, "but I'm sure Oscar will get on that."

"Poor Oscar," Hawes said. "He never got to say, 'Just one more thing, ma'am' like Columbo."

"He's probably saying it right now," I pointed out. "Besides, he'll get something even better—an arrest."

"Thanks to Ironsides here," my sister said.

Oh, puh-leeze.

Mac, still on wheels, attempted to look humble. That's not one of his best tricks. "There is in fiction the grand tradition of what is called the armchair detective. Perhaps it would not be going too far to say that I solved this case from a wheelchair."

SANTA CRIME

No one should be surprised that Sebastian McCabe was tapped to play Santa Claus for the Christmas party at Serenity House, Erin's premier social service agency. My brother-in-law weighs in at a few dozen pounds north of healthy and hides his triple chins under a beard, albeit an almost black one rather than white. Plus, he's just a big kid himself.

But I just couldn't see myself as one of his elves.

"I'm six-one," I reminded my wife unnecessarily. "You should do it."

And what a fetching elf she would make!

"I'm almost as tall as you are, Jeff." *Only when you're wearing heels, my beloved, like those three-inch Italian beauties you bought on our honeymoon. Which I like a lot!* "Besides, size doesn't matter," she went on. "Think of that movie. You know, the one about the tall elf. I forget the title. Listen, you only have to wear a hat. I'm not asking you to put on green tights. I know that would be too much for you."

Damned right!

Lynda reached across the table and took my hand. "Oh, come on, *tesoro mio*. Humor me."

It was hard not to, considering that it was December 1 and we were in the middle of celebrating the tenth anniversary of Lynda's twenty-first birthday. I'd brought her to dinner at Ricoletti's Ristorante, Erin's finest eatery and Lynda's favorite.

"Well, I know you're going to be busy helping Triple M that day," I conceded. "In the Christmas spirit, I'll do my part. How bad can it be?"

Remind me never to ask that question again.

Serenity House isn't really a house. It's a network of social services located in a number of different buildings. But one of those buildings is a house—a former mansion, in fact—located on Front Street. That's where the agency's annual Holiday Fest is held two Saturdays before Christmas. The craft show is a fundraiser where many clients of the agency sell their work while musicians and singers perform in the background. "Breakfast with Santa," served in a separate room, draws in families with kids. Harvey Duncan had played the Big Guy for years, but he was spending his winters in Florida now that he had retired from teaching. Mac, when asked, didn't even feign reluctance to don the red suit and pointy hat.

The place was in a happy uproar when I showed up about ten o'clock in the morning. Dozens of patrons in the holiday spirit talked loudly over the Christmas singers. Tables displaying locally produced crafts, from jewelry and Christmas ornaments to needlepoint and paintings, lined the sides of the mansion's former ballroom and ran down the middle as well.

"Hi, Jeff," yelled Triple M in her usual cheerful manner. Sister Mary Margaret Malone—Sister Polly to most people, just plain Polly to Lynda, and Triple M to me—had a *Star Trek* coffee mug in one hand and a scarf in the other, which she was waving. She also had two males and a female gathered around her, ranging in age from juvenile to old enough to know better. I sized them up immediately as lawbreakers assigned to do community service with Triple M in her capacity as Erin's volunteer jail chaplain.

One of the miscreants was an African-American teenager who looked like he should have been on a basketball court, one a young woman whose attitude problem could be spotted a mile away, and one a thirty-something guy in need of a shave. Dubbing them in my mind the Three Wise Guys, I wondered whether they wouldn't be more trouble than they were worth. I had no idea. Nevertheless, I knew that Triple M could handle them. Standing about five-six and wearing a denim skirt, chin-length dark hair parted in the middle, she hardly looked threatening. But she possessed both an air of authority and a black belt in taekwondo.

"Ho, ho, ho," I replied grumpily to her merry greeting.

"Why don't you just say 'Bah, humbug,' while you're at it?" said a familiar husky voice behind me.

"Okay. Bah, humbug."

This quick accession to Lynda's request did not meet with the approval that I had expected. She shoved a hat down over my eyes. I removed it quickly. This was just horseplay, of course. She couldn't possibly have been upset with me. I'd been tending to laundry and vacuuming back at our apartment like a good househusband for the past two hours while she'd been here helping Triple M and my sister Kate get the crafters set up. I must say she looked especially comely in that red turtleneck sweater with her dark honey curls sticking out of the Santa hat.

And she expected me to wear the goofy green elf headgear that she'd pulled over my eyes. I held it in front of her. "This doesn't fit."

"It fits perfectly, doesn't it, Nicholas?"

I hadn't noticed the boy next to Lynda. He was about twelve years old, but I only learned that later. He looked younger. His hair was about the same shade of red as mine. The other thing he had in common with me was the way he looked at Lynda adoringly. Now I remembered hearing about him. Nicholas Brandt was one of the Serenity House kids that Lynda had become chummy with in her volunteer work there. With his father in prison and his mother dead, his story was a particularly heart-tugging one. Lynda had described him as a sweet boy.

"I guess so," he said hesitantly.

It would fit you better, I thought. *In fact, you look like an elf.* And that's when an idea began to form in the Cody brain. But before I got very far with it I heard—

"Lynda, my dear, look what I found!"

All eyes turned to Serena Mason, because that's what eyes did when Serena Mason was around. Every male in Erin is half in love with her, not exempting infants and old men, but she doesn't play favorites. Now in her mid-sixties, she's been a widow for more than thirty years. As the chair of the Mason Foundation, she's a major supporter of Serenity House and dozens of other good works around town. Her late husband's great-grandfather, or maybe I'm one "great" off, had been a railroad baron.

Serena held out a long box, the kind that jewelry comes in, and slowly opened it. Nicholas's eyes opened wide. Triple M, who belonged to a science fiction and fantasy book club with Serena, ambled our way for a better look. The Three Wise Guys followed. We were all bunched up near a corner of the room. If we'd been in the dead center we couldn't have attracted more attention.

"How beautiful!" Lynda said.

Serena was holding out a strand of pearls for everyone to see. "Yes, aren't they?" She put them around her neck. By their very simplicity they looked stunning next to Serena's short salt-and-pepper hair and hazel eyes. But then, everything looked good on Serena Mason. She didn't have to dress like an heiress, and she didn't. Today, for example, she was wearing a colorful Christmas sweater over gray slacks. She was probably about thirty pounds overweight according to the insurance company charts, but I bet I'm the only man who's ever noticed. And that's only because I'm kind of focused on health issues.

"I think I'll put this away for now." Serena carefully put the necklace back in the box.

Just then the Bernardin High School band struck up "Here Comes Santa Claus." With a sinking feeling, I knew that the moment of my doom was approaching unless I could implement my plan quickly.

"Merry Christmas! Merry Christmas to all!"

You'd think a guy who's written more novels than I've written Christmas cards could come up with a better entrance line than that. But that's what Santa McCabe was booming as he made his scheduled ten-thirty appearance coming down Front Street.

Afterwards I tried to remember who, besides me, went outside to watch Santa make his dramatic entrance in a horse-drawn carriage, but it was useless. I know that Lynda, Serena, and Kate were with me, and there must have been others. But I was too busy watching the ham of all hams playing the part he was made for.

"Ho, ho, ho!"

"Hey, that's my line," I whispered to Lynda. She poked me in the ribs with an elbow.

I pulled out my smartphone and sent a tweet on my St. Benignus College account: *Santa Claus, AKA Professor Sebastian McCabe, has arrived at Serenity House.* It never hurts to boost the faculty. Then I took a photo for Facebook and the website. About an inch of snow lay on the ground and flakes were falling. Perfect!

Mac waved, he smiled, he held up little babies and posed for pictures. This went on for several minutes as he made his way through the crowd to the big dining room for "Breakfast with Santa." After large amounts of sugary juice and fat-laden donuts were consumed, he would listen to requests and give each child a small gift. At some point I became aware that Nicholas was standing next to me.

"You!" I said.

"Me?" He looked terrified, if not guilty.

"Yes you, Nicholas. You're just the young man I wanted to see. How'd you like to earn some money to buy your girlfriend a Christmas present?"

"I don't have a girlfriend, not really."

"Well, I'm sure you could use five dollars."

"I could use ten even more."

What a cute, enterprising kid! He reminded me of myself when I was younger. Or right now, for that matter. After haggling a little just to show that I was paying attention, I slipped Nicholas the ten-spot and the hat. Then I headed back to the crafts room. I still needed to buy a present for Popcorn. What would my secretary like? Maybe one of those scarves Triple M had been looking at before, or maybe a hand-made blanket with a colorful design.

I'd just stepped back into the former ballroom when I heard Serena Mason say, "Oh, no! I can't believe this."

She was standing about where we'd been before Santa's arrival, a shocked look on her face. Curiosity being one of my favorite emotions, I was at her side in short order. Lynda and Kate were already there.

Serena held up the box with her pearls. Well, no, she held up the box *without* her pearls. "I was going to show Kate, but they're gone! I just put the box down for a second to see Santa Claus and somebody took the pearls out."

"Where did you put the box down?" I asked.

She pointed. "On that empty table. The crafts person assigned there hasn't shown up yet."

"You're sure you didn't just misplace the pearls?"

For the first time in my admittedly limited acquaintance with Serena Mason, I saw the steel beneath the velvet. "I do not misplace things."

Okay, I believe you!

"Then you should call the police, Mrs. Mason."

"What, and spoil the day for everyone else? I won't hear of it."

Lynda suddenly took an interest in my presence. "Why aren't you in the other room elfing, anyway?"

"I subcontracted the job to Nicholas. He'll do a fine job and it'll boost his self-confidence."

If she had a problem with that, she didn't say so. She took my arm and walked me away from Serena and Kate. "This is terrible, Jeff. Serena is the biggest supporter of Serenity House. We've got to get her necklace back. Maybe Mac can help."

Why does everybody always think he's the only one who can solve a mystery? "I'm not sure this is a case for Sebastian McCabe. We probably don't have to look any farther than the Three Wise Guys."

My beloved looked at me quizzically. "I mean those three characters helping Polly," I explained. "They have community service written all over them." I looked around. All three were still in the room. "What do you know about them?"

"Not as much as Polly does."

"That's okay, I don't need complete biographies. And I don't want to talk to the good sister until I have to. She'll think I'm picking on them."

"You are."

"But not without reason. If I'm right, they're all petty criminals. Am I right?"

Lynda sighed. "The tall, skinny black kid wearing the Cincinnati Bengals jersey is Billy Major." He was walking around with his hands behind his back, the picture of nonchalance. That seemed highly suspicious to me. "He took his principal's car for a joy ride. Apparently he was irked at repeated attempts to get him to join the high school basketball team. He's a sophomore and taller than you, but he prefers to play chess. Polly says he's bored."

"Maybe he thought stealing a string of pearls from Serena Mason would be almost as much fun as grand theft auto. Who's the girl?"

At the moment she was sitting at a table with her hands folded in front of her. She had long brown hair gathered back in a ponytail that showed off a huge set of earrings shaped like peace symbols.

"That's Minnie Cooper. She's older than she looks, about twenty-two. This isn't the first time she's been in trouble. She's a repeat customer in Oscar's jail. This time around she was arrested for shoplifting jewelry at Looney Ladies Gallery."

Bingo!

"Come on—one of the suspects has a history of stealing jewelry?" I said. "It can't be that easy!"

"Probably not. The dude in the lumberjack shirt walking behind Polly is Elvis Jones. I like the stubble effect, the two-day growth of beard. You ought to try that, Jeff." I glared. Lynda went on: "He got arrested for Operating a Vehicle Under the Influence, not for the first time. Polly says his wife was furious. They're both trying to talk him into joining AA."

"So he might have lifted the pearls as a peace offering to his wife."

"All three make plausible suspects, all right." I was glad I didn't have to point that out to Lynda. "Which one do you think did it? Assuming for the moment that it's one of them and not one of the other eighty people here."

"Not everybody who was in this room a half-hour ago is a suspect," I protested. "It has to be somebody who actually saw the pearls. The Three Wise Guys qualify."

"So is this a *Murder on the Orient Express* deal?"

We'd been married long enough—seven months now—that the Cody sarcasm was rubbing off on Lynda.

I shook my head slowly, mournfully. "This looks like a one-person job, but which one isn't as obvious as I'd hoped. I hate to admit this, but if we want to resolve this without a lot of accusations and denials and disruption, then I guess it *is* a case for Sebastian McCabe."

First, though, I went back to Serena Mason and asked her permission to see if my brother-in-law could figure out who stole her necklace without causing a disturbance in the process.

She thought it over while I watched her run a hand through her short hair. Have I mentioned that she's a beautiful woman? "Well, I would like to get it back," she said, "as long as you're discreet."

"That's my middle name."

Lynda rolled her eyes.

Santa was tucking into his breakfast of egg casserole with goetta, a southern Ohio sausage treat made of steel-cut oats, ground pork, spices, and about a thousand calories per forkful. Nicholas, sitting next to him, was keeping up, making me wonder how well and how often the boy normally ate.

"We have a problem," I announced. "Somebody stole Serena Mason's pearl necklace here at the house, just a few minutes ago."

Mac put down his fork. For him that was a major expression of interest. "Who?"

For a genius, he could be pretty thick sometimes. "If we knew who, it wouldn't be that much of a problem, would it?"

"It could be, but never mind. So, we have a Christmas mystery on our hands." His brown Santa Claus eyes twinkled like a Christmas tree. "Did you ever stop to think, Jefferson, that every great mystery writer eventually writes a Christmas mystery? I can think of excellent stories by Christie, Stout, Queen, Sayers, and of course Conan Doyle off the top of my head. Mary Higgins Clark and her daughter Carol write one together every year."

I wanted to hit him. This was no time to show off his vast knowledge of crime fiction, what with the kids at a dozen tables around us throwing food at each other and antsy to sit on Santa's lap and demand outrageously expensive electronic toys.

"Gee, that's swell, Professor, but Mrs. Mason refuses to call the police, so I was hoping you could find the light-fingered culprit and get her pearls back without a lot of fuss that spoils the festive occasion."

Mac stroked his beard, which was the real thing dyed white for the occasion, although the long hair on his head was a wig. "Oscar won't like that."

That was not news to me. Erin's police chief, Oscar Hummel, takes a proprietary interest in all crimes under his jurisdiction. He especially sees stars when Mac interferes, except on those increasingly frequent occasions when he breaks down and asks Mac for help.

"Describe the circumstances leading up to the discovery of the theft," Mac said, ignoring Oscar's likely reaction, as I knew that he would. I did my best to give a detailed account of the events leading up to his ostentatious arrival at the front of Serenity House. At the end I tacked on what I had learned about the rap sheets of the Three Wise Guys.

"So which of the three is it, Santa?" I asked.

I figured there was a 50-50 chance he could tell me.

"Your focus on Polly's community service charges is quite understandable, old boy. However, I would like to know who else was present when Serena displayed the necklace."

"As far as I can remember, Polly, Lynda, Nicholas, and I were the only other people close to Serena. Some of the crafters and their customers a few feet away might have also seen it, but Serena wasn't making a major production number out of it."

"You didn't steal the necklace, did you, Jefferson?"

When I responded with stony silence, he turned to Nicholas. "Did you do it, Nicholas?"

The lad's eyes got big as quarters. "Gosh, no!"

Mac turned back to me. "Then you shall have to search your three major suspects."

You've got to be kidding me. "That's it? That's your brilliant idea? I could have thought of that! I was hoping to avoid even raising the issue with Triple M until we had the goods on the thief. You know she never saw a lost sheep she didn't think she could save."

He nodded. "Indeed I do. I find her perpetual optimism most edifying. Nevertheless, a search is necessary. You can blame me, and tell Polly that I said it was for the suspects' own good."

I got a little hot. "Why don't you tell her yourself?"

He spread his hands in a gesture of helplessness. "Obviously, I am otherwise engaged. On this occasion I shall have to function as a literal armchair detective while you function as my eyes and ears."

The armchair in question was just waiting for him to sit in while he took Christmas orders.

"Okay," I mumbled, "but I'm going to hate this."

"What!" Triple M cried. "Do you understand how humiliating and discouraging it is for ex-offenders to be the first ones suspected of a crime? It's just not fair."

"Mac said it's for their own good. I guess what he meant is, it's the only way they can clear themselves."

"It does make sense, Polly," Lynda chipped in, "fair or not."

Serena Mason turned out to be an easier sell than I had expected. "It would be a relief to find out that the thief was one of those three and not, for example, one of the clients at Serenity House." Seeing the look on Triple M's face, she hastily added, "If that turns out to be the case, I mean. Sorry, Polly."

After a little more discussion, we agreed that Triple M and I would approach each one separately except for Minnie Cooper. Lynda would help search Minnie.

We started with sunken-eyed Elvis Jones because he was closest. The hangdog look on his face once we explained the situation was more sad than defiant.

"I never stole anything in my life," he said. "I may be a drunk, but I'm not a thief."

"You are not a drunk," Triple M said with quiet firmness. "You just have alcohol issues."

"You didn't want the necklace as a peace offering for your wife?" I pressed.

"I'm so deep in the doghouse now I don't think it would help if I brought her a diamond tiara," he said gloomily.

We went into a bathroom for the search.

"I've never been searched before," Jones said.

Obviously you don't fly.

"It's no fun," I assured him. "And won't be any fun for me, either. Look, if you took the necklace we can handle this with a minimum of embarrassment all around. Just give it to me now and later on I'll pretend to find it somewhere. There'll be no trouble for you. I promise."

He shook his head stubbornly. "I can't do that, Mr. Cody, 'cause I didn't take it and I don't have it."

When he got down to his undershorts, which had red heart designs all over them, it was pretty obvious that Elvis Jones wasn't concealing anything. I didn't do a body cavity search.

"My wife will kill me if she finds out about this," Jones said as he put his pants back on.

"She won't find out about it from me," I promised. "You really ought to think about joining AA, Elvis. I'm sure it would help you stay out of trouble."

"It's looking better and better."

When I came out I learned that there had been a bit of excitement while I'd been embarrassing both Jones and myself. Lynda and Triple M couldn't find Minnie Cooper at first. They assumed she'd done a bunk. It turned out that she was just outside grabbing a smoke.

Minnie gave a good impression of outrage. "You're harassing me just because I made one little mistake. Thanks a lot, Sister."

Triple M glared at her. I could almost hear her famously soft heart harden.

"Okay, it was more than just one mistake," Minnie allowed. "But how am I supposed to go straight, Sister, if society expects me to be a bad girl?"

Lynda gave her a "gimme a break" look. "You're trying to jive your best advocate, honey. That's bad salesmanship. We could have had the search over by now if you didn't yap so much. I don't know what the big deal is unless you have something to hide."

"I don't." Minnie looked like she needed a cigarette, or maybe two at once. "Oh, all right. Enjoy yourself."

They took her into the ladies' room. You might not think that a nun—sorry, woman religious—would know much about body searches, but Triple M used to work in Army intelligence. On top of that, volunteering at the jail was probably like a post-graduate course in the subject.

"She's clean," Triple M said as they emerged from the restroom.

"Well, not exactly clean," Lynda added, "but she didn't have the necklace."

Minnie stalked off with her nose in the air.

"Why did she put up such a fuss if she didn't have the necklace?" I asked.

"Maybe because her underwear is . . . unsubtle," Lynda said. "Think Frederick's of Hollywood without the class."

I'm thinking, I'm thinking! I hadn't finished shopping for Lynda yet. Maybe she'd like . . . No, probably not. But I would! I dragged my thoughts back to the subject at hand.

"Elvis Jones had hearts on his undershorts," I reported. "Nobody said this would be pleasant."

The youngest of the Three Wise Guys, Billy Major, was the last up. That had me worried and excited in equal measure. This could be it. But if it wasn't it, what then?

Not surprisingly, Billy initially declined the honor.

"You can't force me. I know my rights, man."

I held up my hands. *Hey, I'm cool with that.* "Absolutely, Mr. Major." I was showing respect. "You certainly don't have to cooperate. It's just that I think this would be better than calling Chief Hummel, don't you?"

"I ain't afraid of him."

Nobody is, kid. He's a teddy bear. "Of course not. But you've got this community service gig and the judge who sentenced you—"

"Oh, man!" He said a few other words. "Let's just get it over with."

Wow! That was easier than I expected. Was it my technique?

Close up, I could see that Billy Major had valiantly but unsuccessfully attempted to evoke a manly mustache. This kid wanted badly to be a grownup, but he was sure going about it the wrong way.

Inside the restroom, I had him take off his Cincinnati Bengals jersey and his jeans. Except for his wallet, his pockets contained nothing but a Christmas tree ornament for which he had a receipt. "How tall are you, Billy?" I was just making conversation as I held up the pants to make sure nothing was taped inside.

"Five-twelve." I sensed a certain sensitivity on this subject.

"And you don't play basketball, huh?"

"Hate it."

In five minutes of searching, I found nothing.

Billy looked frustrated and angry at the end, a skinny kid stripped of his dignity and in his underwear. I didn't blame him.

"I'm sorry to have put you through this," I said. "But at least we know you didn't take the pearls."

He grabbed his jeans. "I already knew that."

Lynda, Triple M, and Serena Mason were waiting outside the restroom. I shook my head, not saying a word.

"I hope Mac has another idea," Lynda said.

He always does, and sometimes it's a good one.

"Breakfast with Santa" was over, and the big man was enthroned on a chair listening to the three-year-old girl on his lap tell him she wanted an elephant for Christmas. On one side of him was a giant Christmas tree loaded down with ornaments, lights, popcorn, and garlands. Nicholas the Elf stood on the other side, his green elf hat cocked at a rakish angle.

I approached Mac from the tree side. "We did the searches," I said in a low voice while the girl climbed off his lap. "None of the suspects had the necklace."

"Aren't you going to search me?" Nicholas asked. He didn't look me in the eye exactly, but more like past me.

I chuckled. "I don't think that will be necessary, buddy."

"The result is exactly as I expected," Mac said.

"Oh, come on!"

After a boy of about seven or eight put in his order for some death-dealing weapon, Mac turned his attention back to me. "I know who stole Serena Mason's pearl necklace and where it is now. Come see me after Nicholas and I have finished our duties here."

Nicholas's jaw fell open. Knowing my brother-in-law as I do, I was less impressed.

"You're bluffing," I said. But I didn't believe it. I was just goading his ego to see what I could get him to spill.

"I assure you that I am not. You know, Jefferson, of all the many Christmas mysteries I have read, my favorite remains 'The Adventure of the Blue Carbuncle.' Please bring Serena with you when you return."

Sebastian McCabe's laundry list of faults does not include talking in non sequiturs. So he wasn't just informing me about his preferences in crime literature by mentioning the Sherlock Holmes story; he was tossing me a clue. But what was it?

My own mystery reading tends to hard-boiled private eyes like Mike Hammer and Spenser, but I also turn to my *Complete Sherlock Holmes* occasionally in self-defense. Mac has long been deeply involved in the world of Holmesmania, and now my bride had dipped a toe into it as well. At the latter's urging, I'd recently re-read the blue carbuncle story. That's the one where the gemstone of the title is hidden by the crook inside a Christmas goose.

Hidden . . .

So that was it! The body searches had come up dry because the thief had hidden the necklace somewhere, and Mac thought he knew where. I spent about ten minutes trying to figure out who and where before I gave up and decided to do some Christmas shopping. First I picked up a brightly painted wooden box for Popcorn. Then, looking around carefully to make sure that Lynda didn't see me, I bought her a painting of Main Street in Erin. Neither of us had been born in the town, but it was our home now and always would be. The painting would fill that spot over our couch that Lynda always complained looked too bare.

Shopping completed, I circled around to Serena Mason.

"Mac says he knows who stole the necklace and where it is now," I informed her.

She smiled, her hazel eyes showing relief. "And Mac's always right, isn't he?"

"That's a bit of an exaggeration." *He has terrible taste in neckwear, for one thing. He likes bow ties.* "But he does have a good track record as an amateur sleuth."

"I bet he couldn't do it without you."

"That's an even bigger exaggeration." *Actually, I'm just being modest. You're quite perceptive, Serena, in addition to all of your other admirable qualities.*

Mac's tour of duty as Santa ended at one o'clock, although the craft show continued until four. I rounded up Triple M, Kate, and Lynda on the stroke of one.

"This should be interesting," Serena said.

"I'll be glad when it's over," Triple M said glumly. She must have been thinking something along the lines of "nothing good can come of this."

We filed into the back of the room where Santa was holding forth, with Nicholas at his side, just as my nephew climbed onto his father's lap. His siblings were too old for this. Rebecca, thirteen and a half, was out caroling with a boy. Amanda, two years younger, was probably pouring over college catalogues or inventing time travel.

"I want a BB gun," Brian announced.

This struck me as a poor opening gambit for such a good chess player. Most Santas would have responded by telling him he'd shoot his eye out with such a present.

"Handgun or rifle?" Mac asked. I was too wrapped up in looking at my sister to hear the answer. From the look on her face, father and son were both in trouble.

Brian wasn't the last supplicant, although we were already past the official closing time for "Breakfast with Santa." Mac stayed to hear three more kids while I became increasingly impatient to hear his solution to our little mystery. Lynda, sensing my angst, took my hand and squeezed it.

Finally, with a wave and a parting "ho ho ho," Santa made it clear that he was finished until the next Holiday Fest. Parents and children exited. Kate said she would take Brian home. I suspected that he was in for a lecture on the way.

"Hello, Serena," Mac said as the other three of us gathered around him next to the Christmas tree.

Serena shook his hand. "Hello, Mac. You were a wonderful Santa, and I know you're a great detective, too."

Wasn't it a work of art the way she delivered the compliment and the prod in a single sentence? No wonder she's the town sweetheart.

"I asked Jefferson to bring you here because I wanted to deliver your necklace to you from its place of concealment myself," Mac said. "Consider it a Christmas present."

"Thanks. So . . . where is it?"

Mac turned to the Christmas tree. Or, to be more precise, he turned to Nicholas, who was standing in front of the Christmas tree. "Excuse me, Nicholas."

The lad moved over, his freckled face turning red.

Mac reached his hand into the branches of the tree and pulled out a rope of pearls. At a casual glance, all that anyone would have given, they blended in with the popcorn. "It's been here ever since I suggested that you search your suspects, Jefferson."

Call me dumb, but I didn't get it. "How could any of the three come in here and put the necklace in the tree without being seen?"

"None of them did. Nicholas did."

The twelve-year-old's face went through a range of emotions before settling on panic. "Did not!" he yelled. "Why are you picking on me?"

Lynda and Triple M were crestfallen. Nicholas didn't do injured innocence with any conviction at all. For myself, I was too stunned to be disappointed. His mother was dead and he had said he had no girlfriend. Who would he have given the necklace to? Or was he under the illusion that he could sell it?

"When I asked Nicholas whether he stole the pearl necklace, his affirmation of innocence was totally unconvincing," Mac said. "I only asked the question pro forma, but his reaction screamed guilt. Having a son and two daughters of my own, I know the signs.

"When you went away to search the suspects, Jefferson, Nicholas—consumed by the guilt feelings natural to most first-time thieves—assumed that we would eventually suspect him after that proved fruitless. So he had to get rid of the necklace. As I turned my attention to my duties as Santa, I must confess that I did not see him place the necklace on the tree. However, I noticed that when you made your report, Nicholas never looked at you. He looked past you—at the Christmas tree."

"You can't prove it!" Nicholas cried.

Mac shrugged. "I suppose that is not necessary. Serena primarily wanted her necklace back, which she has. She was not so interested in assigning guilt or prosecuting the offender. However, I will note that the necklace was placed just on a level with your arms, Nicholas."

"Oh, Nicholas," Lynda said. "Why?"

He bit his lip, eyes downcast. "I wanted it for you. I didn't have enough money to give you a present."

For Lynda? You little home-wrecker!

Lynda bent down, held his shoulders, and looked him in the eye. "No girl worthy of a gift would want one that's stolen, Nicholas."

Nicholas looked up. "Am I going to be arrested?"

"You should be so lucky," Serena said. "You're a ward of the court, if I remember correctly." She glanced at Lynda, who nodded. "I think I can arrange it so that you and I are going to spend a lot of time together. You may wish you were in jail."

Somehow I doubted that.

That night Lynda and I decorated the tree in our apartment, accompanied by Frank Sinatra singing Christmas carols. It was a real tree, at Lynda's insistence. My cost-benefit analysis of buying an artificial tree and amortizing the cost over ten years as compared to buying a new one every Christmas had made no headway at all.

It was our first Christmas as a married couple, and would turn out to be my last in the apartment where I had lived alone for so long before we married. The ornaments that we had acquired as single people over the years would join forces on the tree, along with new ones that we had bought as a couple.

"The ironic thing," Lynda said, adding an ornament of a goose with a blue gem around its neck as Frank urged us to have ourselves a merry little Christmas, "is that Serena would have given him the necklace if he'd asked. Or, if he insisted, Nicholas could have bought it from her for what you paid him. The pearls weren't real. She just bought the necklace today at the craft show."

I shook my head. "The poor little guy wasn't exactly Raffles, was he?" Maybe it's because Nicholas was a redhead like me, but I was in a bit of a "there but for the grace of God" mood.

"Mac said the fact that he's such a terrible liar means that he doesn't have much practice at it. He's lucky that he picked Serena to steal from. She'll give him so much love and discipline that he won't go wrong again."

"I guess I should be jealous of my rival for your affection," I said lightly.

"In that regard you have no rival, Jeff Cody."

That called for a non-verbal response on my part. I moved toward Lynda, but she was looking around distractedly. By this time the small tree was laden down with ornaments and we had moved on to the rest of the apartment. Empty boxes were all around us on the floor. "I can't find the mistletoe," Lynda said.

I wrapped my arms around her womanly form and whispered in her ear. "Who needs mistletoe?"

A COLD CASE

I

"And this is the kitchen."

That explains the refrigerator, the stove, the microwave . . . Why do real estate agents always feel they have to point out the obvious? I made a mental note to ask my father.

Cecily Almond, a tall, willowy woman with café-au-lait skin and golden hair done up in a Cleopatra hairdo, ignored my unspoken sarcasm. "All the appliances are staying. The owners have already moved into a condo. That's why they're so motivated to sell. I'm also the listing agent on this one, so I know the situation very well."

"I love the island," Lynda said.

This was looking promising. It's not often you find a beautifully preserved arts and crafts house in Erin, Ohio, with a state-of-the-art kitchen. In fact, this was the twenty-seventh house we'd looked at since getting serious about finding a home of our own. And it was conveniently located on Campion Lane, only about a ten-minute bike ride to my office at St. Benignus College and an even faster drive for Lynda to get to her workplace downtown.

Lynda and I had agreed early on in our engagement to live in my carriage house apartment on Sebastian McCabe's property for a transition period, and then buy a place. Now it was late April, we'd been married almost eleven months, and we were looking for a house big enough to hold the children who so far had stubbornly refused to make their requested appearance. This one had four bedrooms and two baths.

Call it superstition, but I had a nagging feeling that our first kid was waiting for us to get a house before showing up. So that was a strong incentive to buy sooner rather than later. Besides, the housing market was starting to pick up a little bit, and prices with it. If we waited too long, we might miss that sweet spot of low prices and low interest rates that homebuyers had been enjoying over the past few years. So we called Happy Homes Realty, the biggest locally owned real estate brokerage in Erin, and started spending a lot of evenings and weekends house hunting with the energetic Cecily Almond. We were already pre-approved for a mortgage loan at Gamble Bank.

It was a beautiful spring day, just made for cold drinks on the porch and baseball on the radio. Lynda was dressed in a bright yellow blouse and short white culottes. The effect against her dark skin and honey-blonde curls pulled back in a ponytail was stunning. I also looked rather cute in my "SARCASM—Just Another Service I Offer" T-shirt and shorts, if I do say so myself.

As the son of a Realtor—my dad owns his own firm in Virginia—I've always been interested in old houses. Lynda doesn't care much, so long as the insides are new. So this looked like it could be the perfect domicile for Jeff Cody, Lynda Teal (Cody), and To Be Announced.

"There's even a big freezer chest in the utility room," Cecily said, with a "surely that seals the deal" attitude.

"You should like that," Lynda to me. "You always want to save money by buying in bulk."

Don't act so enthusiastic! That pumps up the price! I tried to look skeptical.

"Here, take a look," Cecily pressed.

She marched into the little utility room, just off of the kitchen. We followed. We were standing right behind her as she opened the freezer chest . . . and screamed at the top of her lungs.

The body of a woman lay crammed within, on her side, in a fetal position.

II

"Her name was Olivia Wanamaker," I said, "and she was another Happy Homes Realty agent."

"That name sounds familiar somehow," Sebastian McCabe rumbled.

"She was also a member of the Erin City Council," Lynda informed my notoriously apolitical brother-in-law, "and not the most shy. Where Olivia went, controversy was sure to follow. And men, too."

Meow.

We had assembled late Sunday afternoon for cocktail hour, along with my sister Kate, in Mac's study. I've spent a lot of time in that man-cave over the years, some of the happiest moments of my bachelorhood, and wedding bells haven't changed that.

"Oscar said there's not much doubt she was bludgeoned to death with a frozen fish," I said. Lynda and I had only looked at the body long enough to see that she was petite, well dressed, and a bloody mess before we phoned 911. We'd stayed at the house another hour or so after Erin's chief of police arrived on the scene, and then we'd made a beeline for the McCabe house.

Mac, his bulky frame settled into his favorite wingback chair, apparently found this thirsty work. He took a pull on his mug of dark ale before he spoke again. "What kind of fish?"

You're just showing off! I refused to ask why he wanted to know.

"Salmon," Lynda supplied. "Why do you want to know?"

"I like fish. I have even gone fishing." *I know. I was with you. It wasn't a pretty sight.* "The murder weapon suggests an unpremeditated act, of course. The murderer apparently struck with whatever happened to be handy—'apparently' being the key word."

Kate got up to get dinner started, but paused in the doorway. "Didn't the *Observer* have a string of front page stories a while back about Wanamaker tweeting jibes at the mayor and other City Council members during their meetings?"

Lynda set down her Manhattan. "Yeah. It was about a three-day wonder—at least, as far as the paper goes. I doubt if the mayor ever forgot, though. For all her perfect coiffure, she's not a 'forgive and forget' type."

Mac, knowing Her Honor quite well, raised an eyebrow as if he had just been given a five-course meal for thought. But he didn't comment on that. Instead, he asked, "Who owned the murder house?"

"We don't know," I said. "Cecily just said it was 'a motivated seller,' which means somebody who needs to sell in a hurry and is willing to let the house go at a good price." I brightened. "Hey, Lyn, maybe we can get an even better price because of the murder."

She rolled her eyes.

"Well, at least this is one murder where you three don't have to get involved," Kate said. She disappeared into the kitchen.

"Yes." Mac stroked his beard. "We don't have to get involved. What a relief."

I would have bet my 403(b) and my IRA that he was trying to think of a way to get involved. But as it turned out, that was no trick at all.

We were just inside the door of our apartment after a dinner of overcooked spaghetti and turkey meatballs when Lynda's smartphone rang, a very no-nonsense ringtone that sounded like a telephone. She looked at it before answering. "It's Rawls."

Johanna Rawls, a young member of the small reporting staff of *The Erin Observer & News-Ledger*, was working on the paper's story about the body in the freezer. She must have wrestled news editor and former crime reporter Ben Silverstein for the honor. Although Lynda was no longer on *Observer* masthead, having moved up the corporate ladder, Tall Rawls looked up to her as a role model and kept in close contact.

"Hi, Johanna. Great idea! I should have thought of checking that myself. And what did you find? What? Well, yes, that is interesting, and good to know. Thanks for calling."

Lynda had the strangest look on her face, as if she didn't know what to think. "Johanna checked the county auditor's online records to find out who owns the house with the body. The names on the deed are Ralph and Grace Pendergast."

III

"April is the cruelest month." T.S. Eliot wrote that. He must have known Ralph Pendergast.

On Monday morning, the day after discovering Olivia Wanamaker's brutal murder, I was stewing in my office about Ralph's most shameful move yet, and I don't mean owning the murder house: He wanted me to fire Popcorn, my indispensable administrative assistant.

I should have seen it coming. We'd gone through round after round of budget cuts since Ralph arrived at St. Benignus College two years earlier as provost and academic vice president. He had been brought in by the board of trustees to get the college's fiscal house in order. Ralph is an economist by academic training. (No wonder they call it "the dismal science.") He's also an economizer, with the accent on the "miser." Everybody loved our long-time president, "Father Joe" Pirelli, but even I had to admit that he'd always run a rather loose ship. Eventually the trustees had forced him to turn over the day-to-day operations of that ship to Captain Bligh.

Anyway, the belt-tightening had gotten down to the administrative assistant level. First, retirees weren't replaced. That worked out quite well. For the most part their middle-management bosses took on the extra work without complaint, just happy to have a job in this bad economy. The next step was to offer an anemic early-retirement package. That didn't get as many takers as hoped, so now the Administration (AKA Ralph) was looking at layoffs. Ralph hadn't actually told me that Popcorn's head was on the chopping block, but a sightless person could read between the lines.

He had dropped into my office and closed the door on the previous Friday afternoon, just before the start of the weekend. *Nothing good can come of this*, I thought. Oh, there was a time when Ralph thought I was well meaning and at least semi-intelligent, salvageable if only I could be pulled away from the influence of my brother-in-law. But that time was long since in my rear-view mirror.

"Hello, Cody." He helped himself to a seat. Since it was Casual Day, he was wearing a blue blazer instead of his gray suit. I had on khaki pants and a St. Benignus polo shirt, pushing the brand. "I've been looking at the numbers for your office." Ralph shook his head mournfully, causing the light to glint off of his rimless glasses. "It seems to me that we're spending a lot of money for what we get out of it."

I stifled a laugh.

"You must have the decimal points in the wrong place, Ralph. This is a shoestring operation. You do realize that the Office of Public Relations and Marketing is just

Popcorn and me? And that we handle media relations, marketing, branding, the website, and social media?"

Ralph seemed to study the pencil that he held between his two hands. "Oh, yes, you're in charge of that weeter, or whatever it's called."

I could feel my face turning the same shade of red as my hair.

"Well, I'm sure you're a busy fellow," he went on, "although I've never kept it a secret from you that I feel you could do a better job of media *relations* given your *connections*." Low blow. I've never been able to convince Ralph that Lynda's position as editorial director for Grier Ohio NewsGroup, immediate parent company of *The Erin Observer & News-Ledger*, doesn't give me the ability to kill stories that spoil his breakfast. I mean, how in the heck was I supposed to suppress the one about the tenured finance professor who was arrested for passing more than a hundred bad checks? (She's now undergoing therapy for a gambling problem.)

"At any rate, Cody, a lot of people around here have learned to answer their own phones and type their own letters."

But not you, Ralph.

"I already do that!" I exploded. "I can see where this is going and you'd better not go there." Sometimes I descend into clichés under pressure. "Popcorn runs the Facebook Fan Page and posts about half of our tweets. Plus she keeps track of everything so we know what to tweet about." *Women's basketball, for example, a major program about which I am clueless.* "It would be physically impossible for me to do everything I do without her."

That was all true, but it wasn't the whole truth. I didn't have the nerve to say that Aneliese Pokorny also covers me when I'm out of the office in the middle of the day on some madcap assignment for Sebastian McCabe, and that she could—truly, no exaggeration—run the office much better without me than I ever could without her. In fact, maybe I should resign and become a full-time househusband, a stay-at-home dad to those kids who would appear once we had the house. Surely Ralph would see that Popcorn was my natural replacement.

Lynda makes more money than I do anyway. Popcorn, on the other hand, is a self-supporting widow, though how she does it on her meager salary I'll never know.

"Well, perhaps you need to set priorities." I noticed that the point on Ralph's pencil was almost as sharp as his nose. I felt like yanking it away from him and drawing a mustache on his face. Okay, that's pretty weak, but I'm not a violent man. I don't even write two-fisted private eye novels anymore. "Perhaps not everything that you're doing needs to be done," Ralph forged on. *Yeah, try being a college, even one as small as ours, without a Facebook page.* "I haven't made up my mind yet, I'm still looking at the budget, but I didn't want you to be surprised when I do."

That means he's made up his mind, I reflected gloomily on Monday morning. Well, maybe the murder in his empty house would keep him too busy to move forward with the plan. *Fat chance, Jeff.*

"A penny for your thoughts, Boss," Popcorn said as she set a mug of decaffeinated coffee in front of me.

"You'd demand your money back."

"I know what you're thinking about."

"You do?" I looked at her carefully. Almost fifty-one years old, dyed blond hair, just under five feet tall and just this side of plump, Popcorn didn't look worried.

"Sure. It's in the paper."

She sat on the chair in front of my desk and handed me the day's edition of *The Erin Observer & News-Ledger*, with the seventy-two-point headline: **A COLD CASE** and the more informative subhead: ***Councilwoman's Body Found in Freezer.*** The story carried Johanna Rawls's byline. I call her Tall Rawls because she's very Nordic, at least six feet tall even without her three-inch heels.

"The fully clothed body of controversial Erin City Councilwoman Olivia Wanamaker, bludgeoned to death by a frozen fish, was found Sunday by a real estate agent and her two clients in the freezer of a home for sale," the article began.

"According to county records, the home belongs to . . ."

The color photo accompanying the story showed a woman in her late twenties, with dark hair and a self-assured look. Although not beautiful, she was certainly attractive. The photo looked more like the woman I'd met once or twice at social functions than did the body in the freezer.

I only glanced at the paper, having seen it at home and having read the online version of the story late last night. Tall Rawls quoted me as being "shocked" and Lynda as "saddened," while carefully noting that Ms. Teal (retained as her professional name) was employed by the parent company of the *Observer*. Most of the quotes were from Oscar, however, and he hadn't held back much.

"It's accurate enough," I said, "and she spelled our names right."

Popcorn laughed right on cue, knowing full well that Lynda is Tall Rawls's hero and mentor. "So what do you think—did old Ralph do it?"

I had no opinion about that. I didn't even know what I *wanted* to believe. On the one hand, it was tempting to wish that he'd done the deed. Ralph Pendergast has been a pain in the posterior ever since he became provost. A murder rap would take care of the Ralph problem for good. On the other hand . . .

"That would be horrible publicity for the college," I said, not really answering her question.

"But at least you might get a good price on the house."

"Popcorn, you've been around me too long." *But I'm afraid that might be just a short-term problem.*

Before she could offer a loyal reply, the sound of "You're So Vain" exploded in my pocket. I took out my smartphone and answered Mac's call.

"Cody's Circus, ringmaster speaking," I answered.

"Good morning, Jefferson. I have someone in my office with me who would like very much to speak to both of us."

I knew it wasn't Ralph because the "Jaws" theme wasn't playing in my head. I have something of a sixth sense about him.

"Do I have to guess?"

"I doubt that you could."

"I'm on my way." I disconnected. "Popcorn—"

She stood up to her full four-foot-eleven. "Your calendar is as empty as my checkbook. If anything comes up, I'll put it off or deal with it. For the record, I'm guessing the mystery guest has two X chromosomes."

"How do you figure that?"

She shrugged. "That's the way I'd write it."

Popcorn is addicted to the racy romance novels of one Rosamund DeLacey, with titles like *Love's Dying Ember.* It's a mild vice and the only one she has, but I fear that it does rather color her outlook on life.

Racked with guilt that I was once again deserting my post and leaving my job-endangered administrative assistant to handle whatever came in the door, I nevertheless ducked out and hoofed it over to Mac's office in Herbert Hall.

Well, he calls it an office. I call it a disaster area—an overflowing ashtray here, a set of bagpipes there, and books everywhere (not a small number of which he wrote). Mac's gargoyle of an administrative assistant, the humorless Heidi Guildenstern, was absent from her guard post, so I barged right in.

Mac was at his desk, behind the little sign that says "Thank You For Not Breathing While I Smoke." (Yes, the whole campus is non-smoking.) Compared to him, the desk looks small. Popcorn was right that it was a woman sitting in one of his two visitor chairs, and Mac was right that I never would have guessed who. When I entered the room, she stood up and faced me. She was about a head shorter than my six-one.

"I believe you know Mrs. Pendergast," Mac said grandly.

She was a trim, attractive woman in her mid-fifties, with chin-length frosted hair and clear gray eyes behind her glasses. I decided that Lynda would have approved of the red scarf she had chosen for a splash of color to accent her white blouse and tan slacks.

"Grace," she said, putting her hand out. "We met once."

"I remember." And I was quite sure I'd never forget. It was during one jazz night at Beans & Books, our locally owned coffee house. That was the first time I'd ever seen her, and the only time until she accompanied Ralph to my wedding and the reception afterward last May. I'd been surprised that first time because when I saw the two of them sitting together across the room she didn't look like my idea of Mrs. Ralph Pendergast. In fact, I'd had the unworthy thought that perhaps Ralph was stepping out on his wife.[3] Possibly the fact that I was there with a young female who was not Lynda planted the idea in my head. But that's ancient history. I've completely forgotten the whole business.

"Grace has a problem," Mac said.

"And I think you two can help," she added quickly.

Have you ever been in a situation where you could see the lights of the metaphorical freight train that was

---

[3] See *Holmes Sweet Holmes*, MX Publishing, 2012.

bearing down on you at, well, freight train speed but you just couldn't get off the tracks? I sat down. Mac and Grace followed suit.

"I'm sure you know that Ralph and I own the house where that horrible murder took place—or at least where the body was found. I don't know why we ever bought such a large place, other than Ralph thought our children would visit more often than they have. We put the place up for sale four months ago and moved into a new condo in the River Heights development." This was all fascinating intel, no doubt, but I was stuck on her highly perceptive first sentence. It had never occurred to me until now that the murder might have taken place somewhere else. How clever of Grace to spot that. But of course Ralph would marry someone with a logical mind. I seemed to recall that she was a high school teacher by training.

"This has put us in a very embarrassing position." Hands in her lap, Grace Pendergast looked embarrassed.

"Well, embarrassment isn't fatal," I pointed out.

She didn't return my smile. "As I told Professor McCabe, Chief Hummel already called Ralph early this morning. I'm concerned that he may jump to the silly conclusion that my husband has something to do with this awful thing."

"And you are convinced that he did not," Mac said, making it sound like a statement. But it was a question.

"Of course he didn't! Ralph wouldn't hurt a fly." *But he might lay it off.*

"Would Ralph have any reason for killing this woman?" Mac pressed it. "Did he even know her?"

She made a show of thinking about it. "I believe that in her capacity as a City Councilwoman she was quite critical of some of the landlords who own homes and apartment buildings rented by students. That would include us. We have a small building, eight units, that I inherited from my parents."

"They lived in Erin?" I'd always thought of Ralph as a recent carpetbagger. Although I'm not a native myself, I've been in Erin since I came to St. Benignus as a student more than twenty years ago.

Grace nodded. "I was born here. I'm a Shayne." That was a prominent family in Erin—not particularly wealthy or influential, but plentiful. I'd had no idea that Grace Pendergast was one of them. Now that I knew, I immediately began to worry that I might have said something true about Ralph to one of his in-laws. Oh, well, they already knew. "When Ralph was approached to take the position here, I knew I wanted to come home."

"No doubt you used your wiles to convince Ralph that was a good idea," Mac said.

Now she did smile. "I can talk Ralph into anything. He's such a softy." *Ralph—a softy? Ralph Waldo Pendergast? What is this, Bizarro World?*

Somebody had to bring this conversation back to real life, so I nominated myself. "Let me summarize the situation, then: Ralph had a conflict with Olivia Wanamaker in her City Councilwoman role over tenant-landlord issues. He's afraid this looks bad for him, since her body was found in a home you two own, so Ralph sent you to get our help because he couldn't bring himself to ask."

"Oh, no!" Her gray eyes popped wide with horror. "Well, it's true that he'd never ask for your help. I mean, that's just not Ralph. But he wouldn't approve of me asking you for it, either. So, will you help?"

It would be uncharitable to say that her tone was wheedling, so I won't say it. But it was. I liked her anyway, I have to admit. She was standing by her man, in spite of him.

"By 'help,'" Mac said, "I assume you want us to convince Oscar that Ralph is guiltless?"

She stood up. "That's the outcome, of course, but I assume that to get there you'll have to find out who did commit the murder. If I'm not mistaken, you just agreed to do that. I'm very grateful, Professor McCabe, Mr. Cody."

"Jeff," I said numbly. *Wait a minute. How did he agree to what? What did I miss?*

"Just don't tell Ralph I put you up to it. He'd be upset with me."

She gave us her cell phone number on the way out.

IV

"This is priceless," I said acidly. "We not only have to save Ralph's bacon, but we have to do it without telling him we're doing it, which means we don't even get brownie points for the effort!" *As if Ralph Pendergast ever gives out brownie points.*

Mac pulled an unlit cigar out of his mouth. "Hell and damnation, Jefferson, how was I supposed to say no to someone who expressed such utter confidence in our abilities?"

"The technical term for that is 'stroking the immense McCabe ego.'"

He ignored my observation. "There is also the small matter of justice. However much you might relish the removal of Ralph as our bête-noir, you do not in your heart of hearts credit the convenient notion that he killed Mrs. Wanamaker—and you know that it is all too likely that Oscar will."

I was saved from answering that by the Indiana Jones ringtone of my smartphone. When I looked at it, the cheerful face of Cecily Almond stared back at me— Cleopatra with golden hair and light brown skin. I hadn't talked to her since we had gone our separate ways on Sunday afternoon, leaving Oscar's crew and a dead body behind us. I tapped "Answer."

"Hi, Cecily. How are you doing with all of this?"

"Thanks for asking, Jeff. I'm still kind of shaken up. Finding a dead body is a once-in-a-lifetime experience, thank goodness." *Speak for yourself, Cecily.* "The reason I'm calling is to see whether you and Lynda are still interested in the house."

Mac drummed his fingers on the paper-strewn desk. I paid no attention.

"I won't kid you, Cecily, we'd be very interested at the right price. I know you have a exceptionally motivated seller"—Grace said they'd moved into a condo four months ago; plus, Ralph would have lawyer's fees to pay if he got arrested—"but it might be harder now to find a motivated buyer. Not everybody likes the idea of living in a house where a murder took place. There could be, you know, ghosties and ghoulies, and things that go bump in the night. Lynda might be scared."

The agent snorted. "Lynda Teal wouldn't be scared by a grizzly bear armed with an assault rifle." *You know her better than I thought.* "I think I'd better talk to both of you. Why don't you two stop by my office this afternoon, say around two o'clock?"

Mac gave a "thumbs up." Apparently he wanted me to say yes, although I didn't know why. I was pretty sure he wasn't that eager to get rid of me as his tenant and near-neighbor.

"I don't know Lynda's schedule for the day, but I'll make a leap of faith and assume she can make it," I told Cecily.

As soon as we disconnected, I sent Lynda a text message before I forgot: *How about lunch at Daniel's at 1? Then meet Cecily at 2 to discuss house?*

"I'm sure you have more than just price negotiation in mind for Cecily," I told Mac as I tapped out the text.

"By that time I hope we will have formulated some questions for her about the murder. If Ralph is innocent, someone else must be guilty."

I couldn't argue with the logic, just with the premise. As far as I was concerned, the jury was still out on Ralph's innocence. I left that alone for the moment, though. "But you're not going to be there at our appointment with Cecily, Mac. See, the idea of Lynda and I buying a house is that we're not going to live with you anymore."

Mac chuckled. "Watson also deserted Holmes for a wife on at least two occasions, old boy. That did not, however, break up the partnership. I will stop by Happy Homes Realty around two o'clock."

I didn't know how I'd break that to Lynda, so I quickly decided that I wasn't going to. She'd find out soon enough.

"Let's get back to the part about how in my heart of hearts I know that Ralph didn't do it."

Mac raised an eyebrow. "Surely you do not dispute that?"

"I admit I find it hard to believe that the Ralph we know and love quashed a woman with a frozen salmon. It's not his style—not devious enough. But that doesn't mean he didn't do it. Let's leave our feelings out of this and look at what's possible instead of what's likely." *Dang, that sounded pretty good. Maybe I should be the detective this time.* "Anybody, even a bloodless pencil-pusher like Ralph, could get angry enough to hit somebody too hard in the heat of an argument."

Mac stroked his beard. "True enough. That would mean that the killing was unpremeditated, just as it seems on the surface. If so, why were Ralph and Mrs. Wanamaker in that house together?"

I shifted gears. "Okay, maybe it wasn't an argument over the city housing code or whatever. Maybe the two of them were involved in a sordid affair. That's why they were meeting in the empty house. And she'd come to her senses and wanted to break off the relationship."

"You astound me, Jefferson! Sherlock Holmes on more than one occasion indicated that imagination was an indispensible tool in the arsenal of a good detective. Once again you have proved that you have that aplenty."

Was that a compliment or an insult? I was still trying to decide when I heard the little pinging noise that told me I had a text message. It was from Lynda, a response to my text about lunch and a meeting with Cecily: *Works for me. Meet u at my office.* Lynda still hangs her hat at the *Observer* offices, right next to Daniel's Apothecary. *Excellent!* I texted back.

Mac stood up. "Data, data, data—we must have data. And for that, we shall have to descend to the belly of the beast."

V

So we trekked over to Ralph's office in Gamble Hall, discussing on the way how we would approach Ralph. A delicate touch and a little bit of subterfuge were called for when interviewing one's boss as a potential murder suspect.

Ralph's administrative assistant was away from her post when we got there, so we were able to duck in unannounced. Ralph's walnut-and-hardwood office looked like digs of a Fortune 500 CEO, all hundred acres of it. Okay, I'm exaggerating, but it's several times larger than my little hole. I felt a twinge of anger. With all the budget-cutting that had been done at St. Benignus—and Popcorn now in the crosshairs—Ralph hadn't skimped a bit on keeping his office maintained. The walnut was well polished, and he didn't do that himself.

"Good morning, Ralph!" Mac boomed.

Ralph tore his eyes away from the computer on his desk to look our way. "It was." It took him a second or two to realize that Mac wasn't alone. "If you've brought McCabe with you to plead your budget, Cody, I have to say I find that highly inappropriate and I assure you it will be unfruitful."

"You amaze me, Ralph." I actually meant it as a compliment. "How can you stay focused on the college's bottom line when a dead body was found in your home yesterday?"

He looked as startled as if I'd just asked him why he breathes. "Because it's my job." *The show must go on!* "What happened at the house on Campion Lane was very unfortunate." He made it sound like a minor social gaffe. "But it had nothing to do with me. That isn't even our home anymore. We merely own it. Mrs. Pendergast and I moved out late last year." *We know. Your wife told us.*

"I'm afraid the news media won't see it that way, Ralph," I said. Media, as in plural, wasn't an exaggeration. There's only one newspaper in Erin, but we're only forty miles upriver from Cincinnati, and occasionally the Cincinnati TV stations and newspaper notice. This would probably be one of those times, given the dramatic nature of both the homicide and its discovery. I went on with the line that Mac and I had agreed on, playing to Ralph's paranoia. "You know how sensationalistic they are. They may ask some tough questions about you and the dead woman, questions that will plant ideas in people's heads— even the trustees of St. Benignus—if they aren't answered properly. I'm here to help you prep for that by brainstorming the likely questions so you can get the answers ready."

He narrowed his eyes, not quite buying that I was offering what amounted to a favor. After all, this wasn't college business—not from his perspective. I looked at it differently. Any news involving an employee of St. Benignus affects the school, and I really did think the media might be interested. So I wasn't entirely serving up Ralph a hearty dish of baloney stew. I just left off the part about how we

were also hoping to get information from him that would
eliminate him as a suspect in the murder.

"Most generous of you, Cody," Ralph finally said,
barely moving his thin lips. "But why do I have to talk to
those busybody reporters at all?"

"You don't," I assured him. "Feel free to just say
'no comment'—if you want to look like you're trying to
hide something. You can't do that to Oscar and his cops,
though. Sooner or later you're going to have to answer
somebody's questions. I can help you with that."

This was proving to be an even harder sell than I'd
expected.

"Well, I certainly have nothing to hide," Ralph said.
"If that's what you're here for, why is McCabe tagging
along? Doesn't he have trouble to make somewhere else?"

The Lorenzo Smythe Professor of English
Literature and head of the popular culture program at St.
Benignus ranks high on one of Ralph's lists. I'll leave you to
figure out which one it is. Even though Ralph hadn't
addressed him, Mac answered for himself. "Are you
unaware that today is 'Take Your Brother-in-Law to Work
Day,' Ralph?"

He hates it when we call him Ralph, which is all the
time.

Seeing by the contortions in Ralph's face that Mac's
answer was somewhat less than satisfying to him, and not
wanting him to stroke out, I hastened to say, "I thought
he'd be better off with me here than playing bagpipes in the
Quadrangle. He tends to do that at this time of the year, you
know. And he might even have an idea or two. We need all
the help we can get."

"Sit down." Ralph pointed to a group of padded
leather chairs gathered around a round table a few yards
from his desk. We sat and he joined us.

"What exactly do you mean by 'tough questions'?"

"You knew Olivia Wanamaker," Mac said, "and your relationship with her was one of open conflict. To a suspicious mind, it seems a rather curious coincidence that she should be found dead in a house you own. The fact that you no longer live there is of little consequence. You still own it and you still have a key."

"So did the real estate company that she worked for!" Ralph calmed himself with a visible effort. "She could have met anyone there, using the key I provided to Happy Homes Realty."

I gave him full points for a good argument. But then, nobody ever said Ralph is stupid. While Mac nodded approvingly, I moved on. "Tell me about your relationship with Olivia Wanamaker."

"Relationship?" Ralph showed his teeth in a grim parody of a smile. "What is the relationship between a dart player and the dart board? Mrs. Wanamaker was a politician, pure and simple. She was trying to capture the student vote by an aggressive campaign against student-housing landlords in general, and against me in particular."

"That sounds rather abstract," Mac observed. "I presume she had some particular, er, dart to hurl."

Okay, enough with the darts metaphors, please.

Ralph sighed, as if begrudging the time spent talking about these murder-related trivialities. "I'm a busy man. Perhaps I don't spend as much time as I ought in supervising the student rental property my wife inherited. Some minor city code violations have accumulated. That was a regrettable mistake, but Mrs. Wanamaker blew it all out of proportion. I can have all of the violations remedied in short order. Then I plan to sell those buildings and get out of the rental business for good!"

Nice plan. Good luck with that, Ralph.

"Picking on me was like shooting fish in a barrel." He had his second wind now, bringing in a new simile. Too bad it was a cliché. "I'm not especially popular with the students. I don't try to be. That's not my job."

"I don't think you need to stress that," I said in full counselor mode. "It sounds like you're bragging. In fact, keep the politics out of it altogether. Emphasize that the issue you had with the deceased was easily fixed—a lot of drama, but not really a big deal."

Ralph surprised me by nodding. "Yes, I see what you mean."

"When was the last time you saw Olivia Wanamaker?" Mac asked.

"I was at last Wednesday's City Council meeting. I got wind that she was going to be grand-standing about student housing, so I thought I should be there to defend myself."

"You're sure that was the last time you saw her?"

"Of course I'm sure, McCabe. What are you getting at?"

"If you mean what am I implying, nothing. However, that will not be the last time you are asked that question, I assure you. Think hard, because if you even occupied the same sidewalk with Mrs. Wanamaker in downtown Erin after that occasion someone will have noticed and you will be seen as deceptive for not mentioning it."

If Ralph had any curl in his slicked-back hair, it probably would have come out at that point. Maybe it would be an exaggeration to say that he turned pale, but he looked like a man who was finally starting to understand the pickle he could be in.

He licked his thin lips. "I'll think about it, but I don't remember seeing her again after that."

Mac leaned forward. "Then, of course, there is the crucial issue of the fish in the freezer."

"Fish?" Ralph blinked like an owl. "What are you talking about?"

"The murder weapon, of course," I said.

"How would I know what the murder weapon was, Cody? I'm not the murderer."

"That wasn't a trick question. Everybody in Erin knows what the murder weapon was. It was in Johanna Rawls's story in the *Observer*."

"Oh. I didn't read the story. My wife read me parts of it and summarized the rest over breakfast. Either she didn't mention the fish or I wasn't paying sufficient attention."

"Then please pay attention now," Mac said with a show of patience. "Olivia Wanamaker was bludgeoned with a frozen fish. Do you remember leaving a fish in the freezer?"

Ralph shook his head. "I would have sworn that we cleaned everything out of the house before we left, including the contents of the freezer. What kind of fish was it?"

Good question, Ralph. The murderer wouldn't have to ask. But a clever killer would realize that and ask anyway.

"Salmon," Mac said.

"We don't eat salmon. I'm afraid of the mercury."

"If you stick to wild-caught Alaskan and Pacific Coast salmon and don't eat it too often, I think you'll be okay," I advised.

"Well, this is rather intriguing," Mac said. "I wonder where the salmon came from if it was not yours."

"What difference could it possibly make?"

"Possibly a great deal."

I figured Mac was just blowing smoke—which he is a master at, even without a lit cigar in his mouth—so I didn't pay too much attention to that enigmatic response as he led Ralph through a few other questions.

"Did you know Mrs. Wanamaker in any other context—social, for example?"

"Certainly not. If I'd seen her at a party, I would have run in the other direction."

Just imagining Ralph at a party was a stretch for me. "You might not want to put it that way on the witness stand," I told him.

The look he gave me was not one of appreciation.

"Had Mrs. Wanamaker ever shown your house to a prospective buyer?" Mac asked.

"Not that I know of, but I wouldn't necessarily know. The house was available to any agent who wanted to show it."

It went on like that for a few more futile minutes.

"I hope this has been helpful," I told Ralph, as we got ready to leave.

"I don't see how."

"Well, maybe you will later."

"Why didn't you ask where he was when the murder was committed?" I asked when we were down the hallway from Ralph's office.

"Because we do not know when the murder was committed. With the body frozen, it could be have been days ago."

"Oh."

Mac pulled out his phone and began punching numbers.

"Who are you calling?" Okay, I should have figured that out, but I didn't

"Mrs. Pendergast." He pressed the last number and put the instrument to his ear. "Grace? Sebastian McCabe here. Fine. I just have a simple question of fact: Are you certain that you cleaned out the freezer of the house on Campion Lane when you moved to your current place of residence? You did not leave a fish behind? Ah, that is what Ralph said but I wanted to be sure. No, no, we employed a subterfuge. He has no idea that we are acting on his behalf."

Actually, we aren't. We're acting on behalf of truth, justice, the American way, and the good name of St. Benignus College. "We have barely begun making inquiries. I will keep you informed. You are most welcome. Good-bye." He disconnected.

I put up my hands in surrender. "I give up! What's the point?"

Surprisingly, he answered me—and without riddles.

"The point, old boy, is that the murder was premeditated, as shown by the fact that the murderer must have brought the murder weapon. However, the nature of that weapon—which looks on the surface like the murderer picked up the first thing handy—means that it was intended to appear spontaneous. We are, as Sherlock Holmes would say, in very deep waters."

VI

"Now what?" I asked Mac. "Or should I say who?"

"Her Honor, the Mayor. She knew the victim. Perhaps she can shed some light on motive."

Still in her first term as mayor of Erin, Professor Lesley Saylor-Mackie had already proved to be an adept politician. I credit those backslapping and backstabbing skills honed during long years in academia. Her gracious manner concealed a tough-when-necessary cookie.

Her office is in Herbert Hall, just two floors up from Mac's. Since the distinguished historian is a tenured professor and head of the history department, we figured the odds were good that she'd be in her office rather than in a classroom. And she was.

She looked up from a book at Mac's rap on her open door.

"Professor McCabe!" she enthused. "And Jeff!" She whipped off her reading glasses, showing her clear hazel eyes to good advantage. "To what do I owe the pleasure?" See, a politician.

Saylor-Mackie stood and smoothed her gray pleated skirt. I can't exactly say why some women are pretty and some are handsome—by which I don't mean masculine— but I'd call her handsome. The gray streaks in her perfectly coiffed hair added to that, and didn't do a thing to hurt either her academic career or her political one.

"This is not a social call, I am afraid, or even St. Benignus business," Mac said. "As you are probably aware, Jefferson and his wife found Olivia Wanamaker's body."

Her face turned solemn. "How awful for you, Jeff. And what a tragic death!"

I made appreciative noises for her concern.

"It will not surprise you to know that we have taken a special interest in the murder," Mac said.

"You take an interest in every murder, Mac."

Good one, Mayor!

Mac nodded in silent acknowledgement of an undeniable truth. "In your capacity as mayor, you obviously knew Mrs. Wanamaker in her position as a member of City Council. What can you tell us about her?"

The look on Saylor-Mackie's face was hard to read, but I suspected that she was struggling with the old "speak no ill of the dead" tradition. She sat down and so did we.

"Olivia was certainly . . . tireless in pursuit of her objectives, which may have included the mayor's office. It never hurts to have the student vote in this town, and she's been pursuing that voting bloc with quite a will."

Just ask Ralph.

"That doesn't sound like someone who would be especially popular among her fellow Council members," Mac observed.

"Not especially, no."

A word about Erin politics: City Council and mayoral elections are officially non-partisan. The political parties do endorse candidates, but they don't give them a lot of money. As a result, it's basically every man or woman for him/herself. That applies to the floor of City Council as well as to mayoral elections, so the City Hall is not the friendliest place in town.

"What do you know about her personally?" I asked.

"From what I have heard, she was as aggressive in going after real estate sales as she was in going after votes." *So, not a lot of friends there, either.* Saylor-Mackie looked out the window, mentally taking her leave from us for a moment. She was trying to make up her mind about something, and I was pulling for her to do it right. She did. "I've also heard that her marriage was on the rocks."

"Heard from whom?" Mac asked.

"I don't remember. That's why I hesitate to bring it up, Mac. It might not be true."

This was good stuff. Husbands and boyfriends are always excellent suspects. Maybe Olivia Wanamaker had both.

Mac raised an eyebrow. "I hate to be indelicate, but did what you hear include a third party?"

Saylor-Mackie squirmed. "This gossip is making me uncomfortable. I think you'd be better off talking to somebody who would really know—perhaps her husband. I usually only saw her at City Hall and at press conferences to announce some new development in the city, at which she had a knack for standing in front of me."

"What about at City Hall, then?" Mac said. "Based on your own first-hand observation, was there anyone with whom she had a particularly tempestuous relationship?"

Saylor-Mackie gave Mac a Mona Lisa smile. "Well, she did have a shouting match at the last City Council meeting."

"Ah! With which Council member?"

"None of them. It was with a member of the gallery—Ralph Pendergast."

VII

"What do you make of that?" I said as we headed back across campus.

"I think our mayor's political talent might well take her to higher office, should she choose. Her timing in the way she delivered the swipe at Ralph, letting us draw it out of her, was flawless."

I knew where he was coming from. It was becoming increasingly clear that Lesley Saylor-Mackie would like to add provost and academic vice president to her collection of titles, which made Ralph's existence kind of inconvenient. The provost essentially runs St. Benignus, kind of like an executive vice president. Saylor-Mackie probably thought she'd be good at that, based on her experience as mayor. And I didn't doubt that she was right.

"Still," I said, "I'm sure she didn't make up that shouting match. It would have been nice if Ralph had mentioned it to us."

"Since when is Ralph nice?"

"Good point."

We stopped by my office in Carey Hall. Popcorn was sitting at her desk reading *Love's Forbidden Embrace*, another Rosamund DeLacey romance.

"Slow day?" I asked.

"I'm taking an early lunch break."

"What's going on?" I knew there wasn't much because my smartphone hadn't rung and I'd been monitoring my office e-mail.

"Father Pirelli stopped by." Our octogenarian president, always more of an inspirational figure than a detail man, had taken to sticking his head in offices more than ever since Ralph arrived to take up a lot of the administrative chores. "He said he really liked the commencement address you drafted for him. He only made a couple of changes."

Cha-ching! I'm in the zone!

She handed me the printed manuscript of the speech. Flipping through, I saw three or four changes written in red ink in the great man's neat handwriting. Father Pirelli had never fully gotten into the computer age.

"Also," Popcorn continued as I glanced at the changes, "I e-mailed out that press release about the remodeling of the chapel and sent out a couple of tweets. Other than that, all's quiet on the Western Front, Boss."

Thank heavens Ralph didn't hear that. I keep telling him we're busy, busy, busy. Can't possibly make this a one-person office! Actually, this was probably just the calm before some storm. That's the way it works in my world.

"Good." I handed her back the manuscript. "Mac and I are going to see Chief Hummel."

"Tell Oscar I said hi." Her voice sounded like melted chocolate when she mentioned his name.

"Coffee?"

Mac and I answered simultaneously. "Yes, please." "No, thanks." Oscar poured high-test java into Mac's regular mug, the one emblazoned with the words **I SEE NO REASON TO ACT MY AGE**.

"It all looks pretty simple to me," Oscar said. A Dayton Dragons baseball cap covered the chief's bald noggin as his chapeau-du-jour. "Unlike you, Mac, I like simple."

"I suppose we should call that Oscar's Razor," Mac quipped.

"What about my razor?" The chief unconsciously stroked his smooth-shaven skin.

That sidetracked Mac into a longer-than-necessary explanation of Occam's razor, the fourteenth-century friar William of Ockham's principle that simpler is better. Part of it was in Latin. By the time he'd finished, he'd drunk half his coffee.

"Oh," Oscar said at the end. "Well, like I said, I'm for that. So the simplest thing is if the murderer was the person in whose house the body was found, namely Dr. Ralph Pendergast. Why else would the killer be there?"

"Four reasons come to mind offhand," Mac rumbled. *Showoff.* "Suppose the killer went there with Olivia Wanamaker posing as a potential homebuyer and she caught him looting drugs out of the bathroom cabinet. I am told that such behavior occurs frequently at open houses. Or suppose the killer met Mrs. Wanamaker there for a romantic rendezvous that ended tragically. Or suppose the killer and the victim met there because it was a neutral location, one that both could agree upon. Or suppose Mrs. Wanamaker thought that is why they were meeting there, but the killer's plan was to frame the owner of the house. So you see, while Occam's razor is a perfectly sound starting place, it is sometimes insufficient."

Oscar squinted at Mac. *I think he needs glasses.* "You've been thinking about this, haven't you?"

"Guilty."

"Who had keys to the house?" I asked, trying desperately to get beyond the "supposes" into practical territory.

"The owner, for one," Oscar said.

"Surely that is irrelevant." Mac set down his coffee cup on Oscar's metal desk. "Olivia Wanamaker had access to a key in her capacity as an agent for Happy Homes Realty. The killer didn't need a key if he—or she—had Mrs. Wanamaker open the house."

Oh.

But Oscar barely paused. "Still, the fact remains, it was Pendergast's house and he had a big brouhaha with the victim during the City Council meeting less than a week ago. That's why I'm focusing on him, not his wife."

Mac raised an eyebrow. "So you found out about the blow-up? You are to be congratulated, Oscar."

"Gibbons turned it up." His voice betrayed a certain paternal pride in his assistant chief, the unflappable Lt. Col. L. Jack Gibbons. "Routine solves cases. You never get that right in your books."

Not to take anything away from Gibbons, but I bet Mayor Saylor-Mackie just happened to stop by and let that piece of information be coaxed out of her. Oscar's office and the small city jail are in the bottom of City Hall, several floors down from the mayor's office.

"Did you bring Ralph in for questioning?" I asked. "Third degree, hot lights, and all that?"

"He's coming in this afternoon. There's no hurry. He's a respectable member of the community, not a crazed serial killer. Here's what I think happened: They get together to cool things down, reach some kind of accommodation, but it goes sour. He gets carried away and hits her too hard with the frozen fish, totally unpremeditated. He hides her in the freezer, expecting to come back for her later, never dreaming that some snoop is going to look inside."

Oscar poured himself another cup of coffee from the pot behind his desk, then topped off Mac's mug without asking. "That's a simple, no-frills scenario and it makes sense. Do you see any holes?"

Mac sighed. "It is hard to know where to begin. Your unpremeditated rage hypothesis, although it looks good at first glance, falls doubly short upon closer inspection. First of all, it strains credibility that someone looking for a weapon would think to open a freezer and haul out a frozen salmon."

"The house was empty," Oscar said. "There wasn't a lot to work with."

"Granted. It is barely possible that an agitated person standing near the freezer chest and desperate for something to strike out with might look inside the chest, but not very likely. Already your scenario becomes not so simple. Moreover, Ralph and his wife, questioned separately, both assured me that they left nothing behind in the freezer. The murderer must have supplied it."

Oscar sat back. "Oh, well, by all means, let's take their word for that."

You know, amateurs should leave the sarcasm to people who are really good at it, like me.

Mac wasn't finished. "Another weak point is this: Surely the mutual, highly public animus that Ralph and Mrs. Wanamaker had for each other would preclude them from meeting alone in an empty house? That simply does not pass the common sense test."

"Okay, I'll give you that one. Maybe they had a secret thing going and Wanamaker using Pendergast for campaign fodder was a just a façade to cover it up. In that case, the killing happened during a lover's quarrel. Or maybe it *wasn't* spur of the moment, an accident. Maybe she was threatening to expose him, a respectable, married man."

I snorted, and I don't have a cute snort like Lynda does. It wasn't just that the picture of Ralph as a hot-blooded swain was frying my brain circuits. I was also dazzled by how quickly Oscar had turned his theory around—from impromptu act of anger to coldly plotted murder of a troublesome (ex-?) lover.

"Well, which is it—unpremeditated or planned?" I said. "Pick a scenario."

Oscar shook his head. "Doesn't matter. It fits Pendergast like a glove either way. Why would anybody else leave the body there just waiting to be found? And why bring a frozen salmon, of all things, for a murder weapon?"

"I should think that is obvious," Mac said.

But he would say no more.

VIII

"How'd it go?" Popcorn said, putting down *Love's Forbidden Embrace*. "I want all the details."

"Okay. Oscar was wearing a Dayton Dragons cap. I think it's new."

"No, I've seen it before. You're not very observant."

I just don't have the same kind of interest in Oscar that you do, Popcorn. No forbidden embraces with him for me!

Feeling like a rat for not having the nerve to tell her that her job was in jeopardy, I told her everything else. About halfway through, her mouth fell open and stayed that way.

"This is like some surreal dream," she said. "I can't believe that Dr. Pendergast would do such a horrible thing."

"Of course he wouldn't." *He does other horrible things.*

After a brief fill-in on what I'd missed while I was gone (a visit from a history professor named James Gregory Talton who wanted help publicizing his new book), I headed off to lunch with Lynda.

Daniel's Apothecary seems like a throwback to the late 1950s in every aspect from the malt shop menu to the jukebox (new but with classic rock 'n rock music) to the fact that it's a drug store that serves food. In reality, the Daniel family has been dishing out burgers and filling prescriptions there on Main Street since 1904. I've never asked whether the Daniels froze the look before 1960 or went retro at some later period.

I was studying the menu, sitting under a poster of James Dean looking rebellious and causeless, when Lynda sat down across from me with a deep sigh. Her dark oval face looked weary and her honey-blonde curls hung a bit limp.

"Going for the burger and fries this time?" she said, showing that her sense of humor was intact.

I chuckled. "If I decide to commit suicide by cholesterol, you'll be the first to know. Why the sigh?"

"Budgets. The parent company wants us to put out a good news product but they want the publishers and news directors to keep cutting back on the expense side."

In Lynda's job as editorial director of Grier Ohio NewsGroup, she's a kind of writing and reporting coach to all of the Grier newspapers and TV stations in Ohio. Operating from her base at *The Erin Observer & News-Ledger*, she travels a lot, but not very far.

"Somebody must have cloned Ralph to get your CEO," I said.

And so forth.

By the time our food arrived (the Marilyn Monroe sandwich for Lynda, the slightly less toxic Route 66 for me), we were on to the subject of our own personal budget.

"I still think the price Ralph and his wife are asking for the house isn't bad," I said. "But given the current circumstances, we may be able to get it even cheaper if we play it cool."

"But do we want it? I'm not sure we really talked about that."

Oh, yeah. The body kind of took our attention off of that. We hadn't talked about the murder, and I hadn't warned her that the other purpose of our meeting with Cecily was to ask her about Olivia Wanamaker. What was this lately with me hiding things from the women in my life?

"You know I like it," I said. "It's my kind of house. But what do you think? What's your honest opinion?" You probably think I was adding silently, *as long as it agrees with mine.* But that wasn't the case. I was hoping to make one move and stay put, so it had to be a house where both of us could be happy for a long time.

"I like it better than all of the other houses we looked at, and we looked at an exhausting number. If I had to pick one, that would be the one. But I think I'd like to look at it one more time just to be sure." She reached her hand across the table and took mine. "I want to picture our children in it, *tesoro mio.*"

We finished lunch with time to spare and walked over to Happy Homes Realty, not far away on Market Street. The office is mostly divided up into cubicles, with an agent in each one. Cecily Almond, on the phone when we arrived, waved and smiled from hers. After a few minutes she signed off and gave us her full attention.

"Hi, guys. Good to see you. Nice day, isn't it? So, are you ready to make a bid?"

"Not quite," Lynda said. We'd agreed that she would do most of the talking. "We'd like to see the house again."

"Oh, sure. No problem. Um. Well, actually, there *might* be a problem. I'm not sure the police have cleared away the crime scene tape yet. But after that, no problem!"

Could I ever have a better opening for negotiating a lower price? But before I had a chance to open my mouth, I heard, "Lynda! Jefferson!"

Mac was trying to look surprised as he walked our way, but he isn't as good an actor as he thinks he is—at least, not off stage.

"What are you doing here?" Was that a note suspicion I detected in my beloved's voice?

Mac held up a Multiple Listing Service catalog with photographs of homes for sale in Sussex and nearby counties. "I stopped by to pick up a house-hunting aid for a prospective new professor in the English department."

That may have even been true, though not the complete truth. Mac seldom lies, but often misleads.

"This is our real estate agent, Cecily Almond," I said, as if he didn't know. "Cecily—"

"You're Sebastian McCabe. I've read all of your books."

"Not yet," he assured her. "I have many more to write."

"Then I'll read many more. I just love them."

I know you're in the sales business, networking and all that, but do you have to actually gush?

"Thank you, Cecily. That is very kind of you to say so. Lately I feel almost guilty about engaging in murder for fun and profit in my fiction. I have learned that real-life homicide can be sad, tragic, horrifying, and many other things, but never fun."

Cecily shivered slightly—the real thing, nothing theatric. "No, it's certainly not. I hope I never find another body as long as I live."

I keep hoping that myself!

Mac was all sympathy. "That must have been a horrible experience, especially given that Mrs. Wanamaker was your friend and colleague."

"Friend would be pushing it. In fact, colleague would be an exaggeration."

Mac raised an eyebrow.

Cecily looked around Cubeville and lowered her voice. "Olivia was very hard-charging and not a team player. That didn't win her many friends in this office. In fact, she wanted to start her own team and she asked me to join her. Month after month I'm usually the second ranked sales agent, right behind Olivia. I said no thanks."

"You mean she was planning a new company?" Lynda asked.

Cecily nodded. "She even showed me the logo— Olivia Wanamaker Realty. I thought this was a risky time to be going out on her own, but self-doubt was not one of her handicaps. She thought her name on the door would bring in clients." Cecily shrugged her slim shoulders. "She sold a lot of houses, so maybe she was right. We'll never know."

Mac put the house book under his arm and unwrapped a cigar, not that he could smoke inside Happy

Homes. I think he just likes the prop. "As a mystery writer of some experience who has had several unfortunate encounters with untimely death in real life, I cannot help but wonder who might want Mrs. Wanamaker dead."

Cecily chuckled mirthlessly. "If this was one of your Damon Devlin novels, there'd be no lack of suspects. I've already hinted that she wasn't Miss Congeniality here at the office. Besides that, a lot of folks in the local real estate industry weren't happy with her crusade against student landlords. We sell a lot of properties that are rented to students. And I don't imagine that Margaret and Gordon were very happy about her plans to leave Happy Homes, if they heard about it."

Margaret and Gordon Cole, a couple in their sixties, had founded Happy Homes back in the '80s, riding high in boom times and hanging on through several slumps. The last few years might have been the worst they'd seen. I could imagine that losing their highest-producing agent would be a hard blow.

"Surely not everyone hated her," Mac said, waving his cigar. "She leaves behind a husband. Unless her marriage was . . ." He delicately left the thought uncompleted.

"I don't like to repeat gossip." *So listen carefully the first time.* Cecily didn't say that, but that was the idea. "From what I hear, Sam Wanamaker wasn't the dumb blonde she took him for. Apparently things had been strained at their house lately after he smelled pipe smoke in the bedroom. He doesn't smoke."

"Is that what you talk about at lunch around here?" Lynda asked. "That's pretty personal. I'm surprised you'd know a thing like that if she wasn't that friendly with her co-workers."

I couldn't tell from her tone whether Lynda was offended at the gossip or wanted Ben Silverstein to hire Cecily as a reporter. It could have been either. My wife is an old-fashioned girl in a lot of ways, but she's also a newshound through and through.

Cecily lowered her voice. "Piper Lawrence heard it from Sam. They went to grade school together. A man won't tell a thing like that to another man because he doesn't want to look like a fool, but sometimes he'll tell a woman that he's friends with."

Welcome to small town America, where everybody knows everybody—and sometimes too well.

"I haven't seen Piper since she got laid off at WIJC-FM," I said. She'd been assistant producer at the campus radio station until Ralph had decided in an earlier wave of cutbacks last year that Tony Lampwicke and the other on-air personalities could pour their own coffee. That's not all Piper did, of course, any more than that's all Popcorn does. But when Ralph Pendergast gets a notion in his head it can't be dislodged with a jackhammer.

"Piper works here. There she is over there." Cecily pointed. I could barely see the top of her head above a cubicle on the other side of the room.

"She must have gotten her real estate license after St. Benignus gave her the old heave-ho," I said. "I'm glad she landed on her feet."

"Oh, Piper isn't an agent. She's a stager."

I made a mental note to say hi to her on my way out. She might see me, and I wouldn't want her to think I was avoiding her because of survivor's guilt.

"If you were writing a detective story," Mac said to Cecily, "who would be your favorite suspect?"

She gave that a good ten seconds' consideration. "Me."

Mac almost lost his grip on the unlit cigar in his mouth. Whatever he'd been expecting, it wasn't that. "Why you?"

Cecily smiled. "Because I'm the least likely person. Olivia was a pain in the butt, but I don't have a reason in the world to be glad that she'd dead."

"But with her gone, you'd be the top ranked agent here," I pointed out. "Wouldn't you like that?"

"She was planning to leave Happy Homes and start her own outfit anyway, remember? She tried hiring me."

"Oh, right." I wondered whether Olivia Wanamaker had acquired a real estate broker's license—a step up from an agent's license—which she would need to start her own company. That would indicate how serious she was.

After a few more attempts, Mac finally gave up trying to get Cecily to speculate on who might have done in her personally unpopular but politically successful colleague. I'm sure that Mac found her reticence frustrating, but I thought it was admirable.

He held up the catalogue of homes for sales. "Well, I must get back to the groves of academe and put this into the hands of our prospective new professor."

"*Ciao*," Lynda said.

"*Alla prossima.*"

I hate it when they yack at each other in Italian; it makes me feel like a fifth wheel.

"We're leaving, too," I asserted.

So we all three left together, by way of Piper's cubicle. I called out her name as we got close.

She turned around, saw us, and opened her generous mouth in a broad smile. "Oh, hey Jeff, Professor McCabe. Been a while. And you're Lynda, right?"

At St. Benignus, I was used to seeing her in slacks. Today she was wearing a burgundy dress of some soft fabric with a wide, white belt. Her chestnut hair, previously cut rather short, hung down to her shoulders. When her head moved I saw that she wore silver earrings, the same material she had around her wrists and neck. I wondered whether she took her fashion cues from the Duchess of Cambridge, who is Lynda's age and a little younger than Piper.

"Cecily tells me you've become a home stager," I said.

"Isn't that wild? I'm even certified. Half a year ago I didn't even know what a stager was."

Apparently she could tell from the look on Mac's face that he didn't know either, because she hurried on to explain.

"Staging means that I prepare a home for sale to make it appeal to the largest number of potential buyers, which facilitates the quickest sale at the best price. Research has shown that homes can sell up to twice as fast and for ten to fifteen percent more money if they're properly staged."

She had the pitch down cold.

"No offense," Lynda said, "but the Pendergast house didn't exactly look staged. It looked empty."

Piper exercised her smile muscles again. "I didn't work on that one. I guess the owner didn't want to spend the extra money."

That sounds like Ralph.

"How's business?" I ask that all the time. As an investor in index mutual funds—which had done quite well lately, thank you—I'm always hoping for indications of a strengthening economy. And this time I got it.

"Better," Piper said. "People can see that houses are starting to sell again, and that's encouraged people who've been waiting to sell. So listings are up. But it's still taking longer for homes to sell than it does in a strong economy, so a lot of sellers are seeing the value in getting help from a professional stager."

It seemed that Piper had indeed landed fairly softly after being bounced out of St. Benignus. I was sure that Popcorn would do as well if she got the axe. The question was how I would do without her.

"I suppose a dead body in a freezer is about the worst staging possible," Mac said.

Piper seemed to take that personally.

"Like I said, I wasn't involved in that particular sale." She ran a hand through her hair. "I'm still shocked by what happened to Liv. She was very nice to me and helped me out a lot when I first joined Happy Homes."

Finally! Someone with a kind word to say for the dead woman! But then, why shouldn't Olivia Wanamaker be nice to Piper? The two women weren't in competition for sales or votes.

"It sounds like you were rather close to Mrs. Wanamaker, perhaps closer than most of her colleagues here," Mac observed.

She shrugged. "I guess so." She lowered her voice. "I think a lot of the other agents were jealous of her."

"If you know anything that might help the police find her killer, you must tell Chief Hummel."

Piper's green eyes widened. "I don't know anything."

"Perhaps you don't know what you know." The way Mac said that, his tone of voice, it sounded like the most reasonable thing in the world. "What seems innocuous to you might be significant to the police. And what you may think too personal to share may be critical to the hunt for the killer. For example, if Mrs. Wanamaker had a boyfriend and you knew his—"

"I don't!"

"—name, I am certain the Chief would like to talk to him."

"But I don't!"

"Well, then, that is final." Mac smiled. *He's at his most dangerous when he smiles.* "You do not know his name. What *do* you know about him?"

Well played, Mac.

Piper hesitated. Should she tell or not? *Oh, go on!* "I know that he was quite a bit older than Liv. That created, uh, physical challenges that she described in some detail." Piper colored. "I'd rather not be more explicit."

Uh-oh. An unidentified much older boyfriend would play right into Oscar's lamebrain back-up theory that Olivia Wanamaker and Ralph weren't the enemies that they appeared to be in public.

Piper rushed on, as if afraid that Mac would press her for details. "I also know that she had an appointment with him on the morning of the day her body was found."

"What kind of appointment?" Lynda asked. Her journalism genes were kicking in now.

"I don't know exactly what was going on, but they'd reached some kind of crisis and the purpose of the meeting was to settle it. I thought maybe she wanted to break it off."

"Do you remember her exact words?"

Piper paused. "It was something like, 'I'm going to end this even if it's the end of me.'"

"That sounds definite," I said.

But Mac shook his head. "The 'this' could be the relationship, but it could be something else—it could be a misunderstanding, or a behavior pattern, or a deception, or any number of other things."

"Maybe so," Lynda conceded, "but the 'end of me' part sounds ominous no matter what she meant by the other part."

"Should I tell Chief Hummel?" Piper asked.

Let's see: Do we want Oscar to know that the victim was stepping out with an older man and seemed determined to cut it off at a meeting the day her body was found, fitting in perfectly with his conviction that Ralph was the most likely suspect?

"Only if he asks," Mac advised.

"He probably won't," Lynda added, "unless he gets onto the boyfriend angle and works it, or has Gibbons work it, with everybody associated with Olivia. But Johanna Rawls will want to ask you about it."

"Isn't she the reporter at the *Observer* who wrote about the murder?" Piper shook her head vigorously. "I'm not talking to a reporter. I don't want my name in the paper."

Good girl!

Storm clouds gathered over Lynda's pretty visage. Understandably, she wasn't a bit happy about Piper's professed media shyness. It put Lynda in a pickle. She still had newspaper ink running in her veins instead of blood, but she was a journalist without being a reporter. Anything somebody says to a reporter, unless they've first reached agreement that it's off the record, is fair game for quoting. But etiquette says that rule doesn't apply to talking with people higher up the pay scale.

As an employee of *The Erin Observer & News-Ledger*'s parent company, Lynda was more like the publisher who comes back from the Rotary Club meeting with a heck of a story, but tells the troops they have to confirm it on their own and leave him out of it. That happens all the time, by the way, and not just in small town America. It's even more awkward when the publisher is on the board of trustees of say, a museum, which has done something controversial and nobody at said institution will talk to the publisher's paper.

"Well, gosh, how time flies!" I observed. "I guess I'd better be getting back to . . . whatever I'm getting back to. Nice seeing you again, Piper! Good luck."

Mac and Lynda murmured polite goodbyes and we were soon out of there.

"Cheer up," I told Lynda as we hit the sidewalk. "Johanna is pretty sharp. Maybe she'll get a line on the boyfriend on her own, something even more solid, like a name."

Lynda raked both of us with a withering glance. "It's not Johanna I'm worried about. It's you two."

Mac's *"Moi?"* expression wouldn't have fooled a three-year-old.

"You didn't just happen into Happy Homes today, Mac. You guys have been poking into the murder, probably asking questions all over town, haven't you?"

J'accuse!

"All over town would be a considerable exaggeration," Mac said.

"Don't get all legalistic, Mac!" My beloved whirled on me. "And you! Why didn't you tell me what you were up to?" Lynda Teal (Cody) is the most even-tempered of women, even though she is half-Italian, so I was ill-prepared by experience for this tsunami of emotion. What I saw in her gold-flecked brown eyes wasn't anger, it was hurt. And that hurt me. "Well? What do you have to say for yourself?"

I want a lawyer! At least I had Mac. He broke my awkward silence with our defense.

"I believe that what Jefferson is trying *not* to say is that we were rather boxed in by a request from the person who asked us to make inquiries. This person, our non-paying client as it were, is most eager that our involvement on behalf of a third party not be known."

"That's true," I confirmed. *Although it's almost impossible to follow what he just said.* "Plus, it only happened this morning that this person contacted us. I didn't have time to break down and tell you what I wasn't supposed to tell, which I'm sure I would have sooner or later—probably during dinner or pillow talk. You know I'm terrible at keeping secrets."

Apparently being a good husband is more than just remembering to put the toilet seat lid back down and squeeze the toothpaste from the bottom.

Lynda shook her head. "I should have known you boys couldn't stay out of this."

IX

By the time I got to my office the next morning, which happened to be Shakespeare's birthday, Lynda and I had reached an understanding that she wasn't going to be surprised like that again. Lynda isn't one to stew over things, so that was that. But I decided I'd better make reservations soon at Ricoletti's Ristorante, or at least The Roundhouse, just to seal the deal.

It was the day before Olivia Wanamaker's funeral.

"Oscar knows who did it," Popcorn said with an unmistakable note of pride in her voice as she handed me a cup of decaffeinated coffee. *That can't be good.* "He said he talked to him yesterday."

"Who is it?" *As if I didn't know.*

"He just chuckled and said to ask you."

"How very cagey of him." How much should I tell her? With Popcorn keeping company with Oscar, although she remained coy about that, maybe I shouldn't let her have anything we didn't want the chief to know. But I didn't want to get into the same kind of trouble with her that I was in with Lynda.

"Can you keep a secret? Even from Oscar?"

She sat forward eagerly. "I barely know the man, Boss."

Right. But I told her everything, including the older boyfriend stuff from Piper Lawrence. At the end of my summary of the case against Ralph, Popcorn was gaping.

"I can't believe he'd do a thing like that."

"Mac doesn't seem to think he did. Anyway, I know that Oscar had an interview scheduled with Ralph, but I didn't get debriefed on the outcome. I was tending to the home fires last night, so I haven't talked to Mac. Maybe he knows more."

"Call him."

I did so.

"I was just about to call you, old boy," my brother-in-law boomed. "Yes, I spoke with Oscar. Apparently our beloved provost's stuffed shirt got a little stiffer under Oscar's rather aggressive questioning." Popcorn, who could hear Mac halfway across the room, smirked. "In short, I gather that Ralph's injured dignity did not serve him well and he overplayed his hand."

"And that, naturally, only made Oscar all the more suspicious." I groaned. Obviously, Ralph needed a communications advisor.

"I have a class this morning." *How unusual for a tenured professor.* "However, I am available starting at eleven-thirty. I suggest we both take an early lunch and visit Mr. Sam Wanamaker, the widower."

"The funeral is tomorrow. Isn't that a little tacky?"

"Sadly, there will never be a better time, Jefferson."

I wasn't happy about this little plan, but I agreed to it. Mac was going to do it anyway, and he's even more dangerous if he doesn't have adult supervision.

The Wanamaker house was in a new development just inside the city limits. When I had first come to Erin, it had been farmland. Now it was all McMansions for Altiora Corp. executives and others in their income range. Apparently the Wanamakers did quite well for themselves. Although they had no children, they lived in one of the larger houses on the street, two stories in a mock Tudor style, all brick. The landscaping was flawless, of course. That was Sam Wanamaker's business. He had met Olivia on the job five years ago at the annual Sussex County Parade of Homes home show.

We rang the doorbell, waited, rang it again. Finally a big man answered, not fat but tall and bear-like. He had short, golden hair that glittered in the sunlight, as did the equally golden frames of his glasses. He was wearing a Wanamaker Landscaping golf shirt.

The door was only open about halfway. Mac took the lead.

"Mr. Wanamaker? My name is Sebastian McCabe and this is my friend and brother-in-law, Thomas Jefferson Cody. We are sorry—"

"I know who you are. You're that mystery writer from St. Benignus, the amateur detective." He turned to me. "And you found Liv's body in that freezer." I wouldn't go so far as to say he was choking back sobs, but his eyes were wet and there was a catch in his throat.

"That is accurate so far as it goes, Mr. Wanamaker. Jefferson and I—"

Wanamaker opened the door all the way. "Come on in. I think I could use your help."

Whoa—didn't see that coming!

The Wanamaker residence could have been a model home—or at least, a model house. The chairs, the couches, the little tables, and even the paintings were all showroom quality, and perhaps all for show. It was hard to believe that anybody actually lived there.

"Have a seat." Wanamaker pointed to a pair of sturdy-looking chairs, each wide enough to support Mac, while he arranged himself on a more delicate reproduction antique love seat.

"How can we help you?" Mac asked. When he sees an open door, he barges right through it.

"You've come about Liv, my wife." The Golden Bear apparently was not one to mince words. "You're looking into the murder and it's not hard to guess why." *It's not?* Wanamaker smiled bitterly. "It's irresistible, right? Have you seen what the tabloid TV shows have done with it?"

"Fortunately, no," Mac said.

"They've got a lot of cute names for it, like they're having fun with it. The Body in the Freezer. The Case of the Cold-Cocked Corpse." Wanamaker shook his head, not quite believing what life had brought him. "I talked to Chief

Hummel on Sunday and then again yesterday. I'm sure he's a good man, but I'm not sure he's the right man—not for this case. He seems to be fixed on the idea that the owner of the house did it. The owner's probably just some nice guy who has nothing to do with it." *You may have that half right, Sam.* "I'm glad you want to find the man who killed my wife. Find him, prove it, and make sure he pays."

"We didn't actually say—" I began.

But Mac was in no mood to split hairs.

"Why 'man'?" he asked.

"What?"

"You said 'the man who killed my wife.' Why do you assume that it was a man?"

Wanamaker shrugged. "I don't know. The way she was killed, I guess. I just said it, I didn't really mean anything by it."

"Not at a conscious level, perhaps," Mac conceded. "However, the fact that you dismiss the likelihood of Ralph Pendergast's guilt and yet you automatically used the male pronoun for the killer suggests to me that your subconscious mind has a preferred candidate for that role."

Wanamaker seemed to think a bit before his face brightened. "Hey, how 'bout a beer?" It was a safe bet that he'd already had a few, judging by the rosiness of his face and the overly careful way he was speaking.

I declined with thanks, but not Mac. "I am never one to discourage generosity." Later, he claimed that he'd merely been trying to establish rapport with an important witness. I think it more likely he was trying to establish rapport with a cold bottle of Edmund Fitzgerald Porter.

We followed Wanamaker into the kitchen.

"When a woman is killed, the husband is usually the first suspect," Mac observed. "You are fortunate indeed that in this case Oscar is going down a different road, especially since—forgive me for bringing this up—your marriage . . ."

He left the sentence uncompleted. Wanamaker slapped an opened bottle of beer into his hand. "We had some problems. I guess that doesn't go unnoticed in a town like this. But I loved Liv. She had a softer side that a lot of people never saw." *Like the other side of a nail file?*

"And you think perhaps the other man might have killed her."

Wanamaker gulped his beer. "Oh, jeez, are people talking about 'the other man,' too?"

"Not everybody," I said helpfully.

Mac glared at me. "A woman who shared confidences with your wife told us. She did not know the man's identity. However, she said Mrs. Wanamaker hinted that her paramour was a much older man."

Wanamaker shook his head. "I don't know for sure who it is either. He didn't leave his calling card, and Liv wouldn't tell me. But if you're asking me, I think it was that stuffy, self-important, boring Tony Lampwicke from WIJC. He interviewed Liv on his radio show not long ago. She seemed to be captivated by his phony intellectualism—you know, stuff like 'next week we look at the exciting new generation of Bantu poets.'" Wanamaker's imitation of Tony's cultivated Oxford accent was spot-on and amusing.

But my head was reeling. Could this be true? Sure it could. All of a sudden I had a flashback to Cecily saying that Sam smelled pipe tobacco smoke in the Wanamakers' bedroom. Ralph didn't smoke a pipe (or anything), but Tony did. Tony wasn't exactly an old man, only in his early forties or so, but maybe that was old to Olivia.

Why hadn't Piper known about this from working with Tony? If anybody knows whom a man is seeing, it's his administrative assistant.

"How long do you think this had been going on?" I asked.

Wanamaker shrugged. "It was only within the last few weeks that I felt that Liv was moving away from me emotionally. Then, I guess it was week before last, I smelled this tobacco smoke in our room. It was very aromatic, not like a cigar or a cigarette."

Two weeks ago would have been months after Piper left WIJC-FM and St. Benignus, thanks to Ralph's budget cutting. So the mystery of how Piper didn't know about Olivia and Tony, if there was something to know, was quickly solved: She wasn't working for him at the time.

"Clearly, a discussion with our old friend Tony is in order," Mac rumbled. I wasn't sure whether Mac was talking to me, to Wanamaker, or to himself. But his next words were directed to the grieving widower:

"When did you last see your wife?"

"I made her Sunday breakfast. I always do—did. Even with our problems she liked me doing that. She left right afterwards. That was probably, I don't know, nine-thirty or so."

"Did she say where she was going?"

"No. I just assumed she was showing a house. She did that a lot on Sundays. It was like what she did for church."

"I presume she carried a smartphone?"

"Sure."

"Did the calendar on it show any appointments for Sunday?"

"I don't know. I didn't look. Do want me to? Chief Hummel gave me back all her stuff."

"If you don't mind."

Wanamaker took a long pull on his beer and then disappeared upstairs.

Mac drank his brew more slowly. "We progress, Jefferson. I begin to see some light in the darkness."

It must be infrared because I can't see it. He always says things like that, and then refuses to elaborate. This time I didn't give him the satisfaction of asking what he meant. I looked around. It was a top-notch kitchen, with stainless-steel appliances, granite countertops, and cabinets that I was sure were solid maple. The kitchen in the house on Campion Lane was nice, too, at a less expensive level. Lynda could make good use of it. She's a terrific Italian cook.

"Here it is." Wanamaker was holding out the phone as he walked into the kitchen. It was an iPhone 5G, the latest model then available, with a green and white case. Those were the colors of the Happy Homes Realty logo. I wondered if she had planned to change the case when she had her own logo. That reminded me.

"We heard that Olivia was planning to start her own realty company," I said. "Is that true?"

"Oh, yeah. She had a written business plan, her broker's license, and everything. She was just waiting for the market to get a little stronger. I've owned my own business for a long time, so I was helping her with the business aspect of it."

Meanwhile, she was presumably helping herself to Tony Lampwicke. Nice lady!

Olivia Wanamaker's plans to jump ship at Happy Homes probably had no bearing on her murder. Or did they? At any rate, part of what Cecily had told us was now confirmed, which gave more credence to the rest.

Wanamaker looked down at the iPhone. "She does have a notation on her calendar for ten-thirty Sunday morning, but it's just initials: R.P."

X

"Ralph's middle initial might as well be 'I,' as in 'R.I.P.,'" I said glumly as we left the house. "The case against him looks worse and worse. I guess we have to go back to him and ask him to explain himself."

"Why bother?" Mac said with unseemly good cheer. "Ralph assured us repeatedly that the City Council meeting was the last time he saw Olivia Wanamaker. He could hardly recant now, and if we asked him again he would likely assume an eagerness on our part to presume his guilt."

"Well, then we just tell him that his wife asked us— oh, no, we can't do that. We promised. Damn." This business was like a house of mirrors. There had to be a way out somewhere, but I couldn't see it for the life of me. I was beginning to revisit that nagging fear that, no matter what Mac believed, Ralph *had* whacked Olivia with a frozen salmon—maybe in a fit of temporary insanity.

Mac, meanwhile, seemed to be thinking more like a defense attorney than a detective.

"Your fears about the calendar entry dooming Ralph, while not unfounded, are premature. When Oscar described to me his interview with our beloved provost, he said nothing about that notation on Mrs. Wanamaker's calendar. Perhaps he neglected to look at the calendar while the phone was in his possession. After all, we only did so because Piper told us about the appointment. "

I thought about that. Oscar is by no means stupid, but he's no Sherlock Holmes. He's not even a Columbo (except at that Halloween party). "So we have some breathing room until Piper Lawrence or Sam Wanamaker realizes it would be good citizenship and smart policy to tell Oscar what they know. What do we do now?"

"Visit Tony Lampwicke, of course."

We found him at the WIJC-FM studio on the lower level of Muckerheide Center, where he holds forth on his weekly program, *Crosscurrents*, and reads the local news daily. Tony Lampwicke has a perfect public radio voice, which Sam Wanamaker's mocking imitation had captured to a T. I'm sure a lot of people think Tony hails from the BBC-land because he sounds like it, but he's actually a native of Hamilton, Ohio, about thirty miles north of Cincinnati.

When we arrived in early afternoon, he was off the air and getting ready to go home. His work day started early and ended early. It struck me that those must be convenient hours for a wayward Romeo whose girlfriend's husband was gone all day running a business, probably until late.

Tony was in a little office next to the broadcast studio. The goatee over his sharp chin made him look more like a professor than most of our professors. His trademark cable knit sweater and loafers on this very comfortable day in late April completed the effect.

He looked up in surprise when we entered. "Oh, hello, chaps. What brings you 'round? I haven't seen either of you in ages. Have a seat. Excuse the mess. I don't have much time for housekeeping since I lost my devoted admin."

I feel your pain.

"We've been making some inquiries into the murder of Olivia Wanamaker," Mac said.

He sobered up instantly. Was that a look of real remorse on his face or was he just giving us what he thought we expected? I couldn't make up my mind.

"What a tragedy! I've been working on a retrospective of her political career, using an interview that I conducted with her a couple of months ago for *Crosscurrents*. She was so charismatic, so alive. It's hard to believe she's gone. I must say I found her quite attractive."

"That's what we hear," I said.

He looked at us quizzically. Mac and I didn't say anything. It's an old journalism trick: Keep your mouth shut and wait for the interviewee to fill the silence. I've learned not to fall for that as the one being interviewed, because the natural tendency in that situation is to say too much. That's why it's a trick. It's not one that comes easily to Sebastian McCabe—he's not much into silence—but I'd talked him into it on the way over.

It worked better than I could have hoped. After only about ten seconds, Tony cracked. "I see. Tongues have been wagging, have they?"

Later, I realized that he actually wanted to talk about his conquest of a woman who might have been our next mayor. We were just giving him the permission to do it without feeling guilty.

Mac spread his hands, innocence personified. "Let us say, rather, that Mrs. Wanamaker had a close friend in whom she confided."

If Tony drew the conclusion that Olivia was so head over heels for him that she couldn't help mentioning his name to a gal pal, well, Mac hadn't actually said that.

Tony settled back in his chair, smiling faintly as if at a fond memory, and put a pipe in his mouth but didn't light it. Apparently, unlike Mac, he actually obeyed the rules that banned smoking everywhere on campus.

"I knew her by reputation, of course, but we only met when I interviewed her. I found her not only attractive, but intelligent and driven. She wanted to start her own real estate company, she wanted to be mayor. Her passion, her ambition was quite intoxicating. I was already involved with a woman I won't name and I wasn't looking to complicate my life, frankly." He smiled faintly and shrugged his sweater-clad shoulders. "But I'm only human." *Doubtful.*

"You practically had no choice, right?"

Missing my sarcasm, Tony nodded. "There you have it. What was I supposed to do when she threw herself at me? She told me her marriage was on the rocks. I'm no home wrecker. I was offering a lifeline to woman trapped in a dead relationship."

Right. You're a hero, Tony. You deserve a medal. Actually, I don't think even he was convinced by that self-serving pile of bull. Mercifully, Mac moved on.

"Did you have any indication that she was seeing another man besides you, perhaps someone older?"

"Certainly not." He seemed offended at the notion that Olivia would be unfaithful to him.

"Too bad," I said. "Boyfriends are always good suspects." The situation was bringing out the mean in me. But Tony didn't even do me the favor of looking flustered.

"As it happens," he said, "I have an alibi for the time Olivia was killed. I handle the audio-visuals for the Sunday services at Glad Tidings. I'm there all day." Erin's only non-denominational megachurch, offering gourmet coffee and entertaining services, had been packing in the crowds ever since it opened about five years ago.

Mac regarded Tony shrewdly. "What makes you think Mrs. Wanamaker was killed on Sunday? Her body was frozen. She could have been killed days before."

Tony looked from Mac to me and back again. "Well, I guess I just assumed. I was, uh, with her on Saturday afternoon."

Mac nodded. "As it happens, her husband says he last saw her on Sunday morning. Did you know she had an appointment on Sunday?"

Tony shook his head. "A business appointment? We didn't talk business."

"We don't know that it was business. Do you have any idea who might have wanted to kill her?"

He gave it a thought. "Olivia was a very determined woman. If she got in someone's way, killing her might be the only way to remove her. She really was a fascinating woman. I only hope I can do her justice with the segment of *Crosscurrents* that I'm putting together."

"I have a suggestion on that," I said.

"Yes?"

"Don't bother trying to interview Ralph."

XI

"How about Saylor-Mackie?" I asked Mac as we walked back across campus. "Olivia could have been seriously in her way if she'd run for mayor."

What was I saying? Having one of our most eminent scholars arrested for murder was no better for St. Benignus than having our provost tapped for the honor. But Mac wasn't having it anyway.

"Killing someone is a risky business, only to be undertaken if the benefits outweigh the dangers. Of course, not every killer recognizes that, but Professor Saylor-Mackie would. She is not one to take risks, professionally or politically."

"Well, there's always the jealous husband."

"That possibility should not be dismissed," Mac allowed. "However, her husband was not the only person to whom the victim was disloyal. Her plans for starting her own company cannot have been good news to the owners of Happy Homes Realty. I should like to get their perspective on Mrs. Wanamaker."

Mac called and made an appointment for later in the day. After a few hours fiddling around in our respective offices, we met up with Margaret and Gordon Cole in their quarters at the back of the building on Market Street.

I've heard that if two people are married long enough they start to look alike. The Coles could have been Exhibit A for that theory. Or maybe it was just a case of non-opposites attracting. Both stood about five-four or so, with short gray hair—hers was shorter than his—and big glasses. They were wearing white polo shirts brandishing the company logo of a smiling house, color green. They would have made a nice set of salt-and-pepper shakers.

"Yeah, we knew she was gearing up to jump ship and start her own company," Gordon said in a deep baritone that didn't match his size. "She didn't bother to tell us, but word gets around. I would have fired her on the spot if she weren't our best agent. But I tried to keep an eye on her to make sure she didn't sabotage us on her way out."

"I wouldn't put it past her," Margaret added helpfully.

"She could have taken a lot of clients away from Happy Homes," Mac pointed out. "You must have been quite upset that she was leaving you."

"Yes and no," Margaret said.

"She was our biggest producer," her husband repeated, "but also our biggest management problem. None of the other agents liked her because she was a claim jumper. With her gone, the others might be more productive."

It was hard for me to see the hard-driving Cecily Almond being a better sales agent than she already was, but I'm sure not every agent was like her.

"She was also going to give you new competition with her company," I pointed out. "And she was trying to steal away your agents—she offered Cecily a job."

"The woman has no ethics," Gordon huffed. He seemed to forget for a moment that she was dead.

"Olivia's company, if it ever got off the ground, would have been a disaster," Margaret opined. "She knew nothing about motivating people, training, or how to run a business. And none of our good people would have joined her. The only person in this office she got along with was Piper Lawrence. The agents liked her about as much as Cecily did, which is to say not at all."

Cecily! Our go-getting agent's name hit me with gale force. Why had I not thought of Cecily before? Was it just because I liked her? Or was it because she disarmed us by saying she was the least likely suspect? Occam's razor would say that she was actually the *most* likely to be the killer. She found the body, she was the listing agent on the house (therefore very familiar with it), and she didn't get along with Olivia. Okay, the motive was a little weak, as Cecily had been suspiciously quick to point out. There must have been another reason. Romantic jealousy, perhaps?

"Mac, I'm getting an idea," I said.

"I already have one." He pulled out his smartphone and punched a number out of his "Favorites" list.

"Hello, Oscar. Jefferson and I are at Happy Homes Realty. If you will join us at your earliest opportunity, I think we have something interesting to tell you. Why, the identity of Olivia Wanamaker's murderer, of course."

XII

By the time Oscar arrived, we had moved into a conference room. At Mac's invitation, Cecily and Piper had joined us. We all stood around a conference table, somewhat awkwardly.

"So what's this all about?" Oscar demanded. *I was wondering that myself, Chief.*

"Motive," Mac said. "The key to solving this murder is that the culprit had two of them—a motive for killing Olivia Wanamaker and a motive for framing Ralph."

Oscar patted his pockets until he realized that he was out of cigarettes. He always is. "You're going to drag this out, aren't you?"

"Yes. Everyone seemed to hate or at least dislike Mrs. Wanamaker, with the possible exception of the voters who elected her to City Council. By all accounts she was quite unpopular with her colleagues both at City Hall and here at Happy Homes. The singular exception was Piper." He nodded to the home stager, who seemed puzzled as to why she was in the room. So was I.

"Piper provided us with a huge clue—the information that Olivia's paramour was much older and that he had an assignation with her on the day she died. No one else knew this, although the calendar in her cell phone showed an appointment at ten-thirty with 'R.P.'"

"Ralph Pendergast!" Oscar exclaimed. *No flies on you!* "I knew it! You dragged me over here just to tell me—"

"However," Mac forged on, "an analysis by a computer expert of my acquaintance has determined that the appointment was typed into Mrs. Wanamaker's calendar *after* ten-thirty." This totally had my head spinning around like that girl in *The Exorcist.* Mac had said nothing to me about having somebody look at Olivia's smartphone. Was that what he'd been up to this afternoon while I was slaving away in my office? Well, not exactly slaving away. Mostly I was giving Popcorn a blow-by-blow account, including an excellent (if I do say so myself) imitation of Tony Lampwicke's put-on accent. But still—

"What do you mean?" Oscar demanded. I take it back. He wasn't so quick on the uptake today after all.

"I mean that someone else entered Ralph's initials in the calendar after the murder to implicate him," Mac said.

"Cecily!" I blurted. *Finally, my moment has arrived!* Only it hadn't. I don't know who looked more put out, Cecily or Mac.

The former merely looked at me with a "say what?" expression on her café-au-lait mug.

"By no means, old boy," the latter said in a tone that made me want to hit him with a door repeatedly. "Whatever gave you that idea? If Cecily had invented an assignation for Olivia and Ralph and put it Olivia's calendar, she certainly would have called that appointment to our attention."

"Then who—"

"Sometimes people talk about premeditated murder and *crime passionnel* as if the two categories were mutually exclusive. They are not. This was a premeditated crime of passion. I should have seen that right away. Bludgeoning is not the weapon for a murder of gain, even though in this case the murder was pre-planned."

"You mean this was some kind of love triangle?" Margaret Cole asked.

"Nothing as simple as that," Mac said. *Oh, good. I was really afraid this was going to be a simple solution.* "The *affaire de coeur* that led to this crime was not a mere triangle but a quadrangle. The killer was not the husband, Sam Wanamaker, or the boyfriend, Tony Lampwicke, but the boyfriend's girlfriend."

That's when it clicked for me. The woman who had worked with Tony for years until she got let go by Ralph Pendergast—giving her a major axe to grind against the provost—was also the woman who had filled us in about the older boyfriend and Olivia's plan to meet him on the morning she died.

"Piper," I said, staring at her. There was no note of triumph in my voice this time as shock registered on her face. Actually, I felt damned sad. Strangely, I also experienced a twinge of disappointment that Piper didn't have better taste in men. She'd been dating that insufferable Tony Lampwicke and Olivia had poached on her territory. There was no much-older boyfriend. Piper had made that up as part of her frame of Ralph. It all fit. I was three steps behind Mac, but I was catching up now. Apparently I was the only one, though.

"Are you planning on accusing everybody in the room, one by one, Cody?" Gordon Cole demanded. I guess he was feeling a little touchy because Cecily and Piper were both Happy Homes employees.

It's always hard to tell what's going on behind Mac's beard, but I didn't think he was enjoying this any more than I was. "This time Jefferson is right."

Piper pushed stray strands of chestnut hair back off of her face. "That's ridiculous. You guys are just trying to save Pendergast's hide because he's your boss." *That wouldn't be my preference, actually.* "You can't prove a thing."

"I beg to differ, Ms. Lawrence. Oscar, did you find any unidentified prints in the Pendergast house?"

"Well, yeah, a few, but—"

He was probably going to say that's what you'd find in any house. Everybody who's not a hermit has scores of visitors to his or her home over the years, and it's not like most people's fingerprints are in the FBI database. I've never been fingerprinted. Have you? Okay, maybe you have, but not everybody has, not by a long shot.

"I think you will find that some of those prints belong to Piper Lawrence, who had no good reason for being in that house since she didn't stage it and she was hardly a friend of the Pendergasts." Mac waved a hand dismissively. "Oh, no doubt she attempted to wipe away all traces of her presence, but I am confident you will discover that she was unsuccessful."

It was one of Sebastian McCabe's boldest bluffs in a career that had included some doozies.

Piper sat down hard in the nearest chair. She looked like a deflated balloon. "I was out of work for seven months. Do you know what that's like? I'll never forgive Pendergast for that. I was good at my job at WIJC and he took that away from me. I wasn't going to let that bitch take Tony away, too. Liv and I really were friends, or so I thought. But she didn't know about Tony and me. We'd kept that on the down low because he used to be my boss. When she told me how she seduced him, bragged about it, really, I knew I had to get her out of the way so that Tony and I could be happy. That's all I wanted, just to be happy." She looked around the room at the rest of us. "Is that so wrong of me?"

"If there is any means by which one could ascertain when an appointment was entered in a smartphone calendar, I am unaware of it." Mac looked understandably quite pleased with himself. "I made that part up."

"Good thing Piper doesn't happen to be an expert on smartphone technology in her spare time," Lynda said.

We were relaxing in Mac's study, and she had a Knob Creek Manhattan in her hand.

"So how did you figure it out?" my sister asked—as if Mac wouldn't have held forth without prompting.

Mac set down his beer mug. "I started with the risky premise that Ralph was innocent and someone had framed him. That is why the murder was done in that house, and that is why the highly unconventional weapon of a frozen salmon—to make the murder appear unpremeditated, as if the body had been put in the freezer with the expectation of coming back. That would point to the owner of the house.

"The murderer, then, had animus against both Olivia and Ralph. He or she also knew that Ralph owned the house and that it would be available for meeting Olivia. That directed my attention to Happy Homes. Who was it who told us that Olivia had an appointment, and said that it was with an older man, throwing suspicion on Ralph? Piper Lawrence, who was still upset about being laid off by Ralph. What motive could she have for killing Olivia Wanamaker?"

"Romance rears its ugly head," Lynda said.

"Indeed. When Tony Lampwicke told us that he had been involved with another woman that he would not name, it required but little imagination to speculate who that woman might be and to connect the dots. Tony formerly worked with Piper Lawrence. Piper currently worked with Mrs. Wanamaker and was said to be her only friend at Happy Homes—therefore the one person to whom she might confide her current dalliance, and a person she presumably would have no hesitation in meeting at the house on Campion Lane."

"Too bad," I said. "I always liked Piper. But I'm glad it wasn't Cecily Almond."

"So am I," Lynda said. "I forgot to tell you that she's taking us through the house again tomorrow."

XIII

My visits to Mac's office in Herbert Hall are not exactly rare occasions, so I wouldn't call it surprising that Ralph found us both there the following morning. The expression behind his rimless glasses was that of a man forced to carry out an unpleasant task.

"I'm here to thank you for what you did on my behalf," he said. "My wife told me after the fact. Although I don't approve of her appeal to you, and would have stopped her if I'd known, that by no means lessens my gratitude. Incredibly, Chief Hummel seemed quite serious about considering me a suspect."

"He was dead serious," I assured him.

"Er, yes, well." Ralph licked his lips nervously. "If there's anything I can do to repay you, please let me know."

It suddenly occurred to me that he really meant it. The last thing in the world he wanted was to be under a debt to Mac and, by extension, to me.

"I assure you, Ralph, 'the work is its own reward,' as the Master once said."

That was fine for Mac, but I wasn't going to let Ralph off the hook that easily. "There is something you could do for me."

"I see. I'm afraid the price of the house—"

"No, no, it's not that. We want the house and I'm sure we can work out a fair price." *Two pals like us, why not?* "I had something else in mind."

"I just had a chat with Ralph," I told Popcorn as I breezed in to my office a few minutes later.

"Then why do you look so happy?"

"Are you aware that he's cutting budgets again?"

Her face darkened. "I've heard rumors."

"Well, it's true. You are no longer my administrative assistant."

When I saw the "I've-been-punched-in-the-gut" look on her face, I immediately regretted trying to play cute.

"Your title is now assistant director of the office," I hastened to add, "with a higher salary to match. Ralph is going to cut some other budget instead of ours, probably Mac's." I was sure that Ralph would find a way to win in the end. But I had this round by a knockout.

Popcorn sat down. "Wow, thanks, Boss. Something tells me there's a story behind this."

"Yep." I picked up that morning's edition of *The Erin Observer & News-Ledger* with a Johanna Rawls's account of Piper's arrest blazoned across page one. "It's the story behind *this* story."

DOGS DON'T MAKE MISTAKES

I

"Nine-one-one. What is your emergency?"

"I think someone's in my house. My dog's barking like crazy."

"What is your address?"

"928 Senter Street, with an 'S.' Hurry!"

"We'll send a car right away."

(Loud bang.)

"Was that a gunshot, ma'am?"

(Long pause.)

"Ma'am?"

"Yeah, it was a gun."

"Are you all right?"

"I'm not the one hit. It's a man and I think he's—oh, my God—it's my husband!"

The 911 call played over and over again on the Cincinnati television stations in the week after the shooting of Tim Crutcher. When I first heard it on our kitchen TV, I was fixing myself a yogurt salad for dinner and bemoaning my lonely—albeit temporary—bachelor existence. Lynda was out of town on a business trip for a few days, visiting the Grier Ohio NewsGroup's chain of newspapers upstate in the suburban Cleveland area. I had the TV on to keep me company. Our house seemed so big without her. After more than a year and a half of marriage, I'd gotten used to not being alone. My former solitary ways seemed like an old suit that didn't fit anymore.

Concentrating on building a healthful meal, I wasn't paying much attention to TV4 Action News until I heard my friend Ashley Crutcher's name. It came near the end of a lead-in from the male co-anchor, Brian Rose. I looked up with a jerk at Ashley's name. I saw reporter Mandy Peters, as she now called herself, standing in front of a two-story frame house in a middle-class neighborhood. She was bundled up in a heavy TV4 jacket as insulation against the November cold.

"Well, Brian," she was saying, "neighbors in this quiet, small-town community tell us tonight that they were shocked to learn of the shooting that rocked their street in the early hours of the morning."

Cincinnati hardly ever thinks of Erin, about forty miles upriver from the home of the Reds and Procter & Gamble, except at times of crime, grief, and tragedy. On one such occasion more than two years earlier I'd met Mandy Petrowski, then working as an intern at the same station[4]. She'd just recently rejoined TV4 under her new name, which I happened to know she made up. Her auburn hair was now curly and I think she'd had some work done on her teeth, making them even more perfect. She still had a generous mouth, a cute nose, and a penchant for dramatic pauses.

After the mandatory clips of shocked neighbors ("I couldn't believe it!"), Mandy returned in a live shot to actually start telling the story. "It all began at about two-fifteen this morning with this nine-one-one call."

The audio of the call was accompanied by captions so we didn't miss any of the words.

Back to Mandy on camera:

"Dead tonight is twenty-nine-year-old Tim Crutcher, who until recently lived here with his wife, Ashley. Neighbors say the couple was estranged. I'm told the victim

---

[4] See *No Police Like Holmes*, MX Publishing, 2011.

had been out of work for some time and may have had a drinking problem." *I hope you never ask my neighbors about me, Mandy.* "Ironically"—she tried to look ironic—"his wife is a paralegal for a prominent criminal attorney here in Erin named Erica Slade. Now, we tried to reach out to Ms. Crutcher to get her side of the story, but she told us to talk to Ms. Slade. The attorney was unavailable for comment. No charges have been filed. Live from Erin, Mandy Peters, TV4 Action News. Back to you, Brian."

Brian, who'd been glued to the 6 P.M. anchor chair at TV4 since before I'd come to live in southern Ohio, looked serious. I could feel a question coming on. Anchors always have a question. Sometimes they manage to make it look spontaneous.

"What are law enforcement officials saying about the likelihood that an arrest will be made soon?"

"Erin Police Chief Oscar Hummel declined to speak with us on-camera, Brian, but off-camera he told me that an investigation is underway."

"We'll be staying with this story," Brian assured us. "Thank you, Mandy."

"On a much lighter note . . ." his brunette co-anchor, Tammie Tucker, began bouncily. Deciding that quiet wasn't always such a bad thing, I turned the TV off and went to work on eating my yogurt. I'd barely begun, though, when my smartphone made that pinging noise. *Incoming!* It was a text from Lynda.

What do u know about ashley?

I assumed she meant the shooting, not in general.

Only what I saw on TV just now. I miss you.

She picked up on the second sentence first and we texted for a while in a vein that was highly personal, somewhat amusing, and none of your business. Eventually, we got back to Ashley. I didn't bother to ask how she'd heard about the shooting from up in northern Ohio. News is her business. And from her perch on the Grier Ohio

NewsGroup corporate ladder, she's always trying to help *The Erin Observer and News-Ledger* get a leg up on the other media. So she asked me, *Well, what do u think happened?*

How should I know? My friendship with Ashley was a limited one. I'd only met her husband once or twice. I knew her from our membership in the Poisoned Pens, a group of aspiring Erin mystery writers. We meet monthly at Pages Gone By, a used bookstore on High Street, although I'd been slack in attending of late. Other members include Noah Bartlett, Mo Russert, Roscoe Feldman, and Mary Lou Springfield. Noah owns the store. Mo Russert works there, is passionately devoted to mysteries, but has never actually submitted a story to the group for critique. Roscoe is a sixty-seven-year-old English teacher at Bernardin High School. He's been dating Mary Lou, the school librarian, for seventeen years. Sebastian McCabe drops by occasionally to offer words of encouragement.

What did I really know about Ashley Crutcher? She was younger than me, maybe late twenties. She was nice, smart, and not the worst writer in the group (that would be Roscoe). If I were listing acquaintances of mine most likely to shoot their husbands, she wouldn't make the top ten. It could have been a tragic mistake—her estranged husband returned to the house unexpectedly, and she shot him thinking he was a burglar. But Erica Slade would have been out front with that story practically before the cops arrived on the scene. I feared a darker truth. I texted Linda: *Probably a sad story of spouse abuse.*

That shows you what I know. Ashley had a very different story to tell, one that never entered my head.

II

That was on Monday. The next day I was in my office working on preparations for St. Benignus Day festivities on Friday and Saturday when Oscar dropped into my office.

Not surprisingly, the Feast of St. Benignus of Armagh on November 9 is a big deal at St. Benignus College. This year we were honoring St. Patrick's favorite disciple with a two-day blowout. Friday night was to feature a concert with Irish dancers accompanied by Mac on his execrable bagpipes. Saturday, the actual feast day, the campus would host a Celtic Festival most of the day, then Mass in the late afternoon, followed by an alumni dinner with an address by an Irish-American cardinal who had been prominently spoken of as a *papabile*—potential candidate for pope—in the conclave earlier in the year.

The enthusiasm with which Sebastian McCabe entered into the St. Benignus Day festivities struck me as somewhat lacking in humility, given that November 9 also happened to be his forty-second birthday. But who ever accused Mac of being humble? I was just texting his wife, my sister Kate, to ask whether she could hide the bagpipes when Oscar appeared.

"Howdy, Jeff."

For a moment I was speechless. Oscar's baldhead was covered with a tam-o'-shanter. On his big noggin it looked wildly out of place, like wool socks on a cheerleader. When I finally recovered, I said, "What brings you here?"

He sat down, uninvited but welcome. "Oh, you know, I was in the neighborhood and just thought I'd stop by."

That smelled fishy. "You never stop by."

"Oh, hi, Oscar." Popcorn, who'd been down the hall on a potty break, stood in the doorway. She unconsciously straightened her dyed blond hair. Oscar's eyes lit up. *So that was it!* I knew Oscar hadn't come by just to pass the time of day; he was here to make time with my assistant.

"Hello, Aneliese." He hauled his well-padded body out of the chair.

Aneliese! This was even more serious than I thought.

"Do you want me to leave you two alone?" I didn't try to keep the acid out of my voice. "Maybe draw the shades on my way out?"

"Actually, I'm kind of here on business," Oscar said sheepishly.

"Of course." Popcorn shifted into business mode. "I'll make some fresh coffee."

I'd been trying to convince her for six months that she didn't have to make the coffee now that she'd been bumped up to assistant director of our two-person office, but she insisted that she'd never *had* to make the coffee—she wanted to do it. So she disappeared.

Well, actually, she just walked away. I watched Oscar watching her, almost five feet of feminine wiles and administrative competence. Poor guy. I had a feeling he was going to chase her until she caught him.

"What kind of business, Oscar?"

He dragged his eyes back to me.

"Oh, it's this Crutcher case."

"There's a case?"

"Sure there is. The man was shot dead in his own house."

"Actually, he didn't live there anymore."

"Still, his name was on the mortgage."

"But Ashley must have been making the payments if he wasn't working. TV4 said he'd been out of a job for months."

Oscar waved that away. "Let's not get bogged down in details. I'm taking a more psychological approach here." Good grief! Had he been watching *Columbo* again? "What were Mrs. Crutcher's mystery stories like, the ones she wrote for that writer's club you're in?"

"I wouldn't call the Poisoned Pens a club." What would I call it? I'd never put a noun to it. "And how do you know about that?"

"Oh, you know, small town, word gets around."

He didn't find out from one of the other members or they would have answered his question. I sure didn't want to be the one to tell him about "Die Like a Dog," Ashley's short story about a wife's revenge on her husband's unkindness to their pet. That wouldn't help Ashley a bit. Somebody, especially Oscar, could get the wrong idea. Surely Ashley hadn't intended to kill her husband. *Had she?*

"So what were her stories like?" Oscar pressed.

"They were mysteries."

The chief snorted. "I know that. Oh, thanks, hon."

Hon? Popcorn had handed him his coffee first, in a mug with hearts on it. They smiled at each other like two lovers in a sugary TV commercial. I felt a stab of jealousy, not the romantic kind. Popcorn and I had been working together a long time, like Batman and Robin or the Lone Ranger and Tonto or Sherlock Holmes and . . . Never mind. When she gave me my mug of decaffeinated java, I murmured a "thanks" without looking at her.

"What I mean is this, Jeff," Oscar continued. "Were Mrs. Crutcher's stories the blood and guts kind or the light-hearted murder kind or what?"

I shrugged. *No big deal, Oscar.* "They were the forgettable kind, I guess, because I can't remember them. Why is it important?"

Popcorn sat down in the other chair. Oscar managed to keep his eyes on me.

"The kind of stories that she writes would say something about her mind-set, like whether she had violent thoughts or maybe even how she felt about soon-to-be-ex-husbands. It's important because Slade is hell-bent on nailing Ashley Crutcher for this." That would be Marvin Slade, the Sussex County prosecutor and former spouse of Ashley's attorney.

Shocked is too mild a word for my reaction to this news. "Nailing her? For shooting Crutcher in self-defense? Or is it a battered wife deal?" That still hadn't been clarified in the morning's *Observer & News-Ledger* story. Reporter Johanna Rawls had been no more successful at reaching Erica Slade than TV4 had been.

Oscar shook his head. "Neither one, according to Ashley. She swears up and down that she didn't fire a shot and the gun didn't belong to her."

"What!"

Oscar kicked back the coffee like it was a shot of bourbon. "Yeah. You probably heard the nine-one-one tape. She says was still upstairs in her bedroom, talking to the dispatcher, when the shot went off downstairs. The prosecutor doesn't believe her. Who would?"

"Me, for one," I said. I stick by my friends.

"Why would she make up a wild story like that when all she had to do was claim it was an accident or self-defense?" Popcorn asked.

Oscar regarded her. "Who knows why a dame does what she does? Women are illogical." No, he didn't say it, but he would have if Popcorn hadn't been there. I know Oscar. Instead, he fudged it with, "Obviously, she didn't think this through very well. Nobody's saying she's a master criminal."

"Is it really a smart political move for Marvin Slade to go all hard-ass on this one?" I mused. "His party already has a problem with female voters. If he takes this to court, he'll be going head-to-head with his ex-wife. And Ashley will look very sympathetic in the witness box, whether jurors actually believe her story or not."

But the politics didn't concern Oscar. "I just do my job, Jeff." He looked at Popcorn again and repeated, "I just do my job!"

"Well, I think she's innocent," Popcorn declared, staring daggers at Oscar.

"That's up to a jury to decide, Aneliese."

Ignoring that, she appealed to me. "You're not going to let it get that far, are you, Jeff?"

This looks like a job for Sebastian McCabe! "No, I guess I'd better not."

III

So if I wanted to be a hero to my assistant, I had to get Mac off his duff to find the real murderer (if there was one) pronto. No problem. It would be far harder to stop Mac from getting involved. All I had to do was find him, which proved to be harder than I expected.

Meanwhile, Popcorn and Oscar clearly weren't on the same page regarding the innocence of Ashley Crutcher. Well, that wasn't my problem. Or was it? I didn't want Popcorn grumping around about it; that might affect her office efficiency. More importantly, she was as much my friend as she was my co-worker, and so was Oscar. After he left—the parting was a little stiff, but maybe that's just because they had an audience—I thought of making some insightful comment to Popcorn about the course of true love never running smoothly. (At least, it didn't for me.) Then I realized that she's fifty-one years old, a widow, a grandmother of three, and undoubtedly wise to the ways of love from reading those lurid Rosamund DeLacey romance novels. She should have been giving me advice to the lovelorn back when I needed it.

I tried calling Mac three times over the next couple of hours, both on his office phone and on his smartphone, but without success. I chalked that up to committee meetings because I knew he didn't have a class today. After lunch I tried again. He picked up on about the fifth ring.

"McCabe here."

I know that. I called you. Who else would be answering your cell phone?

The background noise sounded like the Fourth of July.

"What's the racket?"

"Gunfire."

Of course. How did I not know that?

"I am taking a late lunch hour at The Bull's Eye. I have just arrived. Please join me."

I would have argued, but talking over the gunfire was too much effort. I told him I'd be there in five minutes.

The Bull's Eye Gun Shop & Shooting Range is located in a strip mall in the newer part of Erin. It's far enough away from campus that I decided to drive my classic (i.e., ancient) lime green Volkswagen Beetle there instead of pedaling on my bike. Mac puts in an hour or two there from time to time, shooting at a target with his Colt .32, for which he has a concealed carry permit. He says it helps him think when he's plotting a mystery novel. That may even be true. But I think he also harbors the illusion that someday his ability to shoot may actually matter. If it ever does, I don't want to be there when that happens.

It was a crisp fall morning with the sun shining brightly, by no means a bad day to be playing hooky from the office. I wished I could just keep driving along the river—or better yet, north to Cleveland and my true love. But that didn't happen.

At one-fifteen in the afternoon, The Bull's Eye wasn't exactly hopping, but it wasn't deserted either. A handsome woman of about thirty in an expensive leather coat was leaning over the sales counter when I came in, intently listening to a healthy-looking sport with curly brown hair and a faint mustache. He pointed out all the fun features of a .38 that seemed to be scaled down to fit her female hand. Seeing the sales staff was tied up, I looked around on my own. I'd only been here with Mac once before, for research back when I was writing my still-unpublished Max Cutter private eye novels.

The front portion of the business, where I stood, was a sporting goods store masquerading as a cozy lodge. Stuffed heads of deer, moose, and boar looked down from the paneled walls. A television set was mounted in one corner of the room, and an American flag decorated the other. The only firearms on display in racks were the Thompson Center Hawken rifle kits (American-made, the box said) and the long guns (some in camouflage colors). The handguns were behind the counter. But everything else in the store that pertained to weapons, from ammunition and Bianchi leather holsters to pistol perches and recoil pads, were on open shelves. Then there were what you might call accessories—expandable batons, blackjacks, mace, and tie tacks shaped like little handcuffs.

When the man at the counter was finally free (because the leather-coated woman had left with a gun in her purse), I put down the paralyzer tear gas I'd been studying and went over to him. He was wearing a blue polo shirt with the store's target-themed logo printed on the front. The shirt was unbuttoned, leaving tufts of hair sticking out.

"Yes, sir?" he said with a "here to help you" smile.

"A friend asked me to meet him here. He's about this high"—I indicated with my hand—"and about this wide and he has a beard."

He chuckled. "You mean Professor McCabe?"

"That's the one."

He handed me a set of electronic earmuffs and told me to go on back to the target range. I remembered the earmuffs from my previous visit. Ingeniously, they let you hear most sounds, such as conversation or the ringtone of a cell phone, but block out all sounds above 86 decibels, most noticeably gunfire.

There were only three or four shooters on the range, but they'd been busy. The air smelled of cordite, although it wasn't permeated with the foggy haze of gun smoke that you might expect. Apparently that's filtered out these days.

A blond woman with muscles came out of a stall and strode past me, a look of satisfaction on her young face. She was carrying a big gun.

Mac was in the next stall, firing away at a cardboard target bearing the image of a male head and shoulders in silhouette. I noticed that Mac's aim had improved since the last time I'd been here with him. If he ever got attacked by a cardboard target, he'd have nothing to worry about. Now I had a problem. Coming up to him and tapping him on the shoulder didn't seem like a good idea. The man had a gun in his hand! Fortunately, he saw me coming out of the corner of his eye. He lay the Colt pistol down on the counter in front of him and, turning around, motioned at the gun as if offering me an opportunity to shoot. I held up my hands in a protesting gesture. I'd gotten out of here that one time without wounding myself or anybody else, and I don't like to press my luck.

Mac shrugged and made a "follow me" gesture. We went out a side door.

"Are you quite sure, Jefferson, that you do not—"

"I'd love to, but I'm a man on a mission." *Like the Blues Brothers!* Maybe I wasn't working for God, but I liked to think that we were at least on the same side. "Popcorn is counting on us to help Ashley Crutcher. And I guess Ashley wouldn't mind, either."

He raised an eyebrow. "The details in the *News-Ledger* were sketchy, but I assumed the death of her husband was a tragic accident." Mac knew her from the Poisoned Pens, about as well as I did.

"I'm pretty sure you've told me on more than one occasion to never assume anything."

I gave him the lowdown on what we'd learned from Oscar, ending with my quasi-assurance to Popcorn.

"I hope you have not overpromised, old boy." Mac sighed. "Well, the situation is serious, but not urgent. I shall finish shooting."

So, with ear protectors back on, I was forced to watch my brother-in-law darned near obliterate the target, putting holes practically on top of holes. After a half-hour or so of this, we walked out together and turned in our ear protectors.

"How'd it go, Professor?" the guy at the counter asked.

"I had a splendid session, Carson! I finished my next novel. Now all I have to do is write it."

Carson looked puzzled. "Well, that's good, I guess. But the important thing is that you can defend yourself if you ever need to, like Mrs. Crutcher did."

A funny feeling crept up my spine, and it wasn't a pleasant one. "You know Mrs. Crutcher?"

"Oh, sure. She's been a regular in here lately."

IV

We met with Ashley Crutcher and Erica Slade in Erica's office the next day. By then I'd convinced myself that there was nothing damning about Ashley target shooting—lots of women do it. But I wasn't sure I could convince anybody else. Marvin Slade and the entire readership of *The Erin Observer & News-Ledger*, just to pick random examples, might see this as proof of cold-blooded practice for killing her ex after somehow luring him into his former home. For that reason, I'd been careful not to mention The Bull's Eye when I talked with Lynda on the phone before going to sleep.

Erica's office is a former Episcopal chapel on Water Street. Undersized for a house of worship, it had proved too small for its brief incarnation as a trendy pub called The Sanctuary. The pub owner also had a few other problems, legal ones that had caused him to hire Erica. She'd taken his equity in the building as part of her fee. As an office it was spacious for one person, with plenty of room to expand the practice later. The building still had the stained-glass windows—and the bar. Nice touch, I thought.

We sat around an oval table in a conference room.

"Thank you for allowing us to speak to your client," Mac told Erica.

"Yeah, it was really swell of you," I added, "especially since you know damned well we're just trying to save her derriere."

Maybe you can't tell, but I was a bit miffed. Not only was Ashley a friend, but I thought Erica was as well, which is why I called her Erica. Most people call her Slade, which fits her and drives her ex-husband nuts as a bonus. He hates it that she still uses his name. I hadn't known her that well when she defended first an innocent suspect and then the real murderer in that *1895* murder business, but Lynda and I had later enjoyed numerous late dinners and discussions with her at Bobbie McGee's Sports Bar.

"Sorry, Jeff." She didn't look sorry. "No offense. But when a client hires me, she gets all of me. I'm totally committed. That means I'm part of every conversation related to the case and I call the shots, not the client. If the client can't buy that, she's not my client. I refer her to another lawyer."

Even without a jury to impress, Erica was dressed to the nines in a little black dress and silver jewelry. In her mid-forties, she looked younger thanks to an unwrinkled face and bright violet eyes. She wore her dark hair long. If it was a dye job, it was a good one. She probably stood about five-seven, but in those stiletto heels she was almost as tall as me. And she had lovely ankles.

"But we're grateful for your interest," Ashley said. I was proud of her for speaking up, but not surprised. She'd always struck me as the independent sort. Erica looked at her like, "What you mean 'we,' Paleface?"

Ashley was twenty-seven, according to the *Observer*, but she looked older this morning. Her wavy brunette hair was disheveled and her brown eyes made it clear that sleep had been a stranger of late. I'd always thought of her as pleasingly plump but I could imagine that with a few more days of stress her moon-shaped face would be going into three-quarter moon mode.

"I only hope we can help," I said. *Otherwise, Popcorn will give me the cold shoulder for weeks and the Poisoned Pens will be down by one member.* No, that's not really what I was thinking. I was worried for Ashley.

"Many defendants go to extraordinary lengths to mount a claim of accident or self-defense in the face of murder charges," Mac noted. "In this case, invoking the 'castle doctrine' that allows one to kill in self-defense when fearing for her safety inside her own home would seem an obvious and easy course. However, we understand from Oscar Hummel that you have eschewed any such defense. May I ask why?"

"Because I didn't shoot the bastard!" Ashley blurted out.

Surprisingly, Erica didn't object to the undiplomatic noun. "Marvin expected us to cop a plea to involuntary manslaughter, angling for probation and no jail time, but Ashley would have had to plead guilty to a crime she didn't commit. We said 'no thanks.' At that, Marvin made it pretty clear that filing charges is just a matter of getting the paperwork done. So we're going to court and I'm going to wipe up the floor with my ex." *It wouldn't be the first time.*

"Why is he so determined to go to the mat over this?" I asked.

Erica snickered. "Maybe he thinks that killing asshole husbands sets a bad precedent. Not that Ashley did that."

"I didn't!"

Erica's unhappy six-year marriage to the politically ambitious Sussex County prosecutor was one of the frequent topics of those late-night chats we'd had with her at Bobbie McGee's. From Erica's perspective, Marvin Slade had been riddled with insecurities about his wife's career as a gym teacher and Cincinnati Bengals cheerleader, plus insanely jealous for no reason. After the divorce, she'd become a criminal defense attorney in revenge. By her count, she'd bested Slade in court more often than not and walked away with a good deal in every plea bargain.

"A suspicious mind like the prosecutor's is likely to find meaning in the fact that you have recently become a regular habitué of The Bull's Eye," Mac said.

"How did you know that?" The look on Ashley's wide face could have been surprise or something darker, but I would have bet a lot that her attorney wasn't unaware of her newfound hobby. And I'm not a betting man.

"Carson Allen happened to mention it. And if he mentioned it to Jefferson and me, sooner or later Mr. Slade is going to hear about it."

Ashley shrugged. "Well, it's no big deal. I've been doing research. I'm working on a new story about a female private eye. It could be a series. At some point she's going to have to fire a gun. I have to admit, though, I kind of like it. There's a rush when you pull the trigger and you feel all that power, you know?"

Maybe it would be best to keep that to yourself, Ashley.

Erica apparently thought the same thing. She spoke up, taking the floor from her client. "This discussion is irrelevant. Target shooting is a very popular sport, including among women. There are more guns than people in this country."

"And yet you say the gun that killed your husband wasn't yours." Mac had addressed the statement to Ashley, but Erica answered:

"My client doesn't own a gun."

"It didn't seem worth the expense just for research," Ashley said, "so I rent a gun every time I go out to shoot. If I keep it up, maybe I'll buy one."

"Would you mind telling us what happened the night of the murder?" Mac said. "I am calling it murder because you deny accident or self-defense and I presume the coroner's office has ruled out suicide."

"It wasn't suicide," Erica said. "The gun was fired straight at his face and into his brain from at least six feet away. Marvin the Martian told us that." She nodded to Ashley. "Tell Mac and Jeff what happened, just as you told me."

Ashley swallowed. "All right. It's not like I could ever forget. It started with Ranger barking. It wasn't a happy bark. He woke me up out of a deep sleep."

Mac stopped her narrative almost before she started. "As I recall, you once wrote a short, rather violent crime story about a woman taking revenge on her husband for abusing her German shepherd. Was that based on Tim's treatment of Ranger?"

She laughed hollowly.

"Ashley—" Erica began. But her client talked right over her.

"That was pure fiction. You know how that works. I was looking for a motive, and thought, 'What would really piss me off?' No, Tim wouldn't hurt Ranger. He was nicer to Ranger than he was to me! Hell, I was afraid he might try to get custody if we got divorced."

"And I presume the canine reciprocated his affection?"

"Well, he never barked at Tim, just wagged his tail. He only barks when his dog sense tells him something's wrong. Ranger's a sweet dog—better company than Tim, frankly—but very protective. I'm really glad to have him around. Living alone, except for him, every little sound I hear convinces me that somebody's in the house."

"And this time, someone was," I said.

She nodded. "That's what I assumed when Ranger's barking woke me up. I called nine-one-one right away. I was still on the phone when I heard the gunshot. I picked up my mace from the nightstand near my bed—I keep it on my keychain—and I walked downstairs, still talking to the nine-one-one operator. At first all I saw was that a man's body was lying in the living room, not far from the foot of the stairs. The face was covered with blood, but after I stared a minute I knew that it was Tim because I recognized his hair and the jacket he was wearing. I was totally shocked."

If all that sounded a bit rehearsed, I put it down to the fact that she'd already told her story to Erica and to the police, probably more than once.

"Were you more shocked that your husband was in your home or that he was dead?" Mac asked.

Ashley had to work on that one. "Well, both, I guess. I certainly didn't expect to see him there, dead or alive. We didn't part on good terms."

"So you have no idea what he was doing in the house?"

She shook her head, sending her tangled mess of hair flying. "None at all. He took everything that was his when he left."

"Maybe he was trying to steal Ranger," I said. *Hey, that actually makes sense.*

"I guess that's possible," Ashley allowed, "but Tim never said he wanted him. Poor baby must have felt abandoned."

"Did you change the locks?" Mac asked.

"No, I never thought of that."

"So he could have used his own key to enter the house?"

"That's what he did," Erica said, "but it was still a B&E. That's not an issue in the case, but I want to be clear about it. Once Tim Crutcher moved out, he abandoned his place of abode and he had no right to enter without the permission of the person who lives there, even though his name is on the mortgage. It's just like a landlord can't enter an apartment without the tenant's permission. It makes no difference that Ashley and Tim weren't legally separated, just living apart."

Mac rubbed his beard, clearly longing for a cigar. "Do you mind telling us how that came about, Ashley?"

She shrugged. "I'd rather keep my private business private, but I can see that's not going to happen. My life with Tim had become like a bad country-western song: He drank, he gambled, he didn't have a real job, and I suspected he did have a girlfriend. One night, about six weeks ago, after he came home late the third or fourth night in a row, we had it out—screaming and throwing things, the whole bit. I don't remember exactly what I said, but something about how I couldn't live with him like that. And he said, 'All right, if you're going to throw me out, I'll go now.'

"That wasn't what I'd meant. I even tried to talk him into staying, but he wouldn't have it. The next day I realized that the break was for the best. I was only eighteen when we married. I was in college and he was a high school dropout. My parents, who are a lot smarter than I am, helped me with tuition so that I could finish school even though they disapproved of Tim. The marriage was a mistake—that was soon obvious—but I tried to make the best of it."

Erica, proving that she had a tender side when her claws were retracted, put a comforting hand on her client-employee's shoulder. "We do a lot of divorce work between criminal cases. I kept hoping that Ashley would see where all this was going. She was supporting that loser."

The Crutchers had no children. Maybe Ashley wanted to stay together for the sake of the dog.

"Tim had a decent job doing maintenance work for the Sussex County Recreation Department but he lost it earlier this year," Ashley said. "He said he was fired for talking back to his supervisor. I don't know whether that's true or not, but it's certainly plausible. Now he just does— did—odd jobs for Meredith Blake."

She didn't have to explain who that was. Everybody who's lived in Erin more than five minutes has heard of our wayward heiress. The only difference between Meredith Blake and one of those thirty-something Hollywood stars who have never grown up is that she isn't a Hollywood star. I'd heard her called "Meredith Flake" or "Blake the Flake" ever since I came to St. Benignus as a student. I wouldn't lower myself to such cheap wordplay, of course.

"Do you have any idea who killed your husband, Ashley?" I asked.

"All I know is, it wasn't me." She paused, then decided she couldn't let well enough alone. "After all these years of reading murder mysteries, it's weird to be in the middle of one. I'm sorry Tim's dead, I guess, but I'm not sorry to be getting a reboot on my life."

"She didn't say that," Erica said.

V

"What do you think?" I asked as Mac drove us back to campus in his red 1959 Chevy convertible.

"Ashley did not kill her husband."

"Of course not! You had a doubt?"

"I always have doubts, old boy. She would not be my first friend who committed homicide."

Point taken.

"Okay, so what convinced you that she didn't?"

"The dog in the night-time." *Not that again!* "As you well know, Jefferson, one of the most famous passages in the entire Sherlock Holmes canon is the one about the curious incident of the dog in the night-time."

"Yeah, yeah. 'The dog did nothing in the night-time.' 'That was the curious incident.' The dog didn't bark because he knew the intruder."

"Exactly. In this case, the dog did bark. And, as Holmes said in another story, 'dogs don't make mistakes.' Ergo, the dog was not barking at Tim Crutcher. Someone else was with him—his murderer."

That all seemed like a huge load of nothing to me. "Well, sure! The man didn't shoot himself, so there had to be somebody else with him if Ashley was telling the truth."

"Unlike you, however, I did not presuppose her veracity. It was the telling detail of the dog barking that convinced me that she was being truthful. Having read her stories, I do not believe she would have made that up. She is not that subtle."

That seemed like a pretty thin reed to me, but then I wasn't looking to be convinced. "I would have thought the fact that she turned down a sweet deal from the prosecutor was a good argument for her innocence."

Mac nodded. "There is that as well."

"So Crutcher and somebody else enter the house together in the early hours of the morning, using Crutcher's key. And then what—some kind of a falling out that ends in a shooting?"

"Perhaps."

"What were they doing in the house?"

"The answer that springs to my Sherlockian mind is that they were retrieving something that Crutcher had hidden there, à la 'The Adventure of the Three Garridebs,' even though Ashley believes he took everything with him."

"Like what? And if Crutcher did leave something behind, why?"

Mac shrugged his massive shoulders. "The possibilities are endless. Whatever this theoretical object was, it must have been something that he did not want Ashley to know he had, and therefore he could not remove it in her presence."

"So it could be drugs, money, almost anything that could be hidden in a house—if it even exists."

"That is indeed a large *if*, I grant you."

"And it doesn't get us any closer to knowing who killed Tim Crutcher."

VI

Marvin Slade looked a lot different with his clothes on—business clothes, I mean. I'm used to seeing him dressed a lot more casually or not at all at Nouveau Shape, the co-ed gym where Lynda and I work out together most mornings. Maybe that's why he agreed to see Mac and me early that afternoon, but I doubt it. More likely he wanted to find out what Mac was up to, knowing him only by reputation. Maybe, aware that we were in communication with his ex, he also wanted to send back a message to Erica that he wasn't going to collapse like a cheap umbrella.

Instead of gym shorts or a towel, Slade was wearing a brown suit with the jacket off, yellow suspenders, and horn-rimmed glasses. His scant remaining hair was a darker shade of brown. I probably wouldn't have noticed the gray roots if Erica hadn't told us they were there. Slade was only in his late forties, but he'd been doing a comb-over for a decade or more.

He came out from behind his desk and greeted us entirely too effusively. "Jeff! Good to see you!!" *You just saw me in the sauna on Friday, Marv.* "And Professor McCabe—

I've always wanted to meet you." He pumped our hands. I tried to figure out what he was running for. Mayor would be a come down from countywide office. Maybe he wanted to go to Washington.

"Thank you for agreeing to see us."

"Glad to do it, glad to do it. Coffee?"

The pleasantries went on like that for a while. Finally, Slade eased into the reason for our visit with all the smoothness of a riverboat gambler producing a four-ace hand.

"Frankly, fellows, I was really surprised when you called me." He put out his arms in what I took to be a gesture of surprise. "I mean, Professor, you're an honest-to-God amateur sleuth who solves mysteries just like Dan Devlin in your books." *That's* Damon *Devlin.* "I buy every one as soon as it comes out." *Liar.* "But there's no mystery here. Ashley Crutcher killed her husband. Case closed."

"I think not," Mac said cheerfully. "Her attorney seems quite resolved to fight any charge you decide to bring against Ashley."

Slade made an admirable attempt to maintain his bonhomie. If he hadn't raised his voice, he would have pulled it off. "The charge will be first-degree murder. Perhaps Ms. Crutcher would be better served by a different counsel. I offered her lawyer"—he apparently couldn't bring himself to utter the name—"a good deal that would have made this easier for all of us, but she turned it down."

He took a breath. "Look, I'm not happy about going to trial on this. I tried to avoid it. I know that a lot of folks in town will be sympathetic to Ms. Crutcher's situation, being in a lousy marriage." *Erica, for one.* "But she doesn't claim to be an abused spouse, and she doesn't claim that she was defending herself. If she did that, she might walk. No, Ms. Crutcher claims that she didn't shoot him. But nobody believes that. It just won't wash. Why didn't she take my offer of manslaughter, a shooting in the heat of an argument? That would have got all of us out of this mess."

It all sounded so reasonable that I almost jumped up and said, "Yeah, why not?" But a cooler head, that of Sebastian McCabe, prevailed.

"Because, as an innocent woman, Ashley quite naturally balks at the idea of admitting to a wrong that she did not commit."

Slade shook his dyed and combed-over head. "No, no, no. That just won't wash, it just won't. She had motive, means, and opportunity—the classic trio." He held up three fingers in case we missed that. "Let's take them in reverse order. First of all, the shooting took place in her and her husband's house. Nobody else was around."

"On the contrary, Mr. Slade," Mac interrupted. "Someone else was around—Tim Crutcher's murderer, the person who entered the house with him."

"Says who?"

"Ranger, the family dog whose barking alerted Ashley to the intruders."

Slade gave Mac a withering glance. "Let's move on. As for means, the gun was still on the floor when the Erin police arrived."

"Was it her gun?" I asked, knowing the answer.

Slade hesitated. "We haven't been able to find out where she bought it yet. But we will."

Jeez, that's weak. I persisted. "Were her fingerprints on this gun that you haven't tied to her?"

Slade shook his head. "Of course not. That's no surprise. Ms. Crutcher likes to write mystery stories—just like you, Professor, though without your considerable success. In fact, I even got a copy of one of them from Mary Lou Springfield." *Just what I was afraid of.* "It happens to be about a woman who kills her husband, oddly enough. Now, everybody knows to wipe off fingerprints, but especially a wannabe mystery writer."

"Why not simply leave her fingerprints on the gun and plead self-defense?" Mac said. "You yourself indicated that she might have escaped the penalty of the law by doing so, Mr. Slade."

"Well, maybe she panicked. I never met a real-life killer who planned things out quite like Professor Moriarty. That's why they get caught."

"How about gunshot residue?" Mac wondered. "Was there any on Ashley or her clothing?"

Slade wiggled in his chair. His triumphant march through the case against Ashley wasn't going as smoothly as he had expected. We kept asking those pesky questions. "It was so obvious that she'd shot him, the officer on the scene didn't test for that. She could have washed her hands before calling nine-one-one anyway. By the time Chief Hummel arrived on the scene and ordered a test for GSR on her clothes and hands, more than an hour had passed."

"So you're saying there was no residue on her hands or on whatever she was wearing—night clothes, I guess." It was hard to keep the satisfaction out of my voice. I'm not much of an actor.

But Slade allowed himself a supercilious smile. "Correct. But we didn't stop there. We got a warrant to get the unwashed clothes in her laundry on the off chance that she was actually wearing something else when she shot him. Pay dirt! There was GSR on a plaid flannel shirt."

"But Ashley—" Mac kicked me under the table before I could say "frequented the shooting range." That's where she must have picked up the gunshot residue. But Mac, being a genius, quickly calculated that there was no percentage in informing Slade about Ashley's hobby of putting holes in the silhouettes of men if he didn't already know it. We were here to get information, not give any away.

"Go on," Mac said. "You still have to cover motive."

"Ah, yes, motive. There's more than just the obvious there, much more." Braced for a suggestion that Ashley's "Die Like a Dog" short story wasn't just fiction, I was totally unprepared for what Slade actually said: "Ms. Crutcher bought a two hundred and fifty thousand dollar life insurance policy two months ago. That was just two weeks before she and her husband split up."

If Mac had had a cigar in his mouth, it would have fallen out. This was big news. A quarter of a million dollars isn't anybody's idea of a fortune, but it was a lot for somebody at Ashley Crutcher's paralegal pay level.

Mac recovered quickly. I could almost hear the wheels turning in his head. "If her intention in purchasing the policy was to kill her husband, would it not have made more sense for her to preserve the façade of their marriage at all costs? That would have deflected suspicion from her."

Good comeback! But Slade smiled, undaunted. "If she were that clever, Professor, she might be as successful at writing mysteries as you are."

"At any rate," Mac plowed on, "the fact is that the Crutchers were not living together at the time of Mr. Crutcher's death. What is your theory of how he happened to be in his former home at that hour of the morning?"

"Not former—he was still half-owner of the house. Since Ms. Crutcher denies that she killed him in self-defense, I'm forced to conclude that it was cold-blooded murder. Therefore, she must have lured him there somehow."

Mac chuckled softly, provoking a look of irritation on the prosecutor's face. "I have to say, Mr. Slade, that if your theory is correct she must have drawn him to the house without much of a plan considering that she shot him . . . and then wiped her fingerprints off the gun, which she left beside the body . . . and then called nine-one-one with the preposterous story that some third party shot her estranged husband. That simply does not make sense. Why would an intruder leave the gun behind? It would scarcely take a Professor Moriarty to come up with something better than that. That is not even considering the minor matter that a gun went off during the nine-one-one call and you have not mentioned finding a second empty cartridge."

Slade sat back. I sensed a lecture coming on. "I can assure you, Professor McCabe, that in the decade-plus that I have held this office, I have encountered much more irrational behavior on the part of murderers. Sam Klein stabbed his girlfriend seventeen times in their kitchen, then used the same knife to slice himself some ham. He was still eating a ham sandwich when officers arrived in response to a call from the neighbors."

"That's not much of a parallel," I argued. "Sam didn't make the call himself."

For some reason, Slade looked exasperated. "My point is that in real life killers do strange things more often than not." He made a show of looking at his watch. "I don't want to rush you out, but I have an appointment with Ms. Rawls of the *Observer* in five minutes."

He wouldn't find it as easy to charm that young lady as he might expect. Tall Rawls was becoming an excellent reporter, thanks in part to some mentoring from my own true love.

"As an elected official, you certainly have an obligation of media availability," Mac said. "One cannot help but wonder, however, whether media attention might not be the driving factor in your planned prosecution of Ashley Crutcher."

Slade made a good show of looking offended; I have to give him that. "I strongly resent your implication, Professor. I strongly resent it." *That wasn't an implication, Marv; he said it flat out.* "This is all about justice for Tim Crutcher, not publicity for me. You've obviously been paying too much attention to my—to Ms. Crutcher's attorney. Let me give both of you some friendly advice: You run a very grave risk of embarrassing yourselves if you continue down the path you're on."

"That is a risk I am quite prepared to take," Mac said.

"That goes double," I added.

"May I remind you that you're not licensed private investigators?"

"We are well aware of that, Mr. Slade," Mac assured him. "Accordingly, we have never charged a penny for our services. I am sure you will acknowledge that as private citizens we are well within our rights to ask a few questions here and there that might prove useful to the competent defense to which every defendant is legally and morally entitled."

Slade didn't acknowledge anything except that our last five minutes was up. He stood. "Well, it was a real pleasure to meet you at last, Professor McCabe. Jeff, I'll be seeing you at the gym. Have a great day." He pumped our hands as if we were the last undecided voters in the county.

VII

"What do you think he's running for?" I asked Mac when we hit the sidewalk.

He shrugged. "Who knows, old boy? Perhaps even he doesn't. These political types like to keep their options open."

"Speaking of options, what are ours? Do you have a counter-theory?"

"I would not be so bold as to call it a theory. Let us say I have been engaging in a thought experiment. It goes like this: Suppose that Tim Crutcher had a paramour, as Ashley suspects. Suppose they entered the house together to recover something that Crutcher left behind, but they quickly quarreled and she shot him in anger. Or perhaps, although she carried a gun, she was inexperienced at weapons and was startled into firing it when Ranger barked. Either way, she dropped the gun and fled. She left no fingerprints because she was wearing gloves."

Stranger things have happened, I guess. "So how do we find out whether there was a girlfriend and, if so, who she was?"

That question would have been a no-brainer if Crutcher had worked at St. Benignus: Popcorn would have found out for us in five minutes, if she didn't know already.

"Philanderers often confide their misdeeds to someone," Mac said. How would he know? "Perhaps Crutcher shared such a confidence with one of his friends. Ashley can tell us who her husband's friends were."

"If Erica lets her," I mumbled.

But I left that to Mac to work on. Being a full professor, he had plenty of time on his hands. I, on the other hand, felt it was time to put in a guest appearance at my office.

It turned out to be a busy afternoon. My boss, Ralph Pendergast, stopped by to let me know that two students had been expelled for hacking into the St. Benignus computers and adjusting a bunch of grades for themselves and a dozen fraternity brothers. I know how they did it, but I'm not going to tell you. You could be a potential grade-changer, for all I know. An eagle-eyed professor noticed the discrepancy between her own written records and what the computer showed. Campus Police were getting ready to file charges. The miscreants could get as much as a year in prison and a $2,500 fine if they took a fifth-degree felony rap, but I expected Marvin Slade to let them plea down to a misdemeanor, which could still land them in jail for six months and have them paying a $1,000 fine on each charge. They'd have been far better off taking the bad grades.

Always a fast writer, I turned out a press release in about a half hour, expressing the disappointment of our president, Rev. Joseph Pirelli, and detailing the steps St. Benignus was taking to make sure that this didn't happen again. I also produced a series of talking points for me to use when the phone calls started coming in from media who wanted to go beyond the press release. I e-mailed the drafts to Father Joe and, covering myself, to Ralph. Both men responded within the hour. Father Joe called the release "excellent work as usual!!!" Ralph said exactly the same thing in Ralph-speak: "OK."

So I was feeling rather pleased with myself when Popcorn came into my office late in the day. I had the phone in my hand, ready to call the communications director for the eminent Cardinal who would be our St. Benignus Day keynote speaker, when she sat down. I put it back in the cradle. My assistant's facial expression told a tale of woe. For one scary moment I was afraid that her belief in Ashley's innocence had opened up a breech in whatever she had going with Oscar. But that wasn't it.

"What do you think of Oscar's mother?" Popcorn asked.

"I try not to."

Where did that come from? That's not fair. Sometimes I get carried away with verbal gymnastics and forget that words are supposed to mean something. In truth, Mrs. Hummel is a very nice octogenarian whose disapproval of smoking keeps Oscar from doing it even more than he does. It's not her fault that he's a momma's boy. Or is it?

"I don't think she likes me," Popcorn said, her voice on the edge of tears.

I stared. How could anybody not like Aneliese Pokorny? My irreplaceable assistant is attractive, benevolent, competent . . . I could continue through the whole alphabet like that!

"That can't possibly be the case," I assured her. "You must be getting the vibes wrong."

"Oh, yeah? I just talked to her on the phone and she didn't sound warm at all. And whenever I'm around her, she looks at me like I'm, I don't know, a seductress out to ravage her son, maybe."

Well, aren't you? Once, when she wasn't looking, I paged through one of Popcorn's romance novels and quickly decided I wasn't old enough to read it. Anybody who laps up stuff like that must have *something* in mind.

"I'm sure it's just that Oscar's always been there for her," I said. "She's not used to him dating." Approaching delicate territory, I paused. "You are dating, aren't you?" *Not that I'm prying!*

She took a pull on her coffee. At least, I assumed it was coffee. "I guess so. Do they call it that at our age? He's been taking me places."

So that was out of the closet at last! I mentally composed a text message to Lynda: *Oscar is hooked. She just has to reel him in.*

I didn't make that call to the Cardinal's media guru for another forty-five minutes, what with dispensing advice to the lovelorn and then bringing Popcorn up to date on the Crutcher case. Since everything always happens at once (Cody's Law), Mac called when I finally managed to get on the phone. I called him back after a ten-minute chat with a friendly northeasterner.

Ashley had offered two suggestions of where to go for a line on who Crutcher might have been seeing on the sly: Joe Robards, who used to work with him at the county recreation department, and Meredith Blake.

"Oh, come on, Mac!" I protested. "There's no way a fast number like Meredith Blake was comparing lifestyle notes with her handyman."

"Perhaps not, old boy. However, he surely was not in her employ alone. He may have bragged to some of his colleagues about his amorous adventures. That is certainly my hope, for Mr. Robards has not yet returned my phone call. Through the kind intervention of a friend of a friend, we have an appointment at Miss Blake's at six-thirty."

I'm convinced that Mac can connect with anybody on the planet with two or three phone calls, max, so finding somebody to put him in touch with the infamous Meredith Blake must have been a breeze.

I had more than enough time to shave and change my clothes first.

Neither the Blakes nor the Caraways, Meredith's mother's family, had old money on the scale of the Gambles or the Masons. But both of her parents were the ends of the lines. So when their Lexus crossed a double yellow line late one night, making Meredith an orphan during her second year at Vassar, she inherited two small fortunes. She'd been partying and protesting ever since. Her causes changed but her antics didn't. I forget what she was protesting when she was arrested naked in front of the White House in 2006, but I'm pretty sure it wasn't public indecency.

Like much of Erin, I had followed her escapades for years even when she lived on the fringes of the Hollywood crowd in Los Angeles. The headlines on the papers in the supermarket checkout lane kept us posted. But within the past year she had reoccupied the old Blake family manse, which had been empty for some time. Wagging tongues said her journey home was an economy move, necessary because she was spending money faster than her trust funds could dole it out. Maybe so, I thought, as we stood on the porch of the big brick house, but the operating expenses on Chez Blake could not be negligible.

"McCabe? Cody? Come on in."

Yes, ma'am! Even with the high-heeled boots, Meredith Blake stood a few inches shorter than my six-one.

But she wasn't short on authority when she directed us. We followed her into the huge entrance foyer.

Having only seen her once, years ago and from a distance, I expected the party girl lifestyle to have taken its toll on Meredith's face and figure now that she was in her early forties. Well, maybe she had a picture of herself tucked away in a closet somewhere that looked like a hag, but the woman who opened the door for us that night sure didn't. Poured into designer jeans and a tight-fitting red turtleneck sweater, she was still what my father would call "a fine figure of a woman." Meredith wasn't as shapely as Lynda, but nobody would ever confuse her for a boy. And she couldn't have been more than five pounds overweight. Her face didn't have the puffiness that sometimes afflicts heavy drinkers, nor had crows left footprints in the corners of her eyes. I suspected Botox. Her hair, hanging soft and feminine down to her shoulders, was jet black except for a fascinating silver streak about an inch wide running from her roots to her split ends.

She lit a cigarette. "So you want to ask me about Tim Crutcher? That bastard!" She expelled smoke like a steam engine.

"You've come at either a very bad time or a very good time," said a man coming into the foyer from the living room off to the left.

Mac probably recognized him before I did. The synapses of my brother-in-law's brain seem to fire faster than mine, as well as working in different ways. Still, it didn't take more than ten seconds even for me to realize that the dirty blond goatee and the hair tied into a ponytail at the back belonged to Charlie Hayworth. So the gossip was true: Meredith and Charlie were an item. Heaven (or maybe more southern regions) knew that they were birds of a feather, although Charlie was younger by a few years.

He was an Erin boy made good, then bad. After a stellar career with the St. Louis Cardinals, he'd been booted out of baseball about a decade ago for using steroids. Lots of dopers played the diamonds in those days, but Charlie—everybody called him that—was the poster boy for the ones who got caught. He made the cover of *Tick* magazine as well as *Sports Illustrated*. Now he spent a lot of time in casinos around the country, and rumor had it that he had moved on from steroids to other kinds of drugs.

He didn't bother to introduce himself, just kept on talking: "Meredith just realized today that a lot of her jewelry is missing—pearl necklaces, diamond brooches, rings—all quality stuff."

"And Crutcher took it." The lady of the house exhaled more smoke, looking pouty while I tried not to cough. "It had to be him."

"May I ask how you reached that conclusion, Ms. Blake?" Mac asked.

"Hey, it's not like this house is crawling with hired help anymore. I only had Crutcher and a couple of other part-timers. He was my general handyman, doing whatever it took to make the house livable. Since he was here every day doing something or other, I finally gave him a key. And what did he do? He took a haul right out of the jewelry closet in my bedroom!"

"And this happened—when?"

"I don't know. It's been weeks since I've looked at my bling. I don't usually wear the tiara to dinner at the Roundhouse." *Was that sarcasm or irony?* "I went into the closet this morning to pick out a necklace for a party next week in New York. Right away I saw that some of my best pieces were gone."

"Weren't you being a little too trusting in giving him a key, Ms. Blake?" I wanted to know.

"It didn't occur to me that he would rip me off. This is Erin, not Beverly Hills, for crap's sake!"

Point taken. But have you noticed the homicide rate in this burg?

Mac had a different question. "Have you filed a police report?"

"Not yet," Charlie said.

Meredith shot him daggers. Studs should speak only when spoken to. "We're still toting up his take. Once we have a list of everything that's missing, we'll take it to the authorities and our insurance company." *Oh, Oscar will love it. Call him first so he can put on his uniform hat.*

"As I explained on the telephone, we are looking into Tim Crutcher's shooting," Mac said.

Meredith shrugged. "What's to look into? The man was a thief and his wife took him out. Good for her. I wish she'd done it a little earlier."

"She didn't do it at all," I said.

"So she says. I saw that on the news."

Couldn't you go outside and smoke? Oh, wait. This is your house.

"We happen to believe Mrs. Crutcher," Mac said.

"How can we—" Charlie looked at the heiress. "How can Meredith help you, Mr. McCabe?"

"By your own account, Miss Blake, Tim Crutcher spent a lot of time here over the past few months. You may have seen him more than anyone in that period. Did you ever get the impression that he had a paramour?"

"You mean a girlfriend? How would I know?" Her voice was scornful. "We didn't exactly see each other socially." She studied her burning cigarette. Lynda used to do that sometimes when she smoked. I buried the thought. "The only women I ever heard him mention were his wife and his attorney, Erica Slade."

"Erica!" I blurted out.

"She represented him?" Mac asked more calmly.

"Yeah, he got pulled over for drunk driving three or four months ago. His driver's license was suspended for a few weeks and his wife had to drop him off here every day."

VIII

"We knew he drank," I reminded Mac on the way to our respective homes.

He grunted. "The significance, if any, of Crutcher's entanglement with the law may not be immediately apparent, but it would have been nice to know. I wish Ashley had thought to mention it."

"You don't think he was carrying on with Erica, do you?" I said with a chuckle.

"No, I do not. Still, stranger things have happened, and in similar circumstances. File that in the back of your mind as 'unlikely, though not impossible.' Perhaps the mystery woman, if there is one, will show up at the funeral tomorrow."

"Not if she's the killer," I said. "Then she'll stay as far away as she can get so that nobody connects her with Crutcher."

"Possibly." I was glad he didn't say what I thought he was thinking: That the theoretical killer-girlfriend might show up if she was somebody who was known to know him, because it might be suspicious if she didn't. That kind of double-bluff brainwork always gives me a headache, and we don't seem to be able to avoid it every time we get involved in these homicidal high jinks. But Mac went on:

"At any rate, the funeral might also afford us an opportunity to talk with Ashley without Erica in attendance. There are several questions that I would like to ask her."

That evening, before fixing myself another lonely dinner, I texted Lynda.

JEFF: *You'll never guess who I met!*

LYNDA: *Some femme fatale, no doubt.*

JEFF: *Who, me?*

And so forth. Meredith Blake intrigued Lynda. I could tell by the questions she texted.

The next day, Thursday, we caught up with Ashley at Holder & Hawes Funeral Home during the sparsely attended visitation before the funeral. It's true what they say about black clothing—it has a slimming effect. At least it did on Ashley. By no means a merry widow, her mood seemed somber though she shed no crocodile tears.

"May we have a few minutes in private?" Mac asked.

She looked around at the thirty or so friends and relatives talking to each other in clumps, a few of them standing in front of the closed casket. The nature of Crutcher's wound had made an open viewing inadvisable.

"Sure. Let's go in here."

We ducked into an empty side room dominated by an aquarium full of fish.

"So, did you find out anything?" Ashley asked before Mac could get started.

"Several interesting lines of inquiry have opened up," Mac said, not exactly answering the question. "Your husband's former employer, Meredith Blake, has accused him of stealing several valuable items of jewelry."

Ashley stared. "You've got to be kidding. No, of course you're not."

"He didn't give you something shiny as a peace offering or something?" I said.

And I thought she'd been staring before. "I had no idea that Tim had sticky fingers on top of all his other flaws. Not that I don't believe it. At this point I'd believe anything you told me about that man—not to speak ill of the dead."

"Well," Mac said, "it may not be true, although Miss Blake seems convinced. Are you aware that the prosecutor finds the life insurance policy on your husband to be a credible motive for you to kill him, or at least a contributing factor?"

She shook her head impatiently. "I explained that. Tim insisted that we both insure each other."

"Why? The purchase seems rather unusual, given that he was underemployed at the time."

"Life with Tim was always unusual. He said it would help his brother, Tom. I don't know Tom well—he'd already moved out of town when I first met Tim—but he seems to move from sales job to sales job with about as much ambition as Tim. Lately he's been selling term life insurance. Tim said it was a good deal. We were both relatively young and healthy, so it didn't cost very much. At least I'll have enough to bury him."

Bury him? Heck, you could build a mausoleum for him with that death benefit.

"Is it true that Erica defended your husband on an OVI charge?" Mac asked. That's Section 4511.19 of the Ohio Revised Code, "Operating a Vehicle Under the Influence of Alcohol or Drugs."

"Yeah. Losing his job didn't do anything to sober him up. Ms. Slade doesn't do a lot of OVI work, but she took the case pro bono as a favor to me. Why do you ask?"

"I was just verifying something we were told," Mac said. "It is a habit of mine to check everything, even if it seems unimportant. One never knows what *is* unimportant, you see. Is your husband's friend Joe Robards here? I was unable to reach him yesterday."

Ashley pointed across the broad hallway into the bigger room where the casket lay. "That's him over in the corner, talking to my brother-in-law."

There was no mistaking who she meant by the reference to her brother-in-law. Tom Crutcher looked remarkably like the photos of his brother that appeared around the room, except that he had a thick mustache. They were both brawny men, almost my height, with low foreheads and full heads of dark hair. Crutcher was talking to a shaggy-haired little guy, maybe half a foot shorter, with a big nose and small chin.

"Tim was a twin?" I said.

"No, no, Tom is a couple of years older. They just looked a lot alike. Strong genes in that family. That should have told me something once I started hearing about Tom."

"I would like to speak with both of those men," Mac said. "Besides, I see Erica coming in and I am sure she would like to pay her respects to you. Thank you, Ashley. We progress, I think. I will keep you informed."

We ducked quickly into the other room, hoping that Erica didn't notice us talking to her client without legal counsel present.

Interrupting two people engaged in conversation is not something I'm comfortable with, but Sebastian McCabe is a past master at it. He walked up to Tom Crutcher and Joe Robards without hesitation.

"Mr. Crutcher? I am sorry for your loss." He introduced himself and me. Crutcher mumbled his thanks. Robards stuck out his hand. "Joe Robards. I worked with Tim for years. You called me yesterday, right? Sorry I didn't get back to you."

Before Mac could respond, Tom Crutcher fired another question at him: "You were a friend of Tim?"

"No, actually, we never met. Jefferson and I know his wife."

"Oh." Crutcher stiffened. He looked around, apparently sighting Ashley talking to her attorney. "I'm surprised she's here. Takes nerve." *Wow, is it cold in here or is it just you?*

"It is certainly a difficult situation," Mac said. "I am sure you realize that what happened is still in dispute."

"Your friend, my dear sister-in-law, gets a quarter of a million dollar life insurance payout because my little brother is dead. I know that much. Unless, of course, a jury decides that she murdered him. Fortunately, a killer can't profit by her crime. Excuse me."

Crutcher didn't wait to be excused, just turned his back on us and looked around, as if searching for a lifeline—maybe somebody he remembered from the old days in Erin.

"He seems upset," I understated, trying to lighten the mood a little, when I gauged that he was out of earshot.

"Tom always was a little high strung," Robards said. "He was in my year at Malcolm C. Cotton High. Haven't seen him since he left Erin, though. I knew Tim real well, all those years of working together at the Rec Department. Shame he got canned, but he brought it on himself. Still, I felt sorry for him. That's why I let him sleep in my basement when he broke up with his wife."

Clearly, Robards liked to hear himself talk. That was a good thing, from our point of view.

Mac raised an eyebrow. "Indeed? I am surprised that he had to rely on your generosity. I rather had the impression that he was enamored of another."

Robards scrunched up his face, as if thinking hard. "How's that?"

"He had a lady friend, didn't he?" I translated. "That's what we heard."

"He never told me nothing about a woman, but I wouldn't expect him to. A gentleman never tells." Robards chuckled. "He did have a little thing going with Lady Luck for a while, though. Last summer, August maybe, we were out having a few beers at Bobbie McGee's. When Tim got two sheets to the wind and talking more than he should, he told me he'd finally hit the jackpot. He didn't say any more than that, but it wasn't hard to figure what he meant. That was right after the Forty Thieves Casino opened in Cincinnati. He must've gambled it all back, though, 'cause no more than six weeks later, damned if he wasn't asking me for a place to stay."

"I guess his luck ran out," I said.

IX

After the funeral, a nondenominational service ably presided over by Jonathan Hawes with a minimum of sentiment and an appropriate amount of Scripture, Mac pointed his big red Chevy toward campus and our respective offices.

"Now we know where Tim did some of his gambling, if that's any help," I observed. "Maybe a big losing streak is the reason he helped himself to Meredith's sparkles."

"Conceivably," Mac allowed. He didn't say much more.

Casino gambling had long been available in nearby Indiana, originally restricted to boats. Ohio joined the party after voters approved four casinos in the state, including the new Arabian Nights-themed Forty Thieves in Cincinnati. I could imagine Crutcher walking out of there shell-shocked and penniless.

In late afternoon, Mac asked me to go with him to see Oscar. Since I was having a quiet day, without a single student arrested or coach fired, I put Popcorn in charge and told her to call me if she needed me. I left with "Okay, Boss" ringing in my ears.

We arrived outside Oscar's office in the basement of City Hall just in time to see Meredith Blake leaving, with Charlie Hayworth in tow. I hoped she'd at least sent flowers to the funeral since she hadn't sent herself, at least not while we were there.

"Reporting the stolen jewelry?" Mac said after we'd all gotten through the conventional acknowledgements of each other's existence.

"No, we were identifying some of it." Meredith began fumbling with her Coach purse, fingers screaming for nicotine.

"We filed the report this morning and Chief Hummel—" her beau began.

"Let's get a move-on, Charlie," Meredith said, talking out of the side of her mouth that did not hold the cigarette she was lighting.

And they left.

"Charming couple," I muttered to Mac. "You can sure tell who wears the jeans in that duo."

"The one with the money, I suspect."

Oscar beamed when we walked in, appearing inordinately glad to see us. "Well, look who the cat dragged in! What brings you geniuses into my humble quarters?"

Without waiting for an answer, he turned around and picked up the office coffee pot from the credenza behind him.

"Originally, we were going to ask if you had turned up any indication that Tim Crutcher was carrying on an *affaire de coeur*," Mac said.

"I don't even know what that means. Coffee?" He held up the pot.

Mac accepted a cup of the awful stuff and repeated his question in English.

"I'm investigating Crutcher's murder, not his love life," Oscar protested. "Of course, now that you mention it, a girlfriend would give his wife another reason to kill him."

That's not really what we were thinking.

Mac ignored that. "You are also investigating the theft of some jewelry from Meredith Blake, and apparently having some success."

"How the hell did you know that?"

"He has his ways," I said, before Mac could. Why ruin the illusion that he'd done something brilliant?

"I do not know all of it, Oscar. Please elaborate."

Oscar was only too happy to relate his own triumph. "Ms. Blake and her, uh, friend came to me this morning to report the robbery. They gave me a list of the stolen jewelry, with photographs. One of the diamond rings, a round bezel design with a platinum band, reminded me of the one that had been on Crutcher's body."

"His body!" I repeated.

"Yeah. I didn't notice it at the time, but the crime scene photos show that he was wearing it on his pinky finger. I remembered seeing it later, in the envelope that I gave his wife with his personal effects in it. So I called her. I don't think she was especially happy to hear from me. But, sure enough, she said she'd never seen this ring before, figured it must have been something he bought or was given after they split. She drove it over here right away."

"See, she's an honest person," I pointed out.

"And it's the ring in the photos Ms. Blake gave me. She just confirmed that."

"Congratulations, Oscar." Mac sipped caffeine. "You really have done quite well."

"I'm just beginning, Sherlock. I've asked for a warrant for both the house where Crutcher lived with his wife and the one where he'd been staying the past few weeks. I figure he must have socked the rest of the jewelry away somewhere. Maybe that's why Ashley killed him."

But I was thinking of Mac's first off-the-cuff theory, the "Three Garridebs" ploy. Maybe Crutcher and his unknown accomplice, presumably the girlfriend, entered the house that night to recover Meredith's stolen jewelry that he had hidden there and didn't have a chance to recover the night he left his wife. That would answer the big question of what he was doing in the house.

"Really, Oscar," Mac said. "That makes three theories you have offered as to why Ashley took her husband's life with malice aforethought—life insurance money, romantic jealousy, and the stolen gems."

Oscar grinned irritatingly. "Yeah, it's an embarrassment of riches, ain't it?"

"Oh, come on!" I admit to being a bit cross. "You can't be all that confident. You haven't filed charges."

"Just a matter of time, Jeff. It's the prosecutor's call, and he's a cautious dude."

X

"Be of good cheer, Jefferson! All is clear now."

Then you must be wearing night vision goggles. It wasn't that there wasn't anything to go on—there was too much. Ashley had more motives than I had rejection slips, but we didn't believe any of them. Instead, we were looking at a hypothetical girlfriend, maybe somehow connected with a stash of jewelry looted from the infamous Meredith Blake— or not.

"Okay, genius," I snapped, missing my wife to the point of irritation and worn down by all this brainwork. "Who do you figure for the killer?"

"It would be premature to share my thoughts at this point, old boy." As usual, Mac was keeping me in the dark so that I could clap with everybody else when he finally pulled the rabbit out of his hat at the end. Until then, he wouldn't even let me see the tip of the bunny's ears. "Tomorrow, I must venture out for a bit of on-the-ground research."

"Good luck. You'll have to fly solo this time."

He looked at me and raised an eyebrow—not a good move since he was driving us back to campus at the time. "I am lost without my—"

"Can it! Maybe it slipped off your radar screen, but tomorrow night's the St. Benignus Day concert. That might not be a big deal to you—you just have to play your bagpipes." *I prefer to think of them as gagpipes.* "But I've got about a hundred details to take care of, and that's just for tomorrow. Saturday will be even worse. I have to make sure everything goes smoothly with the Cardinal, from picking him up at the airport to making sure he gets the gluten-free dinner."

"I completely understand. Far be it for me to take you away from the responsibilities of your day job."

New policy, Mac? He'd never given up so easily before. I felt a little irked that he didn't try harder to get me to go with him.

"So what are you researching?" I asked.

"I merely wish to confirm a certain suspicion of mine which, if true, would almost certainly validate my theory about the killer." *Oh, now I see.*

"Give me a hint so that I can work on it, Mac. What's this all about? What's the motive?"

"Insurance, old boy."

For the next two hours, after Mac dropped me off in front of my office in Carey Hall, I tried to puzzle that out with half my brain while the other half fielded media calls and tested the live-streaming that we would be doing of the concert and the Cardinal's speech on our website. I'm sure you see the puzzle that Mac had handed me: The insurance angle didn't make sense unless Ashley killed Crutcher. She's the one who benefitted from the policy on his life. But if Mac thought she was the killer after all, he wouldn't be so danged cheerful about it.

Insurance, insurance . . . Whenever the word ran through my head, the one that immediately got in line behind it was "scam." I kept shoving it aside, but it kept coming back. Finally I let it stick around while I gave it a good look.

"What's the matter, Boss?" Popcorn stopped in the middle of asking me which of her favorite dresses I thought Oscar's mother would like better on her. "Your eyes are kind of popping out."

"I just had an inspiration. Suppose Tim Crutcher isn't really dead."

Popcorn chuckled. "Then they'd better not bury him."

I ignored her attempt at levity. "You weren't at the funeral, so you don't know that Tim and Tom Crutcher look almost exactly alike. So suppose it's really Tom who died, and Tim took his place!"

"What would be the point of that?"

"To collect on Tim's life insurance policy, which names Ashley as the beneficiary."

Popcorn frowned. "That would mean that she and Tim were in it together—murder and insurance fraud. And their breakup was just a façade."

"Exactly." And if that's what Mac had deduced, an insurance scam, no wonder he'd been cheerful. He would be patting himself on the back for figuring out the plot, even though it meant that Ashley was a colder-than-cold-blooded murderer. It would be far from the first time that the detective's "client" turned out to be guilty, after all.

But Popcorn shook her head vigorously. "No, no, no. You guys are supposed to prove that Ashley's completely innocent."

"You wouldn't want that if she really *isn't*, would you?"

I can't say she rushed to respond in the negative. "No, I guess not," she admitted eventually. "But she is! Otherwise she would have claimed self-defense, wouldn't she? Or killed him somewhere else."

"I admit I haven't worked it all out yet."

"So you think this is what Mac is researching somehow?"

"I'd bet on it." I thought a minute. "But we can do some research of our own." I leaped up. "Come on, Popcorn! The game is afoot!"

"What?"

I can't believe I said that.

Joe Robards lived in a mid-century modern house, a split-level. I'd called ahead. He opened the door when I rang. I could hear loud voices inside the house.

"Hi, Joe. Thanks for agreeing to see us. Oh, this is my assistant, Aneliese Pokorny."

"Assistant? I thought you were Professor McCabe's assistant."

Why does everybody think . . .

"We work together at St. Benignus," Popcorn explained. "I've taken an interest in the Crutcher case."

"Well, like I said on the phone, I don't know anything more than what I said at the funeral home, but come on in."

We walked into World War III. I'm not sure how many boys of various ages were tearing up the house, but it must have been three or four. I could almost smell the pre-pubescent testosterone. Mrs. Robards, an island of placidity in this turbulent sea, was calmly diapering number four or five in the family room when Joe took us in and introduced us. Toys lay everywhere, at least half of them broken. Looking at all this chaos, I thought: *I want this—a houseful of noisy kids.*

JoAnn Robards, a pleasant-faced brunette in a white sweater over a blue and white polka dot housedress, stood up from a diaper-changing table to welcome us. A slender woman, she topped her husband by about three inches.

"Joe says you're trying to help Ashley." *Well, that was the original idea, at least.* She shook her head. "Well, good luck. I feel sorry for Ashley, whatever happened. Living with Tim Crutcher can't have been easy. I've known him since high school. In fact, I took him to my junior prom."

"I guess that didn't work out too well," Popcorn said.

"Oh, it worked out great! Tim introduced me to Joe that night."

The way she looked at her husband as she picked up the baby, a girl for a change, made me want to shout, "Rent a room!" It also made me miss Lynda.

"This may seem a strange question," I said, "but we were wondering whether Tim and Ashley kept in contact when he was living here. I mean, were they friendly? Did they call each other?" Oscar could know that from checking cell phone records, if he'd thought of it. But there was no reason for him to think of it.

JoAnn looked at me shrewdly, as if to say, "If you're helping Ashley, why don't you ask her?" That was a very good question, but not one that occurred to Robards.

He just snorted. "Not hardly. I never really got the lowdown on who wanted the split, but I tried to get Tim to swallow his pride if he had to and work things out. That went over like a lead balloon. He said something like, 'If she thinks I can't do better than her, she'll find out different.'"

"Sounds like he was looking for a girlfriend," Popcorn said. *Or he already had one.* The hypothetical girlfriend was looking less hypothetical.

"Well, that's that," I said. "I had an idea, but it looks like it's dying a fast death." But just then, another idea took up residence in the Cody brain. "Do you mind if we look in your basement?"

JoAnn looked at me with something approaching horror. "It's a mess down there. And kind of sad—we haven't touched any of Tim's stuff." *Perfect!* "Why do you want to look in our basement?"

"It's a real long shot, but we have reason to believe that Tim hid something before he died, and he may have hidden it in your basement." *And I don't want to wait for Oscar to get his search warrant.*

Robards shook his head. "That's weird. What kind of something?"

"Jewelry," Popcorn said. "Meredith Blake is missing some, and she thinks Tim took it." Popcorn knew the whole story, and now the Robardses did, too. Well, why not? They might as well know. We were asking to search part of their house.

"He was even wearing one of her rings on his pinky finger when he was shot," I said. "Do you know the one I mean?"

"No. If he was wearing it around me, I never noticed," Robards said. "Come on. I'll take you downstairs."

"Ignore the mess," his wife ordered.

The lowest level of the house was outfitted as a kind of man-cave cum guest room, with a bar and a futon. Shirts, slacks, and underwear were hanging here and piled there. Tim Crutcher gave up Ashley for this? What a dolt!

I started my search with the overflowing suitcase that lay open in a corner, looking for jewelry cases or smaller and more easily concealed loose items such as rings and necklaces.

"This is kind of creepy," Popcorn said as she probed the pockets in a pair of pants.

Robards ran his hands along the futon mattress. "Why would Tim be paying me fifty bucks a week to stay here if he ripped off a bunch of diamonds and stuff?"

"Maybe he only did that right before he got killed," I said. "The timeline on that isn't real clear, but Meredith Blake didn't realize the goods were missing until yesterday."

After a half-hour search that included holding up liquor bottles to the light and rattling a Cincinnati Reds bobble head to make sure it hadn't been hollowed out, the three of us surrendered.

"What about upstairs?" I asked. "Could he have hiden the stuff in, say, the living room?"

"Naw. He kept to himself. That was part of the deal. He didn't eat with us or anything, and came and went as he wanted. There's a separate entrance through the garage and he had his own key. That night he died, we had no idea until

Chief Hummel called us. Tim was here earlier that night, but he must have gone out again."

We trooped dejectedly upstairs.

"Did you find anything?" JoAnn Robards asked.

"Not even a dust bunny," I said.

In consolation, I took Popcorn to dinner at Bobbie McGee's.

"Well, this has been exciting," she said as we sat down.

"Sarcasm will get you no raise."

"I mean it! I didn't know when I woke up this morning that by the end of the day I would take part in a treasure hunt and get a free dinner. Aw, don't look so glum, Boss. Your idea didn't pan out, but at least you didn't give Ashley yet another motive."

During breaks from discussing Oscar's mother and the vexing dilemma about which dress to wear to the concert on Friday night, Popcorn ordered a frozen margarita, a plate of chicken wing appetizers, a chef salad, and a main course of ribs. *Please don't get dessert.*

I had a Hudy DeLite beer (a rare indulgence) and grilled mahi-mahi.

"Why do you not weigh five hundred pounds?" I asked as our enthusiastic server hustled off with our orders. Popcorn is only slightly chubby.

"I have a treadmill at home."

"That's bad for your knees. My doctor told me—"

"Hello, Jeff."

No, my doctor didn't tell me "Hello, Jeff." Erica Slade stood at our table, wearing a short orange dress and matching high heels. That dark beverage on ice in her glass didn't smell like tea. I introduced her to Popcorn, whose day had suddenly gotten even more exciting.

"How's it going from your end, Jeff?"

I'm sorry you asked, Erica.

"We're not ready to say."

She moved her lush, dark hair out of her eyes. "Well, I hope you're ready soon. I'm going to try to talk to Mac tomorrow and see what he's got. Ashley was charged with first-degree murder today. I got her out on bail."

"But that's so wrong!" Popcorn burst out. "Nobody in this town thinks Ashley's a cold-blooded murderer, even if they don't exactly believe her whole story." *Don't you believe her whole story, Popcorn?* "Why did the prosecutor have to go for Murder One?"

The prosecutor's ex took a belt of her scotch. Her fingernails were the same shade of orange as her dress and shoes. "He always overreaches when he's between girlfriends. I think he's a little tense, you know?"

Ask a silly question . . .

"The last time I talked to Mac, a few hours ago, he seemed convinced that he was on to something." I said. "That's all I can tell you right now because that's all I know. But all the prosecution has is circumstantial evidence, right?"

"You mean the facts that my client had several reasons to prefer the victim dead, that he was shot in her house, and that she'd been spending a lot of time lately at a shooting range putting little holes into a male silhouette?"

Subtle, but I see what you mean.

"Never mind that," I said desperately. "Mac has a hell of track record. And so do you."

"Sure. We'll make Marvin the Martian eat crow by the end of this." She finished off her drink. "But right now I have no idea how. Goodnight, Jeff. Nice to meet you, Ms. Pokorny."

She went back to the bar.

"Let's look at the dessert menu," Popcorn said.

Not much more than half an hour later, after dropping Popcorn off at her car in the St. Benignus parking lot, I was back in my empty house. Instead of calling Lynda, which would just make me lonelier, I sent a text message:

Counting the hours until you get home.
She texted back:
Me too. 18!
I started humming *Boléro.*

XI

In the middle of the night I sat up in bed. *Maybe it was the Robardses!* They had a lot of kids and probably not very much money. If they found the jewelry hidden in their house, it might have been an irresistible temptation to do away with Crutcher and keep the diamonds and such for themselves. That explained what happened to the jewelry and why Crutcher was killed, totally vindicating Ashley. Brilliant!

But wait a minute. Why would they take him back to his old house to kill him? And how could they get him to go along with it? They might have taken the gems, but killing him didn't seem plausible. Too bad I'd already lost an hour of sleep by the time I figured that out.

So the next morning, when Popcorn handed me a cup of coffee, I almost wished that it was laced with caffeine.

"I've decided to wear the blue dress to the concert," she informed me. "The green shows too much cleavage."

Sorry, Oscar. Apparently my vote the day before had been overruled. Popcorn must have asked her beaux what his mother would think.

"Don't worry," I said. "As soon as Mac starts playing those dreadful bagpipes, Mrs. Hummel will be gawking at the hairy legs beneath his kilt. She won't even notice your dress."

Popcorn's eyes widened. "Really?"

The phone rang.

"Hi, Jeff, this is Johanna Rawls. I'm working on a second-day story about the charges filed against Ashley Crutcher." Her first-day story, spread across the top of that morning's *Erin Observer & News-Ledger*, lay on my desk. **ESTRANGED WIFE CHARGED IN SHOOTING** screamed the headline. "I was hoping to get a reaction from you."

"Good morning to you, too." Popcorn waved and left my office. "I don't think I'd better say anything because of my day job. I mean, I'm quoted so often in the paper as the spokesperson for St. Benignus that it would cause confusion for me to talk as the spokesperson for Jeff Cody. But Mac wouldn't have that problem. Have you tried him?"

"I did, but I couldn't reach him. He doesn't answer his home phone, his office phone, or his cell phone. So, off the record, what's going on?"

"Off the record, Johanna, I wish I knew. Mac has something up his sleeves besides his arms, but I don't know what it is."

"What *do* you know?"

"Except for a couple of harebrained ideas I had that didn't pan out, nothing that you haven't reported already." That included Meredith Blake's stolen jewelry report, which Oscar had quite rightly shared with Johanna since it was a matter of public record.

We chatted socially for a while (yes, I assured her, I was really looking forward to Lynda coming home) and then hung up. The office phone was barely in its cradle when my smartphone gave that little *ping* noise to let me know I had an incoming text message. It was from Mac.

Please meet me at Crutcher house 10 AM. I know where the jewelry is.

I wrote back: *Tall Rawls looking for you.*
I will ask her as well.

By this time I was already out of my office. "Mac just summoned me to meet him at Ashley's," I told

Popcorn. "Since he's inviting Johanna to the party, this may be the end game." Sometimes I mix metaphors when I'm excited. "You should come along. You've been part of this."

She shook her head. "Somebody has to hold down the fort. You can tell me about it later. Good luck."

The Crutcher residence was a story-and-a-half brick Cape Cod house, the kind that had been built by the thousands in Erin and around the country after the Second World War. Oscar, wearing his official uniform hat, stood on the small front porch along with Tall Rawls, Meredith Blake, and Charlie Hayworth.

"What's this all about?" Meredith demanded as Charlie lit her cigarette on the third attempt to make the lighter work.

Am I my brother-in-law's keeper?

"I'm sure that will become clear as soon as Mac arrives."

"It better," Oscar said darkly.

"I'm not standing around here all—" Meredith resumed.

"There he is," Johanna said.

Mac had just pulled up in his boat-sized Chevy. Ashley Crutcher, looking pale, got out of the front seat on the passenger side. She saw me and smiled feebly. Erica Slade hopped out of the back.

"Ah, we are all here, I see," Mac said. "Thank you all for coming."

I'm not going to try to record Oscar, Johanna, and Meredith all talking at once. The cacophony reminded me of the Robards household.

Mac raised his hand. "Please, please. I will explain everything inside. Ashley, lead the way. Miss Blake, please extinguish your cigarette."

Giving Mac a foul look, Meredith ground the butt under her boot heel.

Ashley unlocked the door and went in first. The rest of us followed. Within a few seconds the Hound of the Baskervilles appeared out of nowhere and started barking like mad at Meredith Blake. Okay, it was a German shepherd, but it looked like a hellhound to me, and I wasn't even the one under attack.

"Get that beast off of me," Meredith said.

"Ranger, quiet!"

The hound obeyed his mistress's voice. He sat looking expectantly, a low growl in his throat.

"Nice doggy," Johanna said. She pulled out her notebook and spoke no more as she observed and recorded the drama unfolding in front of her, an objective journalist.

"So, what's this about the jewelry?" Oscar said. "I assume it's here somewhere."

"But I'm sure it isn't," Ashley burst out.

"Indeed it is not," Mac said. "Except for the ring found on Tim Crutcher's corpse, Miss Blake's jewelry is resting comfortably in her own home—unless it has already been quietly sold to a private buyer."

"What the hell?" Charlie exclaimed.

Insurance scam, that's what the hell. But not life insurance. Suddenly, I saw it all—or at least the big picture.

"Spare us the theatrics, Mr. Hayworth," Mac said. "I am reasonably sure that your hands are not clean in this business."

"What business?" Erica demanded, clearly unhappy at being left in the dark until now.

"Meredith Blake, desperately in need of funds to finance her chosen lifestyle, planned to report her jewels stolen, collect the insurance, and then sell the jewels to an undiscerning buyer. Fearing that she would be suspected because of her rather colorful reputation, she groomed Tim Crutcher to be the fall guy. I use the term 'groomed' advisedly, for Miss Blake was the 'other woman' in his life.

He thought he was her love and her co-conspirator in insurance fraud. In reality, he was her victim."

Ashley shook her head. "Of all people, I never even suspected . . ."

Meredith's laugh rang hollow. "That's absurd. Tell me what you're smoking, McCabe, because I want some of it. Tim Crutcher was a flunky, a guy who did odd jobs around my house. He was lucky to have a job at all, but he abused his position to steal from me."

"I have some photos that would indicate your relationship was quite a bit closer than that."

Mac pulled a series of prints out of his sport coat pocket and held them up for all of us to see. They showed Meredith Blake and Tim Crutcher looking more than a little chummy. She hung on him amorously as he fed a slot machine.

"Oh, all right, I was slumming, getting it on with the hired help," Meredith said. She looked as if she'd been caught with her hand in a cookie jar. "Big deal! Charlie doesn't mind that kind of thing. How do you get from there to your pipe dream about the insurance?"

"It does seem kind of a stretch," Oscar allowed.

"You need to learn that sometimes looking a gift horse in the mouth is the only wise course, Oscar," Mac lectured. "What man would be caught dead wearing a woman's ring? Tim Crutcher was. Moreover, no thief, not even one without a previous record, would be so stupid as to wear hot merchandise." *So that's why Joe Robards never noticed Crutcher wearing the ring—Crutcher never really had it.*

"The inference was immediately clear to me: That ring was placed on Crutcher's finger to frame him, and it was placed there by the person who accompanied him across the threshold of his former domicile—the same person who killed him, Meredith Blake."

Mac looked at her. She looked back, maybe trying to figure out if he had any more evidence to whip out of his pocket. "You're just blowing smoke, Fatty. You can't prove anything."

"I have something better than proof—an eye witness."

Charlie edged away from his meal ticket, maybe not even realizing it. That's when I knew we had her.

"There was no— That's just a crock. If there was a witness, we'd have heard from him by now."

"We already did. Would you like to hear from Ranger again—just as you did on the night of the murder?"

At the sound of his name, the German shepherd reprised the low growl. He pointed himself at Meredith like an arrow. Ashley tightened her grip on his chain.

"Hell's bells," Oscar breathed.

Mac smiled grimly. "Sherlock Holmes was right. Dogs don't make mistakes."

Charlie's shoulders slumped as if he'd just struck out. "Oh, shit, I knew this wouldn't work."

"Shut up, you moron!" Meredith shouted at him.

"Actually, that's very good advice," Erica assured the former ballplayer. "You should get a lawyer before you say another word."

"What's the use? I know when my goose is cooked. I've been here before. But it was all Meredith's doing. She needed the money."

"You spineless bastard!"

Oscar moved closer to the heiress, close enough to grab if necessary.

"First, she figured out that she could make twice the dough on her jewelry by both making an insurance claim and selling it. Then she had this bright idea that if there wasn't somebody else to take the rap, the insurance investigators might figure out pretty quick that she still had the goods. That may sound loony, but—"

"The guilty flee where no man pursueth," Mac said. "And Ms. Blake does have a notorious reputation."

"So she got me to look for a scapegoat," Charlie said.

"And you just did it?" Oscar said.

Charlie looked at his erstwhile companion uneasily. "Meredith can be very persuasive. She threatened to deprive me of certain things if I didn't go along. And she didn't say anything about murder at first. By the time she did, I was in too deep.

"Anyway, I struck up a conversation with Crutcher at the Forty Thieves about a week after it opened. He looked like a guy with problems. I found out that he was out of a job and I was sure he was too fond of gambling, just the kind of poor sap we were looking for. After I convinced him that I wasn't Charlie Hayworth, just somebody who looked like him, I gave him a card with Meredith's name and phone number on it. He knew who she was. He called her the next day. By that afternoon, he was working for her. Within a couple of weeks, she had him convinced she was in love with him."

"Poor Tim," Ashley mumbled. "He always was gullible."

"I presume that Crutcher was unaware of your relationship with Miss Blake?" Mac said.

"No, he never saw me again. As far as he knew, Meredith was sex-starved." He chuckled. "Fat chance. Anyway, about the time he was swallowing the bait, Meredith laid the big one on me: She'd decided that as long as he was alive there was a danger that he might be able to prove his innocence and it would all bounce back to her. So he had to go. Meredith figured that if he was shot in his own house his wife would be blamed, and if he was wearing one of the stolen rings it would be easier to hang the heist on him."

"That was your idea, you liar!" Meredith needed a cigarette; I know the signs.

"Oh, right, like Charlie Hayworth would come up with a murder mystery plot like that," Charlie said. "Gimme a break!"

"How did she get Crutcher to return to his house that night?" I asked Charlie, interrupting this mutual blamefest. That had always been one of the big puzzles—what was the victim doing there?

"She told him that if he really loved her he'd prove it by killing his wife."

Ashley's mouth fell open. "What! And he went along?"

Charlie chuckled grimly. "Went along? Honey, he was on it like white on rice. He even bragged that he bought life insurance, but he insured both of you so it wouldn't look suspicious. Of course, we thought that was just the stars aligning in our favor because it also gave you a great motive for doing away with your husband."

"That—that—" Ashley couldn't even find a word for Crutcher's perfidy. I couldn't either. But in the next morning's *Erin Observer & News-Ledger*, Johanna managed to sneak the word "scoundrel" past the copy editor. Good for Tall Rawls!

"He also came up with the idea of moving out of your house," Charlie went on. *Who pushed the "play" button on you, sport? Not that Oscar minds.* "He thought that would divert suspicion from him when she got shot by an intruder. Shows how dumb he was. I mean, being split from the wife would have made a more likely suspect, not less likely. But it suited our purposes just fine, right Meredith?"

"Drop dead, asshole."

"And here's the best part: Meredith said she'd go along with him for moral support. She even offered to hold the gun. I bet he never saw what was coming even when she pointed it at him, poor dope. Of course, I wasn't there. You can't pin that on me. It was all her."

"That's not exactly how it works," Erica informed him as Meredith used some of her most colorful vocabulary to disagree with her accomplice. "An accessory doesn't have to be present. You need a lawyer now even more than you did ten minutes ago, friend. Here, take my card."

She'd just lost a client in the best possible way. Odds were strong that she'd just gained one, too.

The McCabe visage assumed a look of satisfaction akin to that of a man who has just enjoyed his favorite cake piled high with ice cream. *Cake and ice cream!*

"Mac! I forgot!"

He raised an eyebrow. "Yes, Jefferson?"

"Happy birthday."

XII

Lynda returned home to Erin just in time to dash with me that night to the concert, at which Mac squeezed monster-caught-in-the-tar-pit sounds out of his bagpipes for a good (actually, bad) fifteen minutes, though it seemed longer to me. It wasn't exactly *Boléro*. (That came later, after Lynda drove us home.) Wrapped in my own domestic bliss at the concert, I paid scant attention to Oscar, his mother, and Popcorn in her modest blue dress. But Popcorn told me later that they got along like three fingers of a glove. I guess that's good.

The story plastered atop the next morning's newspaper, **HEIRESS ARRESTED IN CRUTCHER MURDER**, filled Lynda with pride in her protégé. And rightly so. Tall Rawls did a great job.

That night, the alumni dinner went off without a hitch or a stitch. The Cardinal's humorous but pointed talk, in particular, registered a big hit. Maybe the next time he goes to the Vatican for a conclave, he won't come home. It could happen.

When a task is high stress, it leaves you drained afterward even if all went well. So with the St. Benignus Day events coming right on top of Mac's virtuoso performance in the case of the dog that *did* bark in the night-time, I was happy to spend Sunday getting reacquainted with my wife. We didn't even have brunch with the McCabes after Mass.

It was the following Saturday night, therefore, before Mac got to hold forth for an audience on how he figured it all out. The now-richer Ashley Crutcher had invited Mac, my sister, Lynda and me, along with Erica Slade, to dinner at Ricoletti's Ristorante. The beaming Ms. Slade, possibly the happiest person at the table, basked in the afterglow of a vindicated client and a totally pissed ex-husband. For her, it didn't get any better than that.

"The coincidence of Crutcher's supposed larceny being uncovered the day after he was shot weighed heavily on me," Mac related, "particularly when the presumptive proof of his thievery was his highly implausible wearing of a woman's ring.

"So I immediately began to believe that the reported jewelry theft was, in fact, an attempted insurance swindle by the fast-spending, high-living Meredith Blake. It was more than that, however. The tell-tale ring had to have been planted on his body immediately after the shooting. Therefore, Miss Blake and her latest paramour were guilty of murder as well as fraud."

"Wait a minute." Lynda set down her Manhattan. "The insurance con and the murder didn't have to be connected. It could have been that Crutcher hid the jewels at his house and Ashley found them. Then she killed him for the jewels. Did you ever think of that, Mac? No offense, Ashley."

"None taken." A financially comfortable widow who no longer faced a criminal trial, Ashley looked about ten years younger than she had ten days before.

"Yes, I considered and rejected that scenario," Mac assured my bride. "Why would a murderous Ashley plant the ring on her husband? She would not want anyone to know that her husband was the jewel thief. She also would have either killed him somewhere far from home or she would have leaped at the chance to claim self-defense."

Erica Slade, sporting some fancy jewels of her own over a low-cut scarlet dress for weekend dining, also had a question. "How did you come up with that picture of Meredith Blake and Tim at the Forty Thieves?"

He'd been waiting all week for somebody to ask, which is why I refused to do it.

"Those who know me only from reading Jefferson's account of our little adventures undoubtedly believe that I farm out legwork to him out of sloth or incompetence in that realm. Such is not the case. I secured photos of Miss Blake and Tim Crutcher, both published in *The Erin Observer & News-Ledger* on different occasions, and took them to my friend Cal Daley."

"Isn't he the security guy at the Forty Thieves?" I said, earning a nod from Mac. Daley, an old friend of Mac's, had been an assistant chief of police in Cincinnati before retiring to take the casino job.

"Exactly, old boy. Cal and I spent more than an hour reviewing the security recordings of patrons until we found one in which our two quarry appeared together."

So that was his research.

"I have to admit I wasn't sure you were going to pull this one off," I said.

"Well, I'm sure glad he did," Ashley said. "I'll always be grateful. It feels so good to just be Ms. Slade's paralegal again, and not her client, too. But I can't imagine how we're going to defend Charlie Hayworth."

"Leave that to me." The sparkle in Erica's eyes gave her diamond earrings competition. "I'll come up with something that will give Marvin fits."

A FEW WORDS OF THANKS

This time special thanks go to my friends Leah Cummins Guinn, Paul Hayes, Roger Johnson, Kathleen Kaska, Marcy Mahle, and Kieran McMullan for their support of this book and of my writing in general.

Additional thanks to the usual suspects:

Ann Brauer Andriacco, for her constant help and encouragement, as well as her readership;

Kieran McMullen again, for being my reliable consultant on all matters involving firearms, animals, and police procedure (among other topics);

Jeff Suess, for proofreading and final preparation of the manuscript; and

Steve Winter, for applying his engineering eye to the text.

I will never stop thanking Steve Emecz for being my publisher and Bob Gibson at Stauch Design for producing yet another outstanding cover.

About the Author

Dan Andriacco has been reading mysteries since he discovered Sherlock Holmes at the age of nine, and writing them almost as long. The first four books in his popular Sebastian McCabe — Jeff Cody series are *No Police Like Holmes*, *Holmes Sweet Holmes*, *The 1895 Murder* and *The Disappearance of Mr. James Phillimore*. He is also the co-author, with Kieran McMullen, of *The Amateur Executioner* and *The Poisoned Penman*, mysteries solved by Enoch Hale with Sherlock Holmes.

A member of the Tankerville Club, the Illustrious Clients, the Vatican Cameos, and the John H. Watson Society, Dan is also the author of *Baker Street Beat: An Eclectic Collection of Sherlockian Scribblings*. Follow his blog at www.danandriacco.com, his tweets at *@DanAndriacco*, and his Facebook Fan Page at www.facebook.com/DanAndriaccoMysteries .

Dr. Dan and his wife, Ann, have three grown children and five grandchildren. They live in Cincinnati, Ohio, USA, about forty miles downriver from Erin.

Praise for the earlier
Sebastian McCabe – Jeff Cody mysteries

"The villain is hard to discern and the motives involved are even more obscure. All-in-all, this (*The Disappearance of Mr. James Phillimore*) is a fun read in a series that keeps getting better with each new tale." – Philip K. Jones

"*The 1895 Murder* is the most smoothly-plotted and written Cody/McCabe mystery yet. Mr. Andriacco plays fair with the reader, but his clues are deftly hidden, much as Sebastian McCabe hides the secrets to his magic tricks under an entertaining run of palaver." – *The Well-Read Sherlockian*

"I loved Dan Andriacco's first novel about Sebastian McCabe and Jeff Cody, and I'm delighted to recommend the second (*Holmes Sweet Holmes*), which has a curiously topical touch." – Roger Johnson, *The Sherlock Holmes Society of London*

"*No Police Like Holmes* is a chocolate bar of a novel – delicious, addictive, and leaves a craving for more. – *Girl Meets Sherlock*

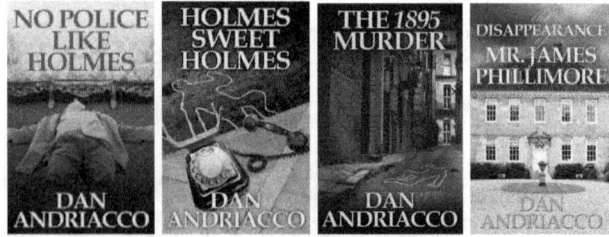

Sebastian McCabe, Jeff Cody, and Lynda Teal will return in
Bookmarked for Murder

Also from MX Publishing

MX Publishing is the world's largest specialist Sherlock Holmes publisher, with over a hundred titles and fifty authors creating the latest in Sherlock Holmes fiction and non-fiction.

From traditional short stories and novels to travel guides and quiz books, MX Publishing cater for all Holmes fans.

The collection includes leading titles such as *Benedict Cumberbatch In Transition* and *The Norwood Author* which won the 2011 Howlett Award (Sherlock Holmes Book of the Year).

MX Publishing also has one of the largest communities of Holmes fans on Facebook with regular contributions from dozens of authors.

www.mxpublishing.com

Also from MX Publishing

Sherlock Holmes Short Story Collections

Sherlock Holmes and the Murder at the Savoy

Sherlock Holmes and the Skull of Kohada Koheiji

Look out for the new novel from Mike Hogan
– *The Scottish Question.*

www.mxpublishing.com

Also from MX Publishing

Our bestselling books are our short story collections;

'Lost Stories of Sherlock Holmes' , 'The Outstanding Mysteries of Sherlock Holmes', The Papers of Sherlock Holmes Volume 1 and 2, 'Untold Adventures of Sherlock Holmes' (and the sequel 'Studies in Legacy) and 'Sherlock Holmes in Pursuit', 'The Cotswold Werewolf and Other Stories of Sherlock Holmes' – and many more……

www.mxpublishing.com